FALLING

IN

LONDON

A Romantic Comedy

Courtney Giardina

Copyright © 2020 by Courtney Giardina

Falling in London

All rights reserved, including the right to reproduce this book or portions thereof in any form whatsoever except in the case of brief quotations embodied in critical articles and reviews.

Falling in London is a work of fiction. Any references to historical events, real people or real places are a product of the author's imagination and used fictitiously. Any resemblance to actual persons (living or dead), events, or locations is entirely coincidental.

This book is licensed for personal enjoyment only. No part of this book, even partial, may be reproduced in any form without permission from the author. The only exception is the quoting of short excerpts in a review. Thank you in advance for supporting and respecting the author's hard work.

Dedication

Jessica – My best friend and travel partner. You have opened my eyes and soul to so many new adventures I would not have been brave enough to experience on my own.

~1~

London's spring weather was not working in Tate Montgomery's favor that morning when she sailed out of her second-story flat. The wind pushed hard against her mid-length black skirt. She could feel the weight on her legs as the heels of her stilettos ferociously hit the cobblestone street. Swarms of people closed in while Tate ruffled through the papers in her hands.

"Don't forget to tell them about the party favors or the music. I love the music."

"I won't forget," Tate muffled into the phone nestled tightly against her shoulder. Genevieve may be more nervous for today than Tate was. She tried to ignore the stutter in Genevieve's voice while fumbling to organize the sheets of paper she'd hastily grabbed off her kitchen counter, but the wind was too strong.

"Crap!" Tate yelled. A single sheet flew from her grasp.

"Are you all right?" Genevieve asked.

Tate didn't answer. Her eyes were locked on the floating paper that had now conveniently wrapped itself around the ankle of a woman walking by. With the risk of breaking an ankle, she lunged over and snatched it.

"Excuse me!" the woman grunted. She glared down at Tate with pursed lips.

hands meant more events, and Tate was happy with how her event planning baby was growing, but this... This could be the event that would send her career soaring. If she booked this, she could afford to hire more employees and take on even more events.

She needed to nail this presentation.

"Oh, thank you!" Tate smiled. She reached out for the door of the coffee shop being held open by a young woman. The aroma of coffee was abundant as Tate stepped inside. Primrose May had become Tate's favorite meeting spot. She didn't even mind that she passed up a dozen other places between her flat and this quaint corner shop; she loved the ambiance here. The white brick walls were painted with inspirational quotes and floral murals. Long bar tables lined each side of the entry along the floor to ceiling windows, and the solid white chairs and wood tables left an opening down the middle of the room, where only a few people stood in line in front of her.

The clock was ticking, but Tate couldn't show up to this meeting without her coffee order. When Tate first started Simple Charms events, she knew standing out would be hard. There were dozens of big-name companies like Rosewood in the area. Her resume wasn't quite as impressive...yet, so she focused on the one skill she did have: hospitality. There wasn't anything anyone loved more in the morning than a nice warm cup of coffee. It took a little research on Tate's part, but she succeeded every time at finding out her clients' favorite type of drink. She'd walk into the meeting, hand it over, and watch the smile grow on her potential client's face. It was her special little touch, and that morning wasn't any different. The only thing out of the ordinary was the new face at the counter.

"Are you okay?" the young girl asked once Tate was at the register.

"I am, thank you."

That question was something Tate had spent a long time getting used to when she first moved here. Every time someone asked her if she was okay, she'd look down wondering what was wrong with her. Did she have mascara under her eyes? Was she bleeding from somewhere? She learned quickly that "Are you okay?" in London meant the same as "How are you?" or "Can I help

He nodded and stepped aside. As the bus slowed, Tate took a few more steps forward, excusing herself until she reached the front platform. When the doors opened, she stepped down into another rush of business suits. That same brisk air hit her again, and her arms tingled. It was a crisp ten degrees across the city today—Celsius, that is. In translation, that was about fifty degrees Fahrenheit. Though not the coldest Tate had experienced since her move to London, her west coast roots were still adjusting to fifty degrees in April. Today was typical of what winter months had looked like growing up in Seattle, but by now, it most likely would be nearing the seventies back home. Tate knew she had another month or so of days like this left here in London before the seventies arrived, but she embraced the cold weather. Cold weather meant a few more months of hot coffee. That was her favorite combination and the first thought in her mind as the bus pulled away.

Tate didn't have time to take in the beauty of the redbrick scaling the nineteenth-century stature of the Westminster Cathedral. She clasped her coat tighter as the wind pushed back. Brick buildings surrounded her as her legs fought through the dense air. Her laptop bag swung heavily at her side, and her heels clicked beneath her as she thought about how she got here.

Two years ago, when she first came to London, she had been lucky enough to land an assistant job with one of the most influential event planning agencies in the city. Rosewood Events was known for hosting some of the most extravagant parties for London's elite. With a degree in hospitality management, it seemed like a logical next step for the girl whose long-anticipated future plans had changed suddenly. The dozens of weddings, galas, and charity functions were a welcome distraction for more than a year. After that, though, Tate decided to step out on her own.

Over the past six months, she'd planned a few small parties and company events. The foundation for Simple Charms was steadily being built. Genevieve, her best—and right now, only—friend in London, had agreed to be her very first employee. Tate still didn't believe that when she said it out loud. She had an *employee*. Someone she actually paid to work for her. Not only that, she was growing so fast, she'd reached out to a local university for internships. More breath before the air brakes burst out in front of her. She pressed her hands quickly against her skirt before the gust of wind revealed what was underneath and then stepped onto the platform.

Her bobby pins had let her down. Tate could now see just how many strands of hair were flying free around her face in the reflection of the bus window as she squeezed her way into an empty seat on the lower deck. Her shoulder rubbed against the man next to her as she attempted to remove her compact out of the front pocket of her laptop bag. There wasn't much wiggle room between the rotund man sitting in the window seat and those standing in the aisle on her other side.

You'd think by now Tate would've mastered this public transport thing. She never drove anymore, but she also was lucky enough to not have to regularly ride during rush hour. It was 9:00 a.m., prime time for the London workforce, which meant for the next few stops she'd be crammed in like a sardine. Her fingertips pressed hard against the compact as she slid it out of the pocket of her laptop case. To get a good look, Tate squeezed the compact between her knees and readjusted a few of those bobby pins in order to hide the disheveled parts of her hair. A few dabs of powder hid the bright red cheeks brought on by the London air, and, for the remaining stops, she closed her eyes and went over her big presentation in her mind.

Tate's eyes blinked open right as the Westminster Cathedral came into view. That meant her stop was next. She reached for the handle above and pulled herself up to stand while eyeing the stunning piece of architecture that dazzled Victoria Street. Westminster Cathedral was not to be confused with Westminster Abbey. That was one of the first things Tate learned when she moved to London. Prince William did not get married at the Westminster Cathedral, and if you messed that up, the locals, understandably so, would be sure to fire their wrath of disapproval for not taking the time to research the details of their beloved city.

"Excuse me." Tate tapped the shoulder of a dapper man with pepper hair who was blocking the aisle beside her. He turned to look over his shoulder.

"Could I squeeze by you?" she asked.

"I'm so sorry!" Tate yelled as she struggled to sprint away in her heels. There wasn't time to absorb the judgment falling upon her. Today was a big day, and if she was late, it would ruin it all.

"Tate? Tate, what happened?" Genevieve nudged.

"Nothing. I'm all right now."

Genevieve let out a sigh of relief and dove back into her list of "don't forgets." "The string lights too—be sure to mention those."

"I've got it all ingrained in my head, Genevieve. I won't forget, but I won't even get a chance if I miss this bus."

If it wasn't for hitting the snooze button that morning...twice, Tate would've had eighteen extra minutes. When preparing for the meeting that could make or break a career, those eighteen minutes, she now realized, were everything. It probably would've been fine if Tate ended up wearing the outfit she originally picked out the night before, but, once she had it on, she didn't think it spoke the right words. Not for her first big meeting as CEO of Simple Charms Events. Thank goodness she ended up buying more than one outfit for today. She was also thankful, after changing out of choice number one, that she left the tags on both. If she had worn the first one and forgone the overanalysis in front of her bedroom mirror, her hair might still be in that neatly pulled-back bun she left the house with. Now, she was blinded by the wisps of hair dangling in front of her face. The wind was exceptionally frigid for a spring morning. So much so that Tate's cheeks burned from the bouts of sprinting she was doing.

"Okay, good luck!" Genevieve yelled through the phone. "And don't forget about the art collections."

Tate shook her head. She knew Genevieve couldn't see her through the phone, yet she couldn't help but laugh. "I won't forget about the art collection, I promise. I'll call you later."

Tate shoved the phone back into her purse before Genevieve even had a chance to respond. The bus stop was straight ahead, and she could see the bus right up the street. Morning traffic was working in Tate's favor. The bus inched slowly toward her as she took the last few bounding steps to the sign where it would eventually come to a stop. There was barely enough time to catch her you?" did back in America. Even now she knew, it wouldn't stop her from looking at her reflection on the way out just to make sure.

"I'll have a half-caff and an Americano, both medium, to go, please." Tate smiled.

"Anything else?"

"I think that's it." She handed over her credit card. "Are you new here?"

The girl slid the credit card into the slot in front of her. "Yes. I started last week."

Tate's eyes squinted to read the name tag secured over the girl's black shirt. One of the reasons she loved Primrose May so much was that everyone there knew her name, and she knew theirs. Now, there was one more to add to her list.

"Well, it's nice to meet you, Isla. I'm Tate."

Isla pulled Tate's card out of the slot and handed it back to her. "It's nice to meet you too." Her cheeks flushed as she rested the card in Tate's open palm.

Tate was thankful for the momentary distraction, but once she stuffed her card back into her wallet, the nerves returned. The vibration was heavy in her hands as she leaned against the counter at the back waiting for her name to be called. The coffee shop was lively with conversation, which, for a moment, distracted her. Two women about her age stared intently at one of their cell phones. Their bellow of laughter almost overpowered Isla when she called Tate over for her order. Luckily, Tate caught her out of the corner of her eye as she slid two cups of coffee onto the bar. Tate's hands were still slightly shaking, but she managed to get a firm grip on both before she jetted back out of the door onto the busy London street.

With only a few minutes to spare, Tate clutched both cups tightly in her hands and walked up the steps to the hotel for her meeting. She stretched out her pinkie as far as it would reach for the handle on the door. This was it. The beat of her heart was now rapidly pounding like a drum solo in her chest. She was only a few steps away from the moment she had been preparing for day in and day out this past week. That door was the only thing standing between her and what would hopefully be victory.

At least, she thought that door was the only thing.

Just as her pinkie was about to wrap around the handle, the door flew open from the inside. A man stepped out onto the steps and right into Tate's path. It doesn't end there. She stumbled backward and lost her grip on one of the to-go cups. A stream of coffee was now flying through the air.

The cup bounced a couple of times before eventually coming to a rolling stop on the ground. Half of what was inside had ended up on the ground with it, while the other half was soaking into the front of Tate's brand-new blouse.

"I am so sorry," Tate heard a voice say once the shock wore off.

The peacoat she was wearing was buttoned just low enough that the coffee had missed it completely, but her blouse, the one she chose specifically to show off at this meeting, had taken the brunt of this unfortunate event.

"Here, let me help you." The man in the suit reached for her hand, but Tate brushed it off. She was too busy assessing the tie-dyed look of her blouse.

"Are you kidding me?" she screamed shaking off the coffee on her hands. "Don't you watch where you're going?"

"I'm really sorry," he said. "I didn't see you there."

Tate looked up at him for the first time. His golden hair was unfazed by the gust of wind that suddenly swept between them. Underneath his gray jacket was an ocean blue tie that seemed only a shade darker than the blue in his eyes. She could see the pained expression on his face, but in that moment, she didn't really care. He would walk out of the hotel as clean and put together as he had walked in, and she was cringing at the wetness of the permanent stain she could feel seeping through her silky white button-up.

"Excuse me," he yelled to the front desk "could you get me some napkins?" He looked back at Tate. "Let me help you."

The man bent down to pick up the empty cup, which, thankfully, ended up being Tate's beloved Americano. The half-caff she'd ordered for her client was still safely in her left hand. The concierge showed up with a handful of napkins, which Tate snatched from him. Her nose scrunched as she patted herself down.

"I think you've done enough," Tate said.

"No, really, at least let me dry-clean it or something. Here, give me your number, and I'll..."

"Seriously?" she snarled and glared at him. "You're asking for my number?"

"No, I didn't mean... I just want to help."

She watched the corner of his eyelids droop and, for a second, thought about accepting his apology. That moment quickly faded as the strike of a clock echoed from the nearby church.

"I'm going to be late!" she panicked.

"Wait—please!" he yelled.

"Sorry, I've got to go." She pushed past him and sprinted into the hotel lobby.

Tate ran to the nearest bathroom to inspect the damage. The coffee hadn't made its way to the white tank top she wore underneath the blouse. She pulled off her coat, unbuttoned the blouse, and shoved it into her bag, then looked in the mirror again and hiked the tank top up a bit higher to hide the lace of her bra before putting her peacoat back on. She fluffed up her coat a little, hoping it would erase the mayhem that ensued at the front door. So much for the CEO outfit she had so gracefully pieced together. She was going to have to present her vision in a full-length brown coat.

Tate looked down at the zebra stripes covering her feet. *At least my heels are cute.* Those were her final thoughts before she pushed through the bathroom door and into the lion's den.

~2~

When Tate walked into the ballroom, she was taken aback. She'd never been in the Gateway Garden room of the Crown Novel Hotel before. She'd never even been inside the Crown Novel Hotel. Next door was a boutique hotel where, a few weeks ago, she'd organized a luncheon for a company whose office was nearby. It had been a quaint room setup for twenty. Pale yellow place cards sat atop black napkins, and when Tate stood back, she couldn't help but be impressed. In that room across the street, she had felt empowered. Her visions were blossoming. Standing in the Gateway Garden, Tate felt as if she was starting over, like a seed amongst many hoping to be sowed. White and gray marble tile lay across the entire space. Gold columns surrounded her, climbing the walls all the way up to the same gold-colored iron arches that lined the roof.

Tate could feel the heat of the sun shining through the glass ceiling. She was happy to have had those moments alone. They had helped her to better understand the space and given her time to breathe and gather some sense of composure. The fact Ms. Donovan had not arrived yet didn't surprise Tate. As the head of some of London's most respected charitable foundations, Ms. Donovan had that luxury.

Tate had first met Ms. Donovan at an event she worked before starting Simple Charms Events. It was at the annual art gala at the Victoria & Albert Museum in South Kensington, one of the many fundraisers Ms. Donovan put on each year. She'd walked through the open archway in a strapless black dress with a ruched bodice, the soft tulle swinging with each step she took. It was half past the hour she should've arrived. Most people were fully engaged in conversation with others, but all of them seemed to hush as their eyes fixated on Ms. Donovan. It wasn't the gown that caught Tate's eye that night, however, but her confidence. Her chin had lifted, lips pursed, and her strides were long and purposeful.

Valerie, the owner of Rosewood Events, had introduced Tate to Ms. Donovan right before the night ended. When Tate shook her hand, her grip was firm, and she looked Tate straight in the eye. Tate had seen her many times since then. Ms. Donovan had even called Tate when she heard she left Rosewood. They'd had a friendly conversation, and Ms. Donovan had hired her for a few small dinner parties at her home. Those dinner parties had kept Tate afloat for the first few months she was on her own. She was sure Ms. Donovan knew because, once business started to pick up, she coincidentally didn't seem to need an event planner for home dinners anymore.

Tate walked over to one side of the room, sweeping her finger across the ribbed column. This space was perfect for the idea she had in mind for the event, the fifth annual Ball of Hope.

The Ball of Hope was an event that helped to raise money for in-hospital experiences for children with cancer. The funds helped to purchase art supplies, books, musical instruments, and more to help bring positive daily activity into children's lives during dark times. When Tate had first received the phone call informing her that she was in the running to plan such an honorable event, she was cooking dinner in her flat. Her knees had buckled, and she'd collapsed against the fridge. The chicken almost slid from her plate, and the sauce on the stove boiled over as she stood there in awe. Ms. Donovan was giving her, Tate Montgomery, a chance to present her ideas. Now, here she was, clinging tight to her tablet that held her vision for the entire night.

"Tate!" a voice called out.

Tate pulled her hand from one of the columns and spun around. She hadn't even heard anyone come in, but strutting through the double doors was Ms. Donovan in a black-and-white polka dot dress, her heels echoing throughout the empty room.

"Ms. Donovan, it's so great to see you again." Tate reached out her hand.

"Please, call me Delaney." She'd asked Tate to do that at least a dozen times by now. Her grip was still as firm as the first time Tate locked hands with her. "I'm so sorry I'm late. I was stuck in horrid traffic trying to get to my first meeting here with a colleague, and then it ran a little late." Her breaths were quick and heavy. Tate could tell by the way her lips pursed she was flustered.

"Oh, no problem," Tate said. She glanced down at the white tank top peeking out from under her coat. It wasn't always something she was grateful for, but that day, she welcomed the heavy London traffic. "This is for you." Tate reached out the coffee cup. "Half-caff, perfect pick-me-up for the gloomy weather today."

"Well, aren't you so sweet?"

"This room is amazing," Tate said. "It's the perfect backdrop for what I have in mind."

When Ms. Dono—Delaney first called to ask if Tate wanted to throw her hat in the ring for this event, she had two simple requests. She wanted the night to be an escape for her guests, one that would take them away from any of their troubles. Her second request was that she wanted the event to support the local arts in some way.

"Well then," Delaney said, "let's get to it, yeah?" She placed her half-caff on the ledge beside her and pulled out a notebook and pen from her oversize purse. She readjusted the thick black frames around her eyes and waited for Tate to begin.

"You said you wanted an escape, something that would take everyone far away for a night. So I was thinking, what is more magical, more sweep-you-off-your-feet, than...*A Starry Night in Paris?*" Tate fanned her hands out overhead and relished silently in the fact she had rolled her "r" perfectly. She'd been practicing all week, saying it just as the French would: *Pah-ree*. It made the whole event title so much more sophisticated than her American accent would.

Tate paused for reaction, but Delaney didn't give her any, so she continued on. "We'll have long tables lining both sides of the aisle. They'll all be draped with white linens. At the end of the aisle, we'll do an extensive photo backdrop of streetlamps over a café, with the Eiffel tower in the background and trees that replicate summer in Paris."

Delaney's gaze was focused solely on her notepad, her pen hastily marking the lines within it. The lack of expression on her face made Tate's palms sweat, but she tried to ignore it and push through.

Continuing with her thoughts, she spilled them out around the lump growing in her throat. "Each place setting will consist of a black charger under white china, and sitting atop will be solid-color French macarons stacked inside a black wire-frame birdcage. I think this will give a unique accent to the tables and a keepsake for each of your guests. String lights will hang above from beginning to end, illuminating the night sky."

Delaney stood scribbling in her notepad as Tate walked around the room pointing out all the ways she'd turn the Gateway Garden into the streets of Paris. Every now and then, Delaney would either nod or let out a "mhmm," but she'd never look up to find where in the room Tate was.

Once Tate was finished presenting the actual design of the night, she came to what she thought would be Delaney's favorite part. If the design didn't warrant any reaction from her, perhaps the use of local arts would.

"Over here in this corner…" Tate squeezed behind Delaney to the right of the entrance. "This is where we'll display local art for auction. All will be French-inspired pieces. I'm thinking paintings, sculptures, ceramics, metalwork, jewelry—art of all kinds. On top of that, guests will be serenaded for the evening with local classical musicians playing music from French composers."

From the corner of her eye, Tate saw Delaney give a nod. Her pen came to a halt before she looked up to see if Tate had anything left. She did. On her tablet, she had put together a vision board for Delaney to see. Slowly, she swiped through the black-and-white scheme of the night intertwined with pops of color, fabric swatches, and photo inspiration to help her envision what Tate saw.

"This is all very lovely, Tate," Delaney said. "Well done. The most important question, though: Can this all be put together on such short notice??"

It was only a week ago that Delaney Donovan had been ready to breathe a sigh of relief. The event was almost buttoned-up. She had hired what she called a "world-renowned" event planner six months ago to put this event together. The choice had thrown Tate for a loop when she heard that it wasn't Rosewood Events, whom Delaney had always used in the past; it was a company she had never heard of before.

Delaney was set to meet with the event planners last week, but they never showed. She made several calls out to them, but none were returned, and she came to find out the planners had filed for bankruptcy and left town, leaving many events in shambles. Delaney wouldn't say when she first called Tate on the phone why Rosewood wasn't on her radar. In fact, she purposely dodged the question. She did, however, emphasize that whoever took over would have only a few weeks to pull off the event of the year and would have to start at square one.

"I have no doubt," Tate answered. She knew the timeline was pushing it, but she had already made some calls prior to the meeting to vendors she knew, to make sure they were waiting in the wings if she so happened to nail this gig.

"Wonderful," Delaney said with a slight smile on her face. "As you know, I've reached out to a few other event companies. I have two other meetings this week, and I'll be making my final decision by Friday. Whoever I choose will need to work very quickly and very closely with our Executive Director of Donor Relations. They know our clients very well, and I want to make sure everything we do here is in their best interest."

"That sounds great," Tate said. "I appreciate the opportunity."

In their silence, she could hear a faint vibration coming from the pocket of Delaney's coat. She reached in and, after looking down, excused herself from the room.

"It was wonderful to see you again, Tate," Delaney said, walking toward the door. "We'll be in touch." She waved, grabbed her coffee from the ledge, and disappeared through the double wooden doors.

~3~

The very first time Tate stepped off the bus in Notting Hill, she had fallen in love. Her heart may have been in a million pieces that day, but as tears streamed down her face, she felt the immediate tug of her heartstrings. She had arrived in London only two days prior and spent both nights in a rented flat up in Camden, all of her things tightly packed into one room while she spent her days searching around for a permanent place to call home. Notting Hill was well-known for the explosion of colors and charming walk-ups that lined the picturesque neighborhood. Tate had only seen it in movies though. Experiencing it in person brought a sense of calm over her that had been lost to her for weeks. She knew right then that Notting Hill was where she would start her new beginning.

It was pure luck finding the flat on the second story of the house with a pink door. She'd walked into a small boutique on the main street and happened to overhear a conversation between two customers about the empty space. Tate had wiped her tears and input herself into the conversation, and, less than a week later, she was lugging what was left of her tattered heart up into her four-hundred-square-foot flat. Luckily, she didn't have much back then, but her tiny new home had accumulated a lot since, including the secondhand couch and coffee table a neighbor sold to her when they moved out. Her bed was new. She bought that once she was settled. Her favorite purchase, though, was the large plant she got for the tiny balcony off the living area. That had become her oasis.

It was where she stood taking in the breeze the following Monday after her meeting with Delaney. One hand rested on the black metal railing, while the other pressed her phone against her ear. Three whole days after Delaney had said she'd be making her decision, and Tate hadn't heard a word. She should've known she wouldn't actually be hearing from her on Friday; that woman had every hour of her days saturated with something. With all she did, and despite her lack of punctuality, Tate never understood how Delaney found time to sleep, yet she never had bags under her eyes.

Tate's thoughts floated off as the ringing in her ear began. She thought about Delaney's work ethic and how it was highly respected and demanded by many within her professional circle—but there wasn't much time to go too deep. The ringing stopped and was replaced by a voice on the other end of the line.

"Buongiorno!" It was never too early in Genevieve's day for such cheer.

Tate had not so patiently made it through the weekend, and with another full day possibly flying by without an answer, she needed coffee and a distraction. Thankfully, Genevieve could provide both.

"Well, hello to you too!" Tate said. "How do you feel about meeting me at Primrose May for our meeting today?"

"Oh, that sounds fantastic!" Genevieve sighed.

"Great. I'm going to hop in the shower. Meet you in an hour?" Tate said.

"Will do. Ciao!"

*

Thirty minutes later, Tate was strolling down Portobello Rd. The bellow of voices from the crowd was engulfed by the music playing through her headphones. The walk to the Tube was only about five minutes, and she smiled when her watch let her know she had time to do a little browsing. Tate had always loved to check out what people were selling at Portobello Market; she was all about filling her home with unique treasures. Most of the trinkets in her apartment were found on these very tables.

"Good morning." Tate smiled at the woman sitting in front of her. She had stopped at a table of homemade jewelry when a yellow pair of dangly, floral earrings caught her eye. "How much?"

"Twelve pounds," the woman said.

Tate pulled a handful of coins from the pocket of her purse and counted them out into the woman's hand. The woman pulled the earrings from the table and slid them into a small paper bag. Tate was always guilty of buying things before she knew what she needed them for. She took the paper bag and slid it into her purse. Someday, she would need a pair of yellow earrings, and when she did, she'd be grateful she swiped these from the market.

Tate took the Tube over to Westminster this time. It was slightly faster than the bus and it would help make up the time she spent on her impromptu shopping trip. Genevieve was waiting outside of Primrose May, oblivious to Tate coming up the street. She was holding her phone out in front of her, trying to find the perfect light for a photo. Tate slowed her pace to observe Genevieve. Her free hand held tight to the brim of her off-white fedora. It perfectly matched the belt that secured her coral sweater dress in place. Tate had always admired Genevieve's sense of style. It drew hundreds of thousands of followers on Instagram, which was why she spent most days looking at her cell phone.

Tate stared down at the outfit she'd put together that morning. She was wearing one of only three pairs of jeans she owned, an oversize sweater tucked loosely into the waistline. Until she saw Genevieve, she was feeling quite confident in her choice. Tate looked at her reflection through the window of the coffee shop and fumbled with her hair until Genevieve finally noticed her.

"Tate!" She ran up and wrapped her arms around her as she air-kissed one cheek and then the other. "How are you? How was the meeting? Why has it been so long since I last saw you?"

Tate laughed as she pulled open the door to the place they met at every Monday. It had only been four days since she met Genevieve for yoga. A few days before that, they were right here for their weekly planning meeting.

Genevieve had a point though: the two of them were in divide and conquer mode with events, making the time they spent together less and less. Genevieve had pulled off a Sunday breakfast event the morning before, while Tate was busy biting her nails in anticipation of Delaney's phone call.

"The meeting went well, yeah?" Genevieve asked. The two of them walked single file through the door.

"I felt pretty good about it," Tate started.

"Oh, thank goodness. When I didn't hear from you, I was terrified you were mulling in self-pity."

Tate laughed. "No, no. No mulling here. I feel really good about the meeting, but you aren't going to believe what happened right before I went in."

Genevieve immediately thrust herself closer to Tate, but she would have to wait. They were next in line.

"Hey, Anya! How are you?" Tate raised her voice.

"I'm doing well, Tate. Good to see you!" Anya was a petite brunette who had worked at Primrose May since before Tate decided to set up shop there. She'd learned a lot about Anya since then. She was working her way through university, and only one more year separated her from a degree in tourism. Anya loved working at Primrose May. With a lot of tourists making their way in after a play at Victoria Palace Theatre or a tour of Westminster Abbey, she learned a lot about what people wanted to do in new cities and what they needed when it came to helpful information before visiting. She credited the coffee shop for her good grades, but Tate was fairly sure it was Anya's hard work and intellect that really paid off.

"One Americano and a caramel latte, no whip, yeah?" Anya asked.

"You got it!" Tate confirmed.

Tate handed over her credit card to pay for both. She'd write it off later.

"Take a seat. I'll have someone bring it over to you."

Tate thanked Anya and booked it to an open table in the corner. She slid into the cushioned seat against the wall, and Genevieve settled into the white chair on the other side. Tate's bag hadn't even hit the spot next to her before Genevieve was begging to hear the story.

"What happened before the meeting?" Her eyes widened as she leaned in as close as she could to the table.

"I was about to walk into the hotel," Tate began, "and this guy barged out through the door and right into me! Coffee went everywhere, including on me."

"Oh, Tate." Genevieve set a sympathetic hand on top of Tate's. "What a jerk!"

"Haha, yeah! I made him feel horrible, but now I kind of feel horrible." She paused to take her cup of coffee from the waitress and started again. "I took my stress out on the poor guy. I mean, I really let him have it."

Genevieve's sympathy turned into amusement, and soon, the two of them were laughing in between sips from their mugs. There were a few times throughout the weekend Tate had relived that moment. She noticed only after the fact how apologetic he'd looked and wished she had been nicer. Accidents happened. It wasn't as if he'd deliberately pushed the door into her. At least, she hoped not.

"Then he asked for my number!" Tate laughed.

"He, what? He hit on you?"

"Technically, he wanted to take my blouse to the dry cleaner."

"Oh, a gentleman. I'm impressed. Was he cute?" Genevieve always said manners trumped allure, but if you could find both, then you won the jackpot.

"I mean…if we were in any other type of situation, I probably would've done a double take. So, yeah, I would say he was good-looking."

Both of their laughs grew louder, to the point they turned a couple of heads in the coffee shop. That didn't stop them though. Every time Tate heaved to try to catch her breath, the sound of Genevieve's laugh made hers even louder. Looking back now, Tate thought the whole debacle seemed hilarious. The coffee flying, the cup rolling on the ground, and her having to show up in an oversize coat instead of her silk white blouse. One of the good things about having to wait for Delaney's phone call was that Tate had time to drop off and pick up the blouse from the cleaners'. The stain had come out, and it was now hanging in the closet ready for another day.

Once the two of them were able to gain their composure, Tate switched to boss mode and pulled out a notebook and planner. "How'd the breakfast go yesterday?"

"It was great! The personalized jam was a hit. They wanted to see what our Sundays looked like in August for another one." Genevieve patted herself on the back. This was the third breakfast Simple Charms had planned for the same company, and Genevieve had run them all.

"Awesome!" Tate flipped open the calendar to August. "We have the second and the last Sundays open. If you want to see what works best for them, then let me know. I can pencil them in."

Genevieve nodded and made notes in her own planner. There were two new events for the fall Tate had received initial deposits for while preparing for her meeting with Delaney. She went over those with Genevieve.

"Do you want to work the Hollister wedding with me, and then I'll reach out to the university for the following weekend?" Tate asked. Genevieve had never passed up an event Tate put in front of her, but she also knew Genevieve's social media influencer role was a full-time job. Tate didn't know how much time it took to run a blog and stay relevant in the digital space until she met Genevieve. There were no weekends in her world; she worked all seven days.

"I can work both. Since we're planning October out,"—Genevieve reached her pen across the table and placed it in one of the squares of Tate's planner—"I'll be out of the country this weekend. I'm meeting my friend Maddie in Cinque Terre."

"I'll cross this whole weekend off then. I'll stuff myself into your suitcase." Tate's eyes brightened as a cackle slipped through Genevieve's lips. "Genevieve OOC," Tate wrote in the boxes for Friday, Saturday, and Sunday of that week. Since starting Simple Charms Events, Tate had learned the magic of color coding and abbreviations. "Out of the country" was too much to fit; "OOC" would have to do.

By the time both Tate and Genevieve's glasses were empty, they had gone through everything on the work checklist and were ready for the week ahead.

Tate appreciated those couple of hours she was with Genevieve at the coffee shop. It had erased from her mind the fact that she was waiting on the fate of her career to be decided by a phone call.

It was barely eleven when she arrived back to her flat, and by then, she expected another day to go by with no word from Delaney. She set her phone on the kitchen countertop and reached into the fridge for the pitcher of water. She was gulping down the last drops from her glass when the phone rang. Tate's heart began to race as she sprinted to it. She was wrong: it wasn't going to be a whole day. Delaney's name was flashing across the screen in big white letters. This was it! Tate snatched the phone off the table and took one big breath before answering.

"Simple Charms Events, this is Tate." She never answered the phone that way, but today, she found it necessary.

"Hello Tate, this is Delaney Donovan."

"Delaney!" Tate acted surprised, as if she hadn't been counting down the hours to this very phone call. "How are you?"

"I'm doing well, thank you. Listen, do you have a minute to chat?"

"For you, Delaney, of course!"

"Wonderful! I wanted to let you know that I shared all ideas with the board last week, and they loved yours. We're very excited to work with you if you're still willing?"

Me! They picked me! Tate celebrated internally. She shook her fist in the air and opened her mouth in a silent scream. Simple Charms Events was officially in the event planning game! Tate did a few more fist pumps before calming herself down to answer.

"I would be honored to be a part of such a great cause. Thank you so much."

"Oh, how lovely," Delaney answered. "Are you free tomorrow? Around...let's say, half past two in the afternoon?"

Tate ran quickly to the coffee table in her living room to flip through her planner. She had an appointment for an eyebrow wax at eleven, and dinner plans with Genevieve at six, but her afternoon was wide open. To be honest, she would have cleared it even if it wasn't. Tate took the pen lying on her coffee table and, in big bold letters, wrote "PM WITH DELANEY" right in the box with tomorrow's date. "PM" meant "planning meeting." That was a staple abbreviation in Tate's book.

"Yes, it looks like I have two-thirty open tomorrow afternoon."

"Wonderful! We'll meet at the office, and you can meet Mr. Walker, our executive director. It's right up the street from the Crown Novel, only two blocks. See you then. Cheerio!"

Suddenly, it was silent, which finally gave Tate permission to celebrate. "Ahhhhhhh!" she screeched as she began to jump up and down on the shaggy gray area rug that covered her tiny living space. She then threw herself back onto the white cushions of her couch and gave a few swift kicks with her heels.

I did it, Tate thought. She had secured her first official "big girl" event. To think, when she originally came over to Europe, she had no idea what she was going to do! She'd left her job, her home, and her family to follow her happily ever after. Then, when that all fell apart, she'd thrown a dart at a map—literally—to figure out where to go next. Tate didn't want to go home; she thought that would mean admitting defeat. She wanted a new beginning, and two years after working late nights and long hours for somebody else, she finally felt as if her life was heading in the right direction.

Here she was, living in London, starting her own business, and answering the phone like she was someone important. Well, today, she was. Today, Tate Montgomery was the official event planner for one of Delaney Donovan's largest charity events of the year. An event she would have to pull together in only a few short weeks. That meant she needed to get started on all the details, and she certainly would. Right now, though, she was going to revel in the bliss of her big win for the remainder of the day—even if that meant acting like a five-year-old in the middle of a temper tantrum. She screamed again and thrashed her limbs across the surface of that poor white couch.

~4~

When Tuesday morning came around, Tate set her alarm for much earlier than she did the day of her first meeting with Delaney. She'd needed those extra eighteen minutes that morning even though there was no second-guessing her outfit. She slid on a pair of dark gray high-waisted pants and let the waves of her brown hair fall over the white blouse she didn't get to show off at her first meeting.

Instead of marching through the crowded streets in heels, this time, Tate opted for comfort and a little flare. She always loved the neutral-toned events she planned. Here and there, she'd throw in a pop of color just like she was today with a pair of forest green flats. She always said it was that little bit of color that brought everything together and made people say "wow"!

Tate caught the bus to Westminster and arrived at Primrose May with plenty of time to go through her binder. Even though she already had the job, she still felt the need to impress Mr. Walker. She wanted to assure him Delaney had made the right choice. Not that anyone doubted her decisions, but Tate still felt as if she had something to prove even if, maybe, deep down, it was more for herself than anyone else.

Anya was working again that morning. As usual, she told Tate to take a table and they'd bring her order over to her. Tate slid into the same cushioned seat she had the last time she was here with Genevieve. She flipped through a few pages in her binder before her coffee arrived. After a few sips and a little people-watching, she turned over a few more.

Ten minutes later, Tate's eyes were burning. She rubbed her fingers over them and glanced toward the front door just as the bell rang to motion a new customer. At first, it was only the suit she noticed: a charcoal gray. Behind the suit, a cold breeze followed, and she suddenly felt the thinness of the material covering arms. Goosebumps rose, as did her eyes as she traced his manly physique. It only took half a breath before she recognized him. Staring toward the front counter were the same pale blue eyes that had looked into hers only days before—the ones that had apologetically offered to help fix the mess he'd made with a spilled cup of coffee.

Tate quickly glanced back at her binder, but the double take she didn't steal only days before, she took now, hoping he wouldn't notice her stare. His eyes were like magnets; she couldn't pull hers away. She observed his stance. His well-fitted suit was neatly ironed, his hands folded in front of him, and Tate liked the way a faint smile rested on his face. She knew when they collided that his features left nothing to be desired, but looking at him now, as he stood across the room, she couldn't help but notice his poise. He stepped so effortlessly over to the counter, and Anya's face lit up as he greeted her.

Tate felt Anya had to be a good judge of character. The way her lips curled and her eyes brightened as she started to talk gave Tate even more reason to feel bad about the way she had scolded the man.

With the bustle of conversation around her, Tate couldn't hear his order, but she recognized the deepness of his voice. He didn't have an accent, she remembered now, as she captured bits and pieces of the conversation. For a second, her weakness for the familiar sound of home took over, and she leaned against the table to draw herself closer, examining the trail of darkness that lined his chin and surrounded his lips as he laughed. She assumed it would feel like sandpaper if he rubbed it against another's cheek. Tate continued to watch as her fingertips stroked her jawline. When they reached the bottom of her chin, she suddenly realized where her mind had gone. *He is so damn sexy.* Thoughts like that flooded her mind as she stared intently at the stranger in front of the counter.

Tate watched as he handed over a note to pay for his order. He strummed his hands on the countertop while Anya counted out his change, and Tate was finally able to rip her glance away from him when she noticed his head turning in her direction.

"Stop it, Tate," she whispered sharply, yanking her hair across her temple and skimming her finger across the words she'd already read. She was too afraid to look up again, but the strands of hair covering her face let her eyes peek through enough to see his movement.

The guy waved at Anya before stepping to the other side of the counter, further from the table where she was sitting. Tate let out a heavy breath. She was in the clear. There was no way he'd see her now, through the stacks of cups and espresso machines lined up in front of him. She reached over and pressed her lips against the warmth of her coffee mug for another taste.

The racing of her heart was evident through her pulsating fingertips as they pressed against her forehead. She tried to quiet the beating with slow breaths, but as the *thump, thump, thump* grew louder, she realized the sound she was hearing wasn't her own heartbeat. A shadow covered the table where she sat. It was followed by a voice from above.

"Hi."

The voice was deep. Tate lifted her head in the direction of the person standing beside the table. Slowly, she slid her fingers to rest on her chin. Her eyes followed the tip of his tie all the way up to the smile on his face.

"Hello," she said. She wrapped her free hand over the top of her mug.

"I don't blame you," he said. "I'd protect it too." She stared blankly into his eyes. "We met last week, right? Outside the hotel?"

Tate waited a minute before she gave a response. She didn't want to give away the fact that, clearly, he had made a lasting impression.

"Oh, right," she said. "Bumped into each other is more like it."

Her eyes wandered. The tight fit of his gray jacket around his biceps pulled her away from the words coming from his mouth. This time, a mint green tie hid underneath the double buttons. It looked good on him. Tate wasn't sure if it was the color or the way it fell against his muscular chest that was forcing her to no longer be a part of the conversation, but, thankfully, his hands readjusting on his to-go cup brought her back to the present.

"Anyway, I am really sorry about that," he said. "I'm glad to see the stain came out though." He pointed down at Tate's blouse. She followed his gaze and then rolled her eyes in embarrassment but quickly shook it off. She liked that he was intuitive. She'd never known a guy to remember what she was wearing the day before, let alone almost a week ago.

"You're forgiven." She smiled. "The stain came out, I wasn't late to my meeting, and everything else worked itself out." Tate gritted her teeth. She knew what she needed to say next. "I'm really sorry for snapping at you. It was a stressful morning." She paused for a moment, watching his blank expression. He didn't seem to be paying attention. That was what she got for trying to be nice? She continued anyway. "Although, you are still making me slightly nervous standing so close to me with that coffee."

He had a dimple on only one side of his mouth. Tate saw it appear when he started to laugh. The cup in his hand shook slightly as he chuckled. Once he noticed, he drew it back.

"Maybe sometime, we'll meet under circumstances that don't involve coffee," he said. His face stiffened. He was waiting for a sign that might allow him to throw out an invitation.

"Maybe," Tate said.

She leaned back against the wall. A part of her—a very small part of her—wished she had given him some inclination she *might* be interested. But the part of her that was intrigued and somewhat optimistic about the tall figure standing in front of her was overshadowed by the broken parts that still remembered how she'd stood in an empty apartment watching the person she thought was the love of her life walk out the front door. Tate would never forget the sound of that front door closing. He'd never even looked back.

"Well, it was nice to see you again…" He paused, waiting for a name to finish his sentence. Tate obliged.

"Tate." She reached out her hand for his.

"Tate," he repeated. "It's really nice to see you again. I'm Leo."

"Nice to meet you, Leo."

Tate let the firmness of his grasp hold onto her for longer than she normally would. By now, she'd usually have pulled back and begun a conversation, but not with Leo. She didn't need to speak a word to get to know him; she only needed him to hold onto her a bit longer. His handshake was strong. The look in his eyes showed kindness, and she could tell by the way his shoulders pulled him upright that he was confident, determined, and successful. Her ex was only one of those things. He was successful, but he lacked confidence, and the only thing he had been determined about was letting Tate go. Leo seemed to be everything a girl would look for in a guy, but, at the same time, he seemed to be everything she needed to run from.

~5~

Brooks Walker almost didn't go to Primrose May that morning. His parents were settling into a new home in Wales, and he had driven there for a long weekend to help them fix up the place. There was a lot to catch up on as the week started, and he was already running behind. He told himself he would skip today, but even with the endless emails he knew would be welcoming him back to work that morning, Brooks was never able to talk himself out of a good cup of coffee. He had been a regular at Primrose May for three years now.

Three whole years it had been since he started working in the high-rise down the street. It was a career change, but it was a choice he hadn't regretted for a second. Not to say he didn't love working in IT, but working from home had him longing for more human interaction. He also liked the fact this new job had a small hand in the greater good.

Don't do it, Brooks, he thought. At least he could say he'd tried. Then he wouldn't feel so bad about the fact he failed miserably as he pulled open the door to Primrose May.

The door hadn't even fully closed behind him when the barista recognized him. A giant smile crossed her face, and she waved frantically from behind the counter. He waved back. While he waited for the line of people to fade in front of him, he looked around the crowded coffee shop. There was a woman scrambling to get the right amount of cream into her coffee cup as she juggled a fidgeting baby in her arms. Next was a group of guys in casual attire undoubtedly getting their caffeine intake before their workday began. Then...there was *her*. He had to do a double take to make sure, but even with her hair down, Brooks recognized her. He'd be lying if he said he hadn't thought about her a time or two since their last run-in and wondered if she had forgiven him yet for wasting a perfectly good cup of coffee.

"Well, hello there, stranger!"

He smiled at the young girl behind the counter who already had his order in the register. Brooks was a simple man. In other aspects of his life, he enjoyed adventure and diversity, but not with his coffee. A medium flat white—that was all he ever needed to get him through the day. He ruffled through his wallet and pulled out a ten-pound note.

"Good morning, Anya. How's your day going so far?" he asked.

Brooks liked Anya. Primrose May was her first job when she moved to London for university. She told him that when he had met her on the day she started. It had to have been more than two years ago now. She was quiet and reserved then—he could tell by the nervous shake of her voice—but not anymore. These days, Brooks would come in and strike up a conversation, and Anya would politely participate. She never forgot his order, and sometimes she, along with a couple of other baristas, would slip him a large at no extra cost.

"It's been great!" Anya took the note and counted out the change from her drawer. While Brooks waited, his eyes wandered around the room, stopping to observe the woman in the corner booth. He tilted his head to get a better look.

"Here you go." Anya placed the change in Brooks' hand. "Your usual will be right up. Have a great day, Mr. Walker."

"You too, Anya," Brooks said.

He stole another glance over to the corner booth before sliding out of the way to wait for his drink. He couldn't see her from where he was standing, but she was vivid enough in his mind. She was dressed a bit more casual this time, her hair draped over her shoulder instead of pulled back from her face, but he knew it was her. Even through the chaos of spilled coffee, he remembered. He took a few steps away from the counter to get a clear look at her between Anya and the stack of coffee cups.

Her sandy brown hair was brushed across her face, one leg crossed over the other bouncing to the beat of the easy listening music that played through the speakers. It wasn't often a girl got under his skin, especially one he didn't know well—or at all, for that matter. Brooks' mom was always hounding him about bringing a good girl home, but he had yet to find one who offered any real substance. This girl, though...there was something about her that drew him in. Their encounter had been brief, but her cheeky responses amused him. He was attracted to her self-assured attitude at the hotel, but the more he stared at her in that coffee shop, he couldn't help but notice the way her pants hugged her minimal curves and the thinness of her lips as they wrapped around the tip of her mug. Yes, she was stunningly good-looking, but he already knew there was more to it than that, and the attraction was strong enough to pull him in her direction and make him do something he wouldn't normally do.

He grabbed his coffee from the counter and slipped the cup into a sleeve to shield his hand from the heat. Normally, he'd then walk out the door, but instead, he found himself heading in her direction. *What's the worst that could happen, right?* he asked himself as he stepped up to her table. He cleared his throat, hoping something a little more clever would come out, but all he could seem to muster was a "hi".

"Hello," she said.

He waited to see if she'd say anything else while he frantically thought of words to continue the conversation. What was wrong with him? This wasn't like him. He never had trouble talking to women. *Say something,* he urged as she looked up at him. He watched her hand slip over the top of her clear glass mug to hide what was left inside. That made him smile. She remembered him.

"I don't blame you," he finally said. "I'd protect it too."

She was staring at him blankly, but Brooks could see the nervousness in the way her eyes wandered in all directions. He decided to play along, though, and pretended to believe she couldn't quite put her finger on where she knew him from.

"We met last week, right? Outside the hotel?" Brooks asked.

That must have helped to jog her memory because she clapped back at him with a sarcastic remark, answering with the same type of spark she did when he'd offered to clean her blouse. He was appeased by her strength and independent manner. He liked her tough personality and her no-fear attitude. He was also happy to see the coffee stain had come out. He remembered the ruffles around her collar that day—the same ones covering her now. He apologized again for spilling the coffee, and this time, she seemed to accept it.

"You're forgiven." She smiled.

Her lips kept moving, but Brooks wasn't quite sure what else she was saying. He was too captivated by the way the outer parts of her eyes crinkled when her lips curled up into that smile. He watched her sweep her shiny hair back, away from her face, and tuck it tightly behind her ear. Even that was sexy. It was all he kept thinking about until her lips stopped moving. When she tilted her head, Brooks came down from cloud nine.

"Although, you are still making me slightly nervous being so close to me with that coffee," she said.

She was sassy. She was challenging him. God, he liked that. Brooks glanced over at the clock on the wall. He had to go but wasn't ready to leave. He wanted to see her again. He offered an invitation, but she didn't bite. She gave him a sly answer, a single word: *Maybe*. Desperation wasn't his thing, and he didn't want to come across that way, so, instead, he waited for her name and hoped she would at least offer up that.

"Well, it was nice to see you again…" He paused, waiting for a name to finish his sentence. Thankfully, she gave in.

"Tate." She reached out her hand for his.

"Tate," he repeated. He liked that name. Not that he knew anyone else with it, but it seemed to fit her well. It was short and to the point…memorable. He wouldn't forget it, and he hoped he could use it again. Brooks introduced himself. "I'm Leo."

Leo always sounded better than Brooks. In school, when the teacher took roll call on the first day, they'd call out Brooks Walker, and he'd raise his hand and politely ask to be called Leo. Brooks was his mother's maiden name. It fit well for their firstborn, but only at work did he ever use it. Leo sounded so much more laid-back. It worked well with him having been born in California, and since it was technically his middle name, he had the right to use it.

"Nice to meet you, Leo."

He liked the way his name rolled off her tongue. This go-around, Brooks felt he had made a better impression, but as he walked out of the coffee shop, his shoulders still sank. His second chance had come and gone, and still, he'd left only knowing her first name. You couldn't even successfully search for someone on social media with just a first name. He was still hopeful, though, as he walked the two blocks into the lobby of his office building. Twice, he had seen her with a Primrose May coffee cup. With how frequently he went there, he was confident he'd see her again.

Next time... he thought. *Next time I see her, I'll be bolder than I was today.* He would be bold enough to ask her out, to get her number, and, who knows, maybe she'd be the girl to turn him into the guy his mom wanted him to be. She was already starting to change him.

~6~

Leo was nothing like Cameron. Not from the outside anyway. With heels on, Tate was the same height as Cameron. From the way Leo had stood in front of her table, she didn't think she'd even come up to his broad shoulders in her highest pair of stilettos. Leo wore his hair neatly cropped, which was the opposite of Cameron's artful mess of brown curls. The feeling in the pit of her stomach as she watched Leo walk out of the coffee shop—it was the same kind she felt the night she first met Cameron at a bar in her hometown. *Cameron.* She hadn't said that name out loud in months. Though, from time to time, it still clouded her thoughts. She'd pass a car that looked like his or hear a song he used to play from their home office while he was working late, and she'd wonder if that song was playing where he was too

—wherever that was. In the two years since she last saw him, she wondered how far he'd ventured from the flat in central Paris they once shared together. Cameron was the reason Tate had ended up in London. He was the reason she was brave enough to pack up over twenty years of memories in Seattle and unpack them five thousand miles away. Tate's friends had loved Cameron, but before she left, they'd asked her if she was sure. They wanted her to be very sure she was ready to close the only chapter of her life she had known for a guy who had yet to put a ring on her finger after five years together. Tate had never second-guessed her decision to follow Cameron to Paris. She didn't need a ring to know life with him was what made sense to her. If his job was going to take him to Europe, then he was going to take her with him. Tate had boarded that plane with no regrets, no uncertainties, and certainly no idea that Cameron's future didn't involve her.

That quick heartbeat and those goosebumps were still lingering as Tate sat at the table with her hands around her coffee mug. She couldn't admit it while he was standing in front of her, but she admired Leo's boldness and his ability to poke fun at himself. It was for those reasons Tate's pulse was still racing even though Leo had left more than twenty minutes ago. She'd probably need at least twenty more to pull herself together. She needed to lose the mind of a girl gushing over a stranger and find, once again, the successful CEO of Simple Charms Events.

It was Tate's turn now to glance at the clock on the wall. She'd have to forget about those twenty minutes; it was time. Her hands whipped the binder closed and tucked it back into her bag. She steadied herself in her seat as her pulse fell slowly back to normal. Delaney's office wasn't far from Primrose May. Tate downed the final drop of coffee from the ceramic mug and ran her fingers through her hair. With her bag hanging heavy on her shoulder, she pushed herself out of her seat, ironed out her blouse with her palms, and headed out the door.

The office was even closer than Tate expected. Two blocks later, and she was spinning in the turnstile to enter the building. A young man with glasses sat at the front desk with a stony expression on his face—which didn't change as she greeted him.

"I have a meeting with Ms. Donovan," Tate said.

"Sign here." He pointed to a lined sheet of paper in front of her, then handed over a badge. "Take the elevator on the left to the fifth floor. Have a seat in the lobby. I'll let her know you're here."

"Thanks," Tate said. She pinned the badge to her shirt while walking to the elevator.

The orange glow of the button on the wall disappeared, and soon the elevator doors opened to welcome her inside. An older man with gray hair and a receding hairline was already propped up against the side wall. He looked over at her.

"Fifth floor, please," she said.

He pulled his hand away without touching a button. It was already lit. Tate smiled and leaned against the wall. She stared at the back of the man's head wondering if he might be Mr. Walker. It seemed like a fitting name for someone of his stature. Trying not to make it obvious, Tate switched to fixate her eyes on the gold tiles that filled the ceiling. The elevator stopped at the second floor, and someone else joined. This time, it was a woman. Tate watched as she pressed the number three. *She couldn't walk up one floor?* Tate thought. She probably wouldn't have either—she just hated the anticipation.

The doors opened again, and the woman stepped off onto the third floor. Once she disappeared, Tate and the gray-haired man were left alone again, and this time, the doors didn't open until they arrived on the fifth floor.

"After you." The man waved his hand.

"Thank you. Have a nice day." Tate waved over her shoulder.

"You as well."

Classical music filled the fifth-floor lobby. Another young woman sat with her legs crossed on a cozy gray chair. She was flipping through a magazine when Tate excused herself to pass by and sit on the love seat on the opposite side of her. She too thought about reaching for a magazine but wasn't sure there was enough time to read about the latest royal gossip. So, instead she strummed her fingers across her thighs to the beat of the music.

A few minutes later, Delaney came around the corner.

"Hi, Tate. Great to see you again." She reached out her hand, and Tate shook it firmly before Delaney led her down the hallway.

They were headed in the same direction as the gray-haired man. Tate was certain now, that was who she'd be meeting.

"Mr. Walker is looking forward to meeting you. I filled him in on our conversation, and he loves your whole idea and can't wait to hear more."

"Oh, good! I am really looking forward to working with him."

"We're going to be right in here."

Delaney turned the knob on the wooden door in front of her and gestured for Tate to enter first. When she stepped inside, she saw someone standing on the other side of a long table. Tate eyed his hands as he quickly readjusted his suit jacket.

"Tate, this is Brooks Walker, our executive director," Delaney said.

Tate should've known when he readjusted his jacket. It was charcoal over a mint green tie. It didn't hit her, though, until she looked up and reached her hand out to meet his. The lump in her throat prevented Tate from saying anything as she stared in his direction.

"It's a pleasure to meet you," Brooks said.

This is not happening, Tate thought as she looked at him smiling at her the way he was. He wrapped his fingers around hers as if thirty minutes earlier he hadn't done the same thing. Why would he lie to her? If he had known who she was, why didn't he tell her? It would've eliminated the awkward silence that now filled the room.

"Yes, Brooks," Tate repeated, "same here."

She wasn't sure if she should be humiliated or furious with him. He had to have known then, standing over her, who she was—Tate was sure of it. Delaney said she had told him all about her; there was no way he couldn't have known. Tate's face was on fire as she slid her hand out of his, but there was nothing she could do except let her body conform to the seat and remember Brooks Walker was the executive director. He was a big deal, and she had to play nice. She refused to take her eyes off him. They burrowed into his while she sat there with her hands folded and her lips pursed, waiting for him to speak.

"So..." He paused and drew a hand to his mouth as he softly cleared his throat. "Delaney has told me a lot about your ideas for the Ball of Hope. I thought it would be good if you and I sat down together to start to organize it all and make sure we're projecting the intended goal."

"Absolutely." Tate leaned closer to the table. "We definitely want to make sure this event is an *honest* representation and that it portrays the *full truth* of the organization." Tate made sure to emphasize all the appropriate words. It was clear she was leaning more toward the furious side.

Brooks cleared his throat again. Silence fell upon the room as he shifted position in his chair.

"I agree," he finally spoke.

"Wonderful." Delaney rose from her seat. "It seems like the two of you already have this under control." She took a quick glance at her watch. "I have another meeting I must attend, but I think you both will make a great team. We'll revisit your progress next week to see where you are and go from there."

"That sounds great," Tate said.

"Great! Well, you two feel free to sit and chat as long as you need. Buh-bye."

Both Tate and Brooks turned toward the door to watch as Delaney walked out. Once her heels had faded down the hall and Delaney had successfully retreated to her next meeting, Tate whirled around and swiftly slumped back into her chair. Her fingers clasped tightly together in front of her, and she leaned into them.

"Well…Brooks," she said. "Where would you like to begin?"

His eyes widened and Tate secretly enjoyed the way he nervously swept his hand across his forehead. She was referring to the details of the event. She was going to remain professional and start going over the logistics, but it was obvious Brooks wanted to clear things up. He could probably see the fire roaring in Tate's brown eyes and needed to put it out.

"You know, my friends…" He pushed his hands against the table and slid out from his chair. "My friends call me Leo. Pretty much everyone calls me Leo outside of work." He walked around the far side of the table and pulled out the chair next to her. "It's short for Leonardo. That's my middle name."

"Leonardo? As in, da Vinci?" Tate asked.

"Padalecki," Brooks said. "Mom was a big fan."

"Leonardo Padalecki? Like, the big Hollywood A-list actor?"

Brooks nodded. Tate's eyes wandered the full length of his stature. She tried to hide her judgement by covering her mouth with the palm of her hand, but her wide eyes gave it away.

"What's so funny?" he asked.

"Oh, nothing," she said. "I just don't see it." She was lying. He stood motionless as she observed his high cheekbones coming together like a crescent moon. The blueness of his eyes exuded the same transparency as a rolling creek. His smile was soft, yet, when it appeared, it radiated a sense of joy. These were all things an A-list actor was known for, but Tate was careful. She claimed to be oblivious as she shrugged and waved her hand over the chair next to her. He laughed, accepting the invitation, and then came around to the front of the chair and lowered himself into it.

For a moment, she let herself slip into Tate Montgomery, the girl in the coffee shop with her snarky remarks, but quickly reverted to CEO. "Did you know?" She looked up at him. "In the coffee shop—did you know who I was?"

Tate watched his hand slowly move toward her knee, but he jerked it back just as it grazed her skin.

"I didn't know," he said. "All of this happened so fast, I was out of the loop until this morning. I had a feeling once Delaney filled me in, though, that it may be you walking through that door."

"And now you know?" she asked.

"Now that I know...I'm not disappointed."

The heat of that "disappointed" was suddenly flush against her cheek as she leaned into her hand. Though the temperature was climbing, her body shivered. Tate turned away from him and adjusted the ruffled collar of her shirt.

"This job is really important to me," she said. Her eyes were still fixed on the papers secured inside her binder.

"I know," Brooks said. He rolled his chair closer. "It's important to me too."

"Good," Tate said. "Now we've got that out of the way, we have a lot to do, and only a few weeks to do it. We have to be professional. Not that we would be...anything other than that. I just don't want to mess this up."

Brooks watched as Tate squirmed in her chair. He liked that he had such an effect on her, but he had to admit, as happy as he was to have found her again, working with her meant pushing his attraction deep down. He could see the determination in her eyes. It roared like a campfire. He knew he would be tempted, he already was, but he was going to hold back. He watched Tate flip through the pages in her binder.

Out of the corner of her eye, Tate saw his hand reaching out. She stopped mid-breath and pushed the palms of her hands harder against the table. His hand came closer, and right before he could rest it on top of hers, she pulled her hands into her lap. Brooks' fingertips didn't stop until they rested on the middle clip inside the binder. He pulled it toward him, and Tate exhaled deeply, hoping he hadn't noticed. She could tell by the way his outer lips curled up that all hope was lost though. He had seen her.

"Professional." He stopped the binder in front of him. "Got it."

Tate watched him continue to smirk as he began flipping through the pages. He'd slide his finger over the top of each photo before turning to the next. She studied his eyes, but they gave nothing away. Sometimes, he would nod, but he didn't say a thing until he came to the last page.

"This really is great stuff, Tate." He slid the binder back to her. "I think our clients are going to love it. In fact, I have a dinner with some of them Thursday night. You should come. It'd be great for you to meet them and learn a little more about the charity."

"Dinner?" Tate said, shrinking back into her seat. She reached down into her bag and gripped her floral-patterned planner. Slapping it down on the table, she flipped it open onto the following day. That Thursday morning, she was meeting with a floral designer for the backyard wedding she was planning for July. After that, her calendar was clear. She needed a manicure, but that could wait for another day.

Tate knew Brooks or Leo—*Oh, gosh, what do I call him now?*—whatever his name was, he was right. She should go and get to know those who would be involved. If anything, it would be a good networking opportunity. If *A*

Starry Night in Paris impressed them all and they were ever in need of an event planner, this would hopefully make Tate their go-to girl.

Stalling no further, Tate agreed. "I can do dinner," she said. "One question though."

"What's that?" Brooks asked.

"What in the heck am I supposed to call you?"

He laughed. "I guess that's up to you, but, for all intents and purposes, Brooks is fine. Let's not confuse any more people."

In the midst of being professional, Tate decided he was right. Leo wasn't going to cut it. They couldn't be the two people inside that coffee shop; Tate needed to come across as serious and established. She needed this. All of her focus had to be on putting on the best charitable function Delaney Donovan had ever seen.

"Okay then, Brooks," Tate said, pulling the cap off her pen. "When and where do you need me?"

"The Lanesborough. Seven o'clock sharp." Brooks' finger tapped the appropriate line in her planner.

"Seven o'clock it is," Tate said. She reached out her hand, and Brooks grabbed it firmly. This time, though, Tate was able to pull herself away quickly. She couldn't afford any distractions. None that came with the name Brooks, anyway. This event needed all of her creative energy and focus.

Yet, at that moment, the only thing she could focus on was the curve of those lips and the stubble around his jaw. She was in so much trouble.

~7~

Tate's fingers pressed heavily against the back of her gold hoop earring. It was the final touch to tonight's dinner outfit. Music played through her flat as she did one final twirl in front of the bathroom mirror, making sure every button was fastened along the back of her gray dress.

Brooks had offered to give Tate a ride to dinner, but she had politely declined. Instead, she told him she'd meet him in the lobby a few minutes early so he could brief her on everyone they'd be dining with. It was a quarter past six when she slipped her toes into a pair of nude ballet flats and headed out the door to the bus stop just off Portobello Road. At this pace, she'd be walking into the Lanesborough about ten minutes prior to everyone's arrival. Plenty of time for Brooks to give her the lowdown.

Portobello Road was lively as ever. Tate peeked at the vintage collectibles laid out atop the tables as she strolled through the streets. The eclectic mix of vendors she eyed along the way tried to lure her in, but tonight, she only admired from afar to be sure she didn't miss the bus that would get her to Hyde Park Corner on time.

*

Brooks was waiting on the top stair outside the hotel when Tate arrived. This time, a navy blue jacket hugged tightly to his chest. She watched him from a distance as he typed vigorously on the screen of his phone, his golden hair slicked back, unfazed once again by the strong winds of springtime in London. She shook off the wonder of what she would find underneath the buttons of his jacket and made her way up the stairs to him.

Brooks' fingers froze as he looked up at who was standing next to him. His eyes wandered, and Tate could see the way they traced every inch of her as she had done to him only moments before. He smiled once his eyes made his way back up to Tate's, and he tucked his phone back into his jacket pocket.

"Wow," he said. "You look amazing."

"Thank you," Tate said. She lowered her glance and strengthened her grip on the black clutch to hide the flush of her cheeks. "You look quite handsome tonight."

The two of them stood there surrounded by the night air as cars rushed by below them. The bustling noises of city living seemed to vanish as they stared into each other's eyes. Brooks had never noticed the way the color in Tate's eyes transformed as the light hit them before. They were smooth at first, like caramel. Then, as she turned toward the glisten of the streetlights, they lightened, and with that came a hint of chestnut that matched perfectly to the same subtle color spread throughout her hair.

It took a group of women exiting the hotel in stark amusement to shake them both from their stare. Once they passed, Brooks reached out his arm.

"Shall we?"

"We shall," Tate said. She wrapped her arm through his.

Tate had never been to the Lanesborough before, though she had passed by it many times during her runs through Hyde Park. The exterior was exquisite, with elevated columns leading up the stairs, but as they stepped into the lobby, Tate embraced a whole different world. They were guided through to the restaurant by a long row of hanging chandeliers and adorned archways.

Brooks was quite familiar with the Lanesborough. His clients had brought him here often when he first started this job. At first, he'd found it stuffy and uptight, but after a while, he had come to enjoy it. It was here he had built the relationships he was so fond of today. These tables were the foundation of his career, and he was thankful for that.

When he and Tate made it to the table he had reserved, Brooks slid out a chair for her in front of the silver rimmed place setting, and she nestled in under the extravagance of the glass chandelier. Brooks slid the strap of her purse off her shoulder and over the back of her chair, then settled in beside her. He ordered two bottles of wine for the table.

"I'll let you do the honors," he said when the waiter returned with them both.

"Oh, gosh, I don't know," Tate said. She was not accustomed to any sort of lavish lifestyle. The bottles of wine hanging on the rack in her cozy kitchen had cost her less than eight pounds at the local grocery store. She didn't think she was equipped to test out a bottle that would be serving some of London's elite.

"I trust you," Brooks said, gesturing to the waiter.

He poured just enough into her glass for her to take in the aroma. Tate lifted the rim to her lips and drank in a sip that probably cost more than her monthly rent alone. The deep plum flavor dissolved smoothly, and she was left with an oaky aftertaste. This was a wine Tate could get used to. Though, her wallet would never be able to afford it even on her best payday.

"That is amazing," she said.

"Wonderful!" The waiter placed both bottles into a bucket in the center of the table, and Brooks began the breakdown of the guests who would soon be arriving.

"Aaron is the big man on campus. Great guy, but he knows exactly where he stands on the corporate ladder and makes sure everyone else does as well. He'll do most of the talking tonight," Brooks said, his voice just shy of a whisper in case anyone decided to arrive early. "Madeline, she's quite reserved. We'll be lucky if she says much more than her name tonight, but you won't find a sweeter soul."

"Arrogant Aaron and quiet as a mouse Madeline," Tate said before taking a sip from her water glass. "Got it. And who's the fifth seat for?"

"I saved the best for last," Brooks said. "Oh, Charlie. No matter what you say, he finds it hilarious. He will laugh the night away. He's done wonders for our children's charity. He's a very giving man."

"Chuckling Charlie," Tate said. "All right then, I think I'm ready."

"Good," Brooks said, sliding out his chair to stand. "Because here they come."

Tate too pushed herself up from her seat and slid her hands down her dress to iron it out. As they approached the table, she took in one deep inhale to prepare herself for blending in with high society. Brooks led the way with introductions, and Tate followed with a firm handshake and a smile. Once everyone was comfortably seated, it was time for the wine. Brooks poured a round for everyone, and the conversation began.

"So, Tate, Brooks tells us you're creating quite the gala," Aaron said.

Tate dabbed her napkin across her lips before offering a response. "I'd like to think so," she said. "The event is going to highlight the local arts while offering up an opportunity to grow an already surmountable charitable contribution. I'm excited for it to all come together."

Brooks sat quiet, his eyes fixated on Tate as she eluded to some of the details she had planned for the gala. He watched as her fingers massaged the earring dangling against her chin. His leg was close enough to her that he could feel the vibration against the floor from her leg. The shaking was the only way he could tell she was nervous. No one else saw it but him. To everyone else around the table, she was undaunted; her chin lifted, and her eyes made contact with each one of them. Her voice was modulated with each word she spoke. Brooks was in awe of the way Tate commanded the group.

Both Aaron and Charlie relaxed into their chairs. Their lips zipped together as they nodded at her words.

"Have you done something like this before?" Aaron pulled himself from the back of his chair and leaned closer across the table.

"My company hosts multiple events each month. I'm grateful for a dedicated team and clients who have held the utmost confidence in us."

"Are your events usually this grand-scale?" Aaron asked.

Tate swallowed hard, trying to come up with something that sounded as prestigious as she knew he was hoping for. Before she could pull any words together, Brooks came to her rescue.

"Delaney has seen firsthand the work Tate has been a part of and was very impressed with her vision. We're thrilled she has considered taking this event under her wing."

"Well then," Aaron said, lifting his wine glass over the table, "I'll cheers to that."

Charlie's laugh rumbled across the room as he followed suit and lifted his glass to meet Aaron's. Soon, all of their glasses were clinking together, and Tate no longer felt like the outcast. She pressed her lips around her glass to take in another sip and turned toward Brooks after she placed it back on the table. She didn't need to say anything.

Brooks nodded at the way her eyes sparkled. A faint smile was noticeable underneath the shine of her lip gloss. Her leg had stopped shaking; his voice had soothed her nerves.

It was as if he had known she was pleading for him in her mind when she fell silent. He'd answered at exactly the right time, and for that, Tate was thankful to have him next to her tonight.

Conversation flowed throughout dinner, and in the moments Tate felt tongue-tied, Brooks once again came to her rescue. Regardless of the success, Tate couldn't help but let out a huge sigh of relief when everyone had said their goodbyes. She and Brooks fell behind in the lobby as the rest of the group headed out the door. They waved to each of them as they dispersed into the moonlit night, and for a moment, the two of them stood quietly next to each other, soaking in what was now an abandoned lobby.

"Can I give you a ride home?" Brooks asked. "The driver is only a few minutes away. He won't mind the extra stop."

"Oh, no." Tate waved her hand at him. "I'm fine taking the bus."

"It's rather chilly out there tonight," he pleaded. "It would also not be very gentlemanly of me to let a lady walk home alone in the dark."

"I can handle it." Tate tried to stand strong.

"Oh, I have no doubt," Brooks said, "but I would feel much better knowing you arrived safely to your door after being in my company."

Tate fought herself hard in the lobby. She knew she should say no. It wasn't exactly unprofessional for Brooks to offer her a ride; it was more the fact the closer he stepped to her, the more rapid her heart would beat. She didn't trust herself being so close to him, but her argument seemed moot when his one-dimple smile spread across his face.

"Okay then," she said. "Let's go home."

"Hey now," Brooks chimed in, "I don't let anyone take me home on the first night."

"Oh, my gosh!" Tate gave him a swift slap to the chest. The firmness hurt her hand more than it did him, but she acted as if her hand didn't sting. "The bus is looking pretty good right about now."

"I'm kidding," Brooks said. "Come on, let's go."

He wanted to take her hand and lead her out of the hotel. He wanted to bring her closer to him and feel the smoothness of her skin, but he had to remember that this wasn't a date; this was a business meeting, and he had promised Tate he would keep a working relationship. So, instead, he placed his hand on the small of her back with enough space between the two of them to hinder the spark and guided her out of the lobby.

Tate still couldn't believe she was walking out of a night she never could've imagined being a part of when she first left Paris for London. Though she had worked hard to get to where she was today, she owed a tiny bit of this experience to Brooks. The man who barely knew her yet was completely confident in what she was capable of. Tate found it so incredibly hard to believe in herself one hundred percent of the time, but she had tried tonight. She was thankful that during the times a small percentage of doubt had started to creep in, there was someone there who had her back.

~8~

Brooks and Tate waited on the sidewalk until a black sedan pulled up. Once the car came to a complete stop, Brooks stepped off the sidewalk and reached for the door handle, stepping back enough to let Tate slide in first.

"Your carriage, mademoiselle."

Tate shook her head and laughed as she bent down and slid onto the warmth of the leather seat. "So, what's your driver's name?" she asked.

"Perry," Brooks said. "He's not technically my driver. It's on the company card tonight."

Tate nodded. Her hand stroked the leather interior of the door, and she sighed. She wasn't quite at a place where she could rent a driver for an evening out. Vans, she rented often in order to get all of her party supplies from one place to another. Maybe someday she'd get there, but for now, she would take the experience of tonight.

"Thank you for everything," Tate said. "For the invitation and for being there when I needed you."

"You don't need to thank me," Brooks said. "You're a natural."

Tate laughed. "I don't know about that. Unlike you, I spend most of my time in sweatpants and a tank top. It took a lot to get me ready for tonight."

Brooks looked over at her as the driver slowed for a red light. He found that hard to believe. It had been difficult enough for him to keep his eyes off her in her casual dress at the coffee shop; she had no idea what she was doing to him showing up in a mid-length dress that exposed her toned legs. What she was wearing didn't matter to him tonight though. He knew from the way all of their dinner guests shook her hand when the night was over that she had impressed them.

"You're not the only one who can't wait to get themselves out of these clothes." Brooks unbuttoned his jacket and pulled his arms out of it. "I spend all day every day in suits and ties. I'd much rather lounge around in plaid pajama pants than tighten these things with a belt buckle. Where I come from, board shorts and tanned skin is the norm."

"Where do you come from?" Tate asked. She had been wondering that since the day he spilled the coffee out of her hands. His voice and demeanor were so familiar to her. Brooks felt like home when he laughed and brushed his hands through his hair. She loved hearing him talk. She was sure he was from the States at least, but he had to be from the west coast. He just had to.

"Well, I was born in San Diego. I called that home until I was seventeen. My dad took a job here right before I graduated high school. My grandparents offered for me to stay in San Diego until I graduated, so I did. I flew over to London for university."

"Do you miss it?" Tate asked. "California... Do you ever get homesick?"

"I miss it, sure. You can't beat sunshine all year round. I went back for a couple of years after I graduated university here, but there's something about London that kept calling me back."

"So you're back for good now?"

"I think so," Brooks said. "My parents aren't far from here. They moved recently to Wales, and my brother's in Reading. We're all really close."

Brooks was becoming more attractive by the minute. Tate missed her family greatly. There were times when she first moved into her flat in Notting Hill that she felt so alone, she would cry herself to sleep wondering if she should go back to Seattle; back to the comfort only a hometown could bring.

Brooks had stayed close because this was where his family was, and Tate liked the sound of that even more than she liked watching his bicep flex as he folded his jacket into his lap.

Cameron hadn't had the best relationship with his parents. They divorced when he was young. He'd lived with his mom for the most part, but she was never home. She went out a lot with her friends and used to buy Cameron's forgiveness with money. His dad had seemed nice the handful of times Tate met him, but he remarried before she met Cameron and spent a lot of his time focusing on what Cameron called his "new family."

"What's your story?" Brooks asked.

That was a good question. Tate's family life wasn't complicated. She too was close to her parents, and although she and her sister Grace had the normal sibling rivalry, they'd grown closer in high school. Grace had even come to see Tate twice since she moved overseas. Once, to help her unpack into her current place, and another long weekend when she was in between jobs. That story was the easy part. The rest of it—how Tate had ended up in London—was the part she was uncomfortable with. Yet the sincerity in Brooks' voice made her feel safe enough to say it out loud.

"I'm from Seattle," she said. "I followed my heart to Paris after college, and it didn't work out, so...now, I'm here."

"Your heart... Meaning, a guy?" Brooks asked.

"Yeah."

"I'm sorry," he said.

"I'm learning to find the silver lining. I'm a firm believer that life will never lead you in the wrong direction. Without Paris, I wouldn't have London, and I think it's turned out pretty great so far."

"I like your way of thinking."

Perry turned onto Bayswater, toward Tate's quaint flat. Up ahead, he made his final turn into Notting Hill. There was a spot on the street a few doors down, which he swerved into, then shifted the car into park and saluted from the front seat.

"I guess this is you." Brooks' voice was somber as he pointed out the window.

"Yup, home sweet home." Even with those words, Tate found herself unable to move. She watched Brooks flick the handle of his door and step out onto the street. Tate's chest grew heavy as her door popped open and Brooks' hand reach inside.

"Thank you," she said.

"Of course. It was my pleasure." Brooks leaned against the back of the car.

Tate gripped her purse tight as she stood in front of him. "I'll see you soon, I'm sure."

"You will," he replied, looking up at Tate.

His eyes still offered the same clarity as they did in the coffee shop.

"Here, let me give you my number." He saw Tate flinch as he pulled his phone from his pocket and tried to settle her nerves. "This is my work phone. You can call me anytime."

"Sure," Tate said. Her phone number spilled from her lips as he typed each digit into his phone. He pressed send, and soon, her phone was vibrating. It would be the only time Brooks' number would come up unknown. Once it stopped ringing, she quickly added him to her contacts, smiling as she slid the phone back into her purse.

Tate's legs were uneasy with each step she took closer to the sidewalk. Her hand slid across the car for balance until she was too far to hold on anymore.

"Goodnight, Brooks," she said, turning back toward him.

He slowly lifted his arms and wrapped them gently around her. Tate rested her hand on his shoulder, sucking in the air when she felt her cheek brush against him. The smell of cedar escaped his neck and intoxicated her. Her fingers gripped tighter when she felt his lips press softly against her cheek. They lingered there for a minute before he pulled himself away.

"Goodnight, Tate," he whispered.

Giving Brooks one last wave, Tate headed up the sidewalk. She could feel his eyes on her as the pink door grew closer. Her legs were numb, so her path to the door probably looked like she'd had one too many glasses of wine. Her weight fell against the cold glass above the door handle when she placed her key in the slot, and a sudden wave of desire overcame her. She wanted to see Brooks one more time, but she fought the urge to look back and instead twisted the key and pushed through the door, falling hard against the inside once it had shut. Listening out, she heard the door to the car close and she felt her chin start to tremble. A lot of firsts happened that night for Tate. One of them she realized when that car door shut.

    This was the first time she had truly felt a sense of contentment since she moved into this flat. Sitting at that table with Brooks by her side, she was able to relax. She felt secure. It dawned on her as the sound of the engine revved back into the street how much she missed that feeling and how much she yearned to have it back as her ear pressed against the door and the screaming of the car faded into the night.

~9~

Tate needed the weekend to cool off from the flames that had ignited between her and Brooks in the front seat of his car. The aftermath had followed her into her dreams every night since. They were so vivid, she could hear his laugh and feel his arms around her hours after she fell asleep. Last night, she'd woken up in a cold sweat after his lips came within inches of touching hers. This hold that he had so immediately been able to place on her was dizzying.

The day before, Tate had made it through booking the centerpieces, the photo booth backdrop, and musicians for the Ball of Hope without needing help from Brooks, but this coming Monday, she would be nailing down all catering, food, and cocktail choices. That was something Delaney very much wanted Brooks to be a part of, but Tate had yet to send an invitation his way. Thank goodness there were two days between Friday and Monday. With a hen party for a bride-to-be on the horizon, she was so happy to have something else to focus on.

The bride-to-be, Natalie, was a lover of the countryside, and Tate couldn't wait for her to see what she had put together, even if the weather wasn't working in their favor. The sky had opened enough to let a drizzle through the grayness on the morning of the party. Tate had rented a car for the day, and the back seat was packed to the brim with decor and favors she'd be setting up for the celebration. She crept slowly through the outskirts of London with the windshield wipers on full blast.

Driving was something Tate had done rarely since her arrival in France, and after a couple of years, she still wasn't any more confident. Driving on the left side of the road was terrifying. She only did it if she absolutely had to. Her hands braced the steering wheel so hard her knuckles began to turn white. She slowed down more than any of the other drivers at the multiple roundabouts in order to figure out which lane to pull into. She held her breath until she made it through each one.

It took a little longer than usual with the rain and Tate's evident fear, but a little over an hour later, she was pulling in alongside a three-story walkup just outside of Greenwich Central Park. She threw the hood of her rain jacket up over her head before stepping out into the steady stream of water that had been pelting the roof of her car for the past fifteen minutes. Susan, the mother of the bride, held the door open for her as she carried all the boxes inside.

"Everything can go in here," Susan said, pointing to the floor to ceiling window-lined living area. "This table over here is for the drinks, and, of course, you can use the kitchen for any preparation."

A long farm table sat to the left side of a brick-lined fireplace. Tate set one of the boxes on top of it and started to empty out the mason jars. She lined them along one side to make room for the pitchers that would hold the grapefruit and rosemary mimosas as well as the peach Bellini's she still had to make.

"Oh, aren't those adorable?" Susan said once Tate had finished placing the green-and-white-striped paper straws inside each jar.

"Thank you!" Tate said. "When I'm done, we'll have turned this place into a little countryside retreat in the hills of Tuscany."

She and Susan both laughed before Tate pulled out the second box, which held the party favors. Susan's house boasted a window seat nook that looked out into her tiny backyard. That was where Tate placed a white wooden basket and filled it with little cubes of organic soap in multiple different colors. Next to the basket, each guest would find a mesh satchel to fill and, of course, a chalkboard that read "Enjoy the sweetest scent-iments as we celebrate Natalie." Once it was all placed in a way Susan approved of, Tate headed into the kitchen to prepare the cocktails.

Peach Bellini used to be Tate's drink of choice. While she was waiting for her visa to be approved to join Cameron in France, she spent many Sundays with her sister Grace sitting under an umbrella on the deck of Harbor 66 overlooking Ellicott Bay. Grace always went for the Bloody Mary bar, but Tate never wavered from the endless Bellini's. It was the first drink that came to mind when Natalie had mentioned she wanted something fruity yet posh for her guests to enjoy.

As Tate stirred the mixture inside the pitcher, she thought back to those days in Seattle. She had been nervous as hell to leave the familiar, but the excitement of a future in France overshadowed all of her doubt. That excitement was short-lived when Cameron walked out. Since that day, she hadn't experienced any real kind of eagerness for something new. Even when she moved to London, Tate's heart was still as gray as the winter skies she drove in under.

During the time she stayed in Camden looking for a place of her own, Tate was still at a point where tears filled her eyes daily, and even when the colors of spring began to bloom, those tears blurred them all together. Her world was more like an abstract painting; it had the potential to be beautiful if she could figure out what she was looking at. She'd been on a few dates in London, and though all of the guys were nice, none of them had turned into anything. One guy, she actually met at Primrose May. He'd chased after her when she was leaving and asked if she wanted to grab a bite to eat. Against all of her inhibitions, Tate had agreed. They'd had a nice time, but, as it turned out, he was only in town for the week on business. Tate met up with him one other time before he went back to Germany. He made her laugh, but even though the two of them exchanged numbers, Tate hadn't heard from him since.

The tapping of the spoon inside the pitcher of the grapefruit mimosa turned Tate away from memory lane long enough to piece the rest of the party together. Everyone was already enjoying morning cocktails in their mason jars when Natalie arrived. The shriek that came from her once she took everything in was proof enough of a job well-done.

"Oh, Tate, thank you, thank you, thank you! Everything is splendid!" Natalie exclaimed.

"I'm so glad you love it! Would you like me to pour you a drink?" Tate asked.

"That would be lovely."

Natalie hugged every one of her friends while Tate snuck off to fill a mason jar to the brim with a peach Bellini. She walked over and placed the cocktail on the small table beside the ottoman where Natalie had set her purse. Natalie was so immersed in laughter and conversation with those around her that she didn't notice. Tate slipped back into a corner of the room and back down memory lane, remembering the time she thought she too would be where Natalie was.

On one of their final nights in Paris together, Tate and Cameron had made a reservation at their favorite bistro. He had been acting strange all week, so Tate made sure to add a little bit of extra color to her lips that night. Her long-sleeved lilac dress accentuated all the right places, but when she walked out of their bedroom, Cameron didn't seem to notice the extra effort. Tate had reached for his hand as they walked to the bistro. He held on, but his grip was weak, and it was evident his mind was somewhere else.

When they arrived, Cameron pulled out the chair for her. That wasn't something he ever did. For the two hours they were in the restaurant, Tate fidgeted in her chair. She held her breath every time he reached under the table, wondering when or if he would ever pull something from his pocket. That was her only thought about why he'd been acting so weird, but he never did pull anything out. He only remained quiet for the rest of the night.

Cameron walked at arm's length from her back to the Metro and stood while she took a seat. The only thing Tate received that night was a quick kiss on her cheek before he rolled away from her in bed. It would be just eight hours later, when she woke up the next morning, that Cameron would say this "just isn't working." The night before had been an attempt to try and see if something was still there—that's what he told her right before she threw the sheets off and jumped from the bed.

"What do you mean, this isn't working?" she screamed.

And that was when he said it. The most cliché words she had ever heard: "I love you, Tate, but I'm not in love with you anymore."

While in her trance in the back corner of the room, while Natalie and her guests enjoyed the party, Tate remembered the heavy footsteps from that morning in her Paris apartment. They'd pounded from the bedroom into the kitchen like a hammer to a nail. She was shaking so hard that when she pulled a glass from the cupboard it slipped through her hands and fell to pieces across the floor. Cameron came running out. Tate stood frozen at the kitchen sink while he swept a broom across the floor. The sound of the glass as Cameron gathered it together sounded eerily similar to the clanking of Natalie's mom's spoon against her cocktail glass as she tried to get everyone's attention, pulling Tate back into the room. She blinked a few times to dry out the tears that were creeping in and listened.

"Thank you, everyone, for coming to celebrate my sweet Natalie today," Susan said. "We're so excited for her and Jack and their happily ever after."

Happily ever after... Was that also a cliché? How did you define the overused line? Tate hated that those words were even running through her mind. Of course, happily ever after was a real thing; she'd planned enough weddings to know that it could happen. Perhaps not in the way the world perceived it, but that was because from a young age, we were programmed to believe a skewed version of it. Happily ever after didn't mean endless days of sunshine; it meant you'd found the one you were willing to commit to, dig through the trenches with, and sometimes push aside your pride for—something Tate had been willing to do, but Cameron obviously was not.

So now, here she was, planning other people's happily ever after while she wondered when hers would arrive. Strange that in the same moment she asked herself that question, she pulled out her phone and scrolled to Brooks' name.

He was the one thing she'd been fighting against all weekend, but, in her weakness, she did what she had been telling herself not to do. She sent him a text.

~10~

It was over a month since Brooks had spent a weekend in London, and this weekend was no different. His parents had recently moved from their Wandsworth home not far from London's city center to Cardiff, on the south coast of Wales. Their new home had a lake view, but it needed some work, so Brooks had been helping his dad to fix it up on his days off. His mom, Kimberly, was overseeing the decorating, and she welcomed the challenge.

Kimberly had left her full-time job as a veterinarian when the family moved to London. She had worked part-time at a local home decor shop in Wandsworth and ended up loving it so much she stayed until Brooks' dad retired. Now, the two were ready to put down roots in a quieter area of the United Kingdom.

Brooks was glad they'd chosen Cardiff. It was close enough that he could visit often, and it was near all the places his family used to visit before he and his brother Garrett were too old for family vacations. Now that he was grown up, he missed the weeks they used to spend in Snowdonia National Park and Pembrokeshire during holidays from university, and he longed for when his work schedule would allow him to go back. *This summer, I'm taking a vacation.* That was what Brooks told himself last year, but the summer came and went, and Brooks never took that vacation. He repeated those words as the New Year arrived, but his workload continued to pile up, and he wondered if this summer would be the same as the last. At least he had his weekends. Even if they weren't used for hiking or relaxing on the coast, he was able to spend some time with his parents.

"I brought you boys some lemonade," Brooks' mom said. She stepped out of the back sunroom onto the cobblestone patio behind the new house.

Brooks and his brother were pulling shrubs that hadn't been tended to in what seemed like ages. From the beads of sweat dripping from their foreheads, it would seem as if it was the height of summer, but it was typical spring weather on the coast, with heavier winds escaping from the lakeside. Brooks had been battling an overgrown shrub for more than ten minutes and finally yanked it from the ground as he heard his mom call out.

"Thanks, Mom."

It's looking really great out here," she said.

His breath was heavy. It'd been a few hours since he started. His side of the patio was just about cleared. He looked over at his brother, who had already finished his side of shrubs and was now replacing loose stone on the patio. To be fair, Brooks' side was much worse.

"Careful where you step," Garrett yelled. "You'll roll your ankle on those stones right there."

Kimberly stumbled to find her footing on the opposite side of where Garrett was pointing. The glasses on the tray shook, but she was able to make it to the black iron table, the only piece of furniture that currently sat outside. She poured each glass to the brim and set them back down.

"I'm making lunch right now," she said. "It should be ready in about ten minutes. I'll yell when it's on the table."

"Okay, Mom. Thanks again," Brooks said.

Brooks wiped his forehead dry and threw the gloves off his hands. He walked over to the table and chugged the glass of lemonade, then poured another and was almost done with that too by the time Garrett made it over to drink his first.

"Working hard out here, Grandpa?" Garrett joked.

Brooks rolled his eyes. He was used to the grandpa jokes by now. There were eight years between Brooks and his younger brother. Garrett may still have a few years before he turned thirty, but Brooks reveled in the fact Garret's head was filled with more gray hairs. It was a heated debate last Christmas when the family gathered for the last time in their London home. Garrett's fiancée had gotten the silent treatment from him for about an hour before dinner when she agreed with Brooks. She even attempted to pluck a few to show him.

"Hey, where's Vera?" Brooks asked. "I thought she was riding down with you this weekend."

"She's wedding dress shopping," Garrett said. "She was supposed to go last weekend, but her mom wasn't feeling well, so they rescheduled to this one. She says hi and asked me to ask you if my best man had a plus-one yet?"

Garrett laughed and ducked as Brooks pretended to take a swing at him. Vera had been "in the family" now for three years. She was born and raised in Reading and was a Year Two teacher at the same school she went to as a child. Brooks was pretty sure Year Two in England was the equivalent to first grade in the US, but he was still slowly learning the differences with all that. Vera and Garrett had met in the parking lot of the restaurant he managed in Reading. She had a flat tire and, as fate would have it, Garrett happened to be leaving his shift at the same time she was pulling in. "He got down on one knee," Vera would always say, "and changed that tire like a champ."

Brooks was fond of Vera. He knew she'd be sticking around the first time he met her. She wasn't timid of his boisterous family, and he wasn't ashamed to admit her sarcasm was a level up from his. Hence her dig about a date to her and Garret's wedding. "You have a whole year," she'd said when they first announced their engagement. "Surely, you won't still be single by then." The wedding was now four months out, and Brooks was still flying solo. Although, after this week, he'd almost convinced himself that may be about to change.

"You tell Vera that just for that, even if I did have a plus-one, I wouldn't tell you," Brooks joked.

Garrett laughed, but from the wonder in his eyes, Brooks could tell there was a part of him that was curious. "Come on, dude," he said. "There's no one special back in London for our boy Leo?"

Brooks' thoughts immediately flashed back to Tate walking up the steps to the Lanesborough. He was mesmerized by the olive-colored skin peeking out of her dress. Her laugh still echoed in his head in the moments he was home alone. Every now and then, when he sat at his desk at work, he'd find her smile in the most natural shade of pink come into view. Talking to her came so easy. He could've sat in the back seat of that car after dinner with her for hours. There was so much more about Tate that he wanted to know.

We have to be professional.

Brooks would remind himself of Tate's words during the moments he picked up his phone to text her. He only wanted to say hi or see how she was doing, which technically wouldn't be unprofessional, but he knew Tate wouldn't see it that way. Instead of texting, he would just sigh and slide his phone into the middle drawer of his desk to fight the urge.

"Work is the only thing I'm taking home with me these days," Brooks said.

"Leo, man, you shouldn't work so much," Garrett said. "I mean, I know you're a big shot and all, but you've got to work to live man, not live to work."

"You're so philosophical, bro," Brooks said.

Garrett slugged Brooks in the arm before taking one last sip from his lemonade glass.

Brooks missed his younger brother. They used to share the flat in London Brooks now lived in alone. For four years, they were roommates, and, as surprised his mother was, the two of them got along quite well in the tiny space. She stopped over every Sunday to bring them a home-cooked meal and had them over to dinner in Wandsworth a few times a month, but other than that, the boys never cooked. They lived on takeout and tap beer from the bar below them.

Brooks had woken up to many girls sneaking out of Garrett's room in the early hours while he was still living his bachelor days. Admittedly, Garrett had witnessed a few of Brooks' one-night stands as well, but he'd had far fewer than

Garrett. The last year they lived together, fewer girls went in and out. They were both in exclusive relationships. Garrett was with Vera and Brooks was with the only girl Garrett ever seemed to remember.

"I'm serious," Garrett said. "You haven't brought another girl around since Mya. That has to be at least four years ago."

Garrett was right. Mya was the last exclusive relationship he'd had when he was still working in IT and had more time for a social life. Brooks had met Mya when he and Garrett were out one night having drinks in Piccadilly Circus. She pushed between the two of them to order a drink at the bar, her curly black hair draped over her warm beige skin, and when she turned to smile at him with a drink in her hand, Brooks let her walk away. His eyes followed her, though, and Garrett was the one who made the move for him.

"Ah, Mya," Brooks said fondly. The two of them had spent seven months together. He would spend a few nights at her place, and on the weekends, she would come to his. Brooks had adored Mya. They had fun together.

"Maybe you should invite her to the wedding." Garrett let out a chuckle, but part of Brooks wondered if he was really kidding. Garrett had always liked Mya. When she left their apartment for the last time, Brooks saw the way his brother's face fell. Both of them felt the sting of that breakup.

"I'm not sure her husband would appreciate that," Brooks said. That was the main reason the two of them hadn't worked out: Mya wanted to get married. She wanted to have kids, at least three of them, and she wanted it all before she turned thirty. Since they were both twenty-eight, Mya's timeline was too fast Brooks.

"She's married? Really?" Garrett's voice rose. "I had no idea."

"Yup, to a lawyer. She has two kids."

Not that Mya had told him that herself. That was the benefit of living in a digital age. They were online friends, and every now and then, her photos would pop up on his screen. Brooks was about to change the subject when his mother reappeared in the doorway.

"Lunch is on the table. Come in and eat," she said.

Brooks let out a heavy sigh of relief and smiled at her standing there in her floral apron. Everyone had always said he could be his father's twin, but he for sure got his golden hair from his mother. His ambition to succeed and love of experiencing the world also was something he stole from her. There were parts of Tate that reminded him of his mother. He saw it in the way she carried herself and her passion for her job. *Man, would Mom love her,* Brooks thought as he made his way inside.

"Sit down," his mom demanded. "Garrett's been here a few days now, so I've already pestered him. Now, it's your turn." She sat down in the chair next to Brooks and rested her hand on his shoulder. "How are you doing?"

Garrett didn't let him answer. "If you're wondering about his love life, Mom, he doesn't have one. I already asked."

"Oh, Garrett, hush now."

Brooks smiled and tossed a potato chip in his brother's direction. Even if he was mocking him, Brooks was happy Garrett had been the one to break the news to his mom. He could already see by the way her bottom lip jutted out that it wasn't what she wanted to hear. Lucky for Brooks, his phone went off right as he was about to take a bite of his sandwich. He wiped his hands on his sweaty shirt and walked back out into the sunroom to grab it. Looking down at the name flashing on his phone, he smiled. It was the weekend. She couldn't be thinking about work. Maybe she was thinking of him too. Maybe she was giving in like he wanted to. He slid open the text from Tate.

Tate: *Meeting with caterer on Monday. Does 1pm work for you?*

He was wrong. It was business as always, but even in that moment, he couldn't help but see a glimmer of hope that maybe in the middle of the day, her mind was clouded with thoughts of him too. That maybe she didn't *have* to send that text right when she did, but she wanted to because she wanted to fill his mind with those same thoughts. She wanted to see his name on her phone. Without hesitation, he sent back his response.

Brooks: *1pm is perfect. See you then.*

He wasn't sure that 1:00 p.m. was perfect. In fact, on a Monday, he most likely had a scheduled meeting or client phone call. He'd move it if he had to.

He wanted to see her, and, technically, this event came before anything else right now. Delaney would understand. Brooks hung around in the sunroom for another couple of minutes, hoping Tate had something else to say, but there was no response. Not even those three tiny bubbles to tease him.

"Leo!" His mother called. She hated interruptions during meals.

"I'm coming, Ma, I'm coming!"

He slid his phone into his pocket and headed to the kitchen for what he was sure would be another round of Garrett's sarcasm. He also knew his mother wasn't done with asking questions.

~11~

Tate was still convincing herself it was just business when Monday came around and she was stepping off the stairs of the bus back to Westminster. Convincing was something she seemed to be doing a lot of lately when it came to her meeting with Brooks. She hated how torn she felt.

Tate wasn't used to liking the company she was around. Not in the "goosebumps appear every time she accidentally brushes up against him" sort of way. She thought the more time she spent apart from Brooks, the less she'd feel that way, but her lucid dreams proved otherwise. On days like today, her feelings were evident. She was happy Delaney wanted Brooks to be heavily involved in the planning even though she knew she could nail down food and drinks on her own; it gave Tate an excuse to see Brooks without him knowing she liked having him there.

Tate wasn't oblivious to the fact she should've respectfully declined Brooks' offer to meet early for coffee, but, instead, there she was trotting along in a new pair of tan wedges. She held her lips still when Brooks came into view and waved at him as if he was exactly what he should be: a colleague.

"Good morning," he said. He was already standing at the door of Primrose May. With a firm grip on the handle, he motioned a few customers in and out before Tate followed.

Almost every one of the white chairs was occupied. Even her little corner booth was stuffed full of people typing away on their laptops. It always amazed Tate that even in the hours like this, when Primrose May was overflowing, the music was still one of the only sounds flooding the space. That was why she liked it so much. Everyone came here to work. They concentrated hard, and she could surround herself with others without distractions.

"Well, hello there, you two!" Anya was behind the counter that afternoon. Tate watched as her eyes ping-ponged between her and Brooks. "I didn't realize you knew each other."

Brooks looked in Tate's direction and met her gawk with a half-smile. "We met recently. We're working on a project together," he said.

"That's so cool," Anya said. She pressed her hand to the side of her mouth and whispered, "You two are my favorite customers."

"Haha!" Brooks leaned in toward her and mirrored Anya's hand placement with his own. "Well, you're my favorite barista." He gave a quick wink and pulled himself back up.

Anya didn't have to ask for either of their orders. Both Brooks and Tate nodded when she read what she'd typed into the register out loud. They'd planned on dining in with their coffee, but the only open seats were a few stools near the window ledge surrounded by a group in a lively conversation. Instead, they took their order to go and tried to think of another way to bide their time.

"We could head over to Piccadilly and walk through the Arcade," Brooks said. "Our meeting is pretty close to there."

Tate shrugged. "Yeah, we could do that."

Brooks was unconvinced by her answer. She focused on the ground while her hands fidgeted around her neck.

"Is there anywhere you want to go?" he asked.

Tate loved the Piccadilly area of London's West End. She and Genevieve had seen more shows than she could count at the Piccadilly Theatre, but that afternoon, she wasn't in the mood for the crowds of tourists she knew would be filing through. There was one part of West End that Tate never could get enough of, and on days like these, when she yearned for serenity, it seemed like the perfect place.

"I have an idea," Tate said.

She reached her hand out for his and maneuvered the two of them through the crowd on the streets that led to the Victoria Tube Station. Less than ten minutes later, the two of them were ascending the stairs from Leicester Square to Tate's favorite place to escape. The hidden alcove of Cecil Court was where Tate went when she wanted to be thrust into other worlds and forget whatever it was that was bothering her. Tate had accidentally stumbled upon it when she first moved to London. She had finished a day of shopping at Convent Garden and was trying to find the right bus to get her back home. A wrong turn had led her down Cecil Court, and since then, it had become her saving grace.

Some days, she would spend hours there without any inkling of time. When she was done, she'd look up, and somewhere along the way, the light had succumbed to darkness, and the moon was staring through the window as a reminder it was time to go home.

"Here we are!" Tate said. She didn't realize she had grabbed Brooks' hand again until she went to turn toward him and it slipped out of his hold.

"Wow," he said. His gaze rose to admire the row of Victorian-inspired architecture.

Cecil Court was Tate's secret hideaway. Never had she brought anyone here before. She always came alone, but not today. Today, she was sharing her secret with Brooks. When they turned into the narrow alley, that same feeling that always came over her returned. Her eyes lit up. The everyday noise of London's streets immediately disappeared, and suddenly, she didn't feel so small.

"Isn't it amazing?" Tate wrapped her hand around one of the lampposts that lined the middle of the street. She stretched her arm and let the black pole hold the weight of her as she twirled around it.

Brooks couldn't believe that in all the time he'd lived in London, he'd never been down this street. When he was younger, Piccadilly was his favorite place to hang out. He loved late nights in Little Italy, yet he had never found himself here. He watched Tate as she twirled around the lamppost. She'd never smiled like that before. He'd paid close enough attention to her to know she had different types of smiles. There was the one she gave when she was trying not to smile. Then, there was the one she hid behind when she felt uncomfortable. Before today, his favorite was when she would smile because she'd discovered something new. There wasn't a smile of hers that he didn't like, but this one, right here in the middle of the alley, was his favorite by far. She seemed so carefree, not so rigid. He liked seeing this side of her.

"What is it about this place?" Brooks asked.

"History, adventure..." Tate said. She let go of the light pole and began to frolic through the doors of one of the places she'd been to so many times before. "Come on!"

Cecil Court was filled with more than a dozen secondhand bookstores. Between all the pages she'd read, Tate had been able to travel back in time, escape to the mountaintops of Iceland, and dive even deeper into the history of London. Reading, for Tate, had not only helped to ease her pain when she arrived here, but it had sparked creativity back into her everyday life. The very idea of *A Starry Night in Paris* was born on these shelves after she discovered a historical romance novel set in Paris.

"Here," Tate said. "This is it." She pulled the tattered book from the shelf. "I've been planning this Paris-themed event ever since I finished this book. Must've been over a year ago at this point."

"Over a year?" Brooks took the book from her hands.

"Yup! It was the scene on page one-eighteen. A young couple strolls down a quaint Paris street lined with cafés. Live music plays, while they admire all the patisserie offerings from the windows."

Brooks flipped through the book, fanning out the pages until he came to one-eighteen. Tate watched his finger glide over line after line. He flipped the page again and continued, while she followed his wide eyes across every word. When his finger found its way to the last line of the scene, he closed the cover.

"I see it," he said. "I really see it."

"Can you?" Tate asked. He nodded. "I've been holding it tightly up in here." She tapped her forehead. "I was waiting for the perfect moment to make it come to life."

"This is really special to you, isn't it?" Brooks asked.

"It really is."

"Well then, I feel honored to even be a tiny bit involved."

Brooks held the book tightly in his hands as the two of them stood quietly in the aisle. His eyes locked on Tate's, and she wondered if the mellow music surrounding them was enough to hide the rapid beating of her heart. The curve of his lips inspired her to do the same, and soon, she realized the both of them were leaning closer to each other. His lips, she wanted to feel them against hers, and she almost gave in to the longing that rose inside of her—but just as her eyes began to close in acceptance, the door opened, and two rowdy kids ran inside.

Tate stumbled backward, letting the bookshelf catch her. A few books tumbled off and landed on the floor between the two of them. Tate bent down first to pick them up, and Brooks followed. Both of their foreheads collided before either of them could grab any of the fallen books.

"Ow!" Tate said. She suddenly felt a sharp pain on her forehead.

"Sorry." Brooks was laughing as he rubbed his own forehead to diminish the pain.

"My bad," Tate said. She looked at her watch. Baguettes and beef bourguignon were waiting for them. "We should probably get going."

"Okay. I'll meet you outside. I'm going to use the restroom quick," he said.

"Sounds good. If you can't find me, there's an antique shop across the street that always lures me in when I'm here."

"I'll be sure to come rescue you."

"Thanks," she said.

Tate's chest brushed up against his as she squeezed past him to the door. She was sure then that he could feel her heartbeat. Brooks stood still as she moved past him, leaving him alone in the aisle. He was still holding the book tight in his grasp as Tate pushed herself against the glass and out into the warm breeze of her favorite cozy street.

Tate walked over to antique shop. She didn't go in, but she did lean her forehead on the window to admire its trinkets. She searched frantically for something, anything, that would make Brooks' eyes disappear from her mind, but everything she looked at only made them more vivid. She saw him as she stared at the blue of the pillar candle and the clear blown glass figurine.

There wasn't a time they'd been together that he hadn't made her laugh. When she talked to him, she could tell by his raised eyebrows and wide eyes that he wasn't only pretending to hear, but really listening to what she had to say. Brooks made her feel like she mattered. She was falling hard, and her flashbacks to Cameron made her realize that her hesitation was about way more than a professional working relationship. She was terrified of letting someone in again. Tate didn't want to allow herself to be vulnerable out of fear that her heart might shatter again like the pieces of glass on her kitchen floor. She pressed her hands against her face and leaned harder into the window, desperate for something to offer a distraction from wanting the thing she couldn't have, but even then, she failed completely.

~12~

Brooks was in awe watching Tate in her element. He sat back for most of the catering meeting while she talked with the chef about different combinations of appetizers and side dishes. She eventually turned to Brooks to ask his opinion on hors d'oeuvres and whether he preferred them passed or stationary. He was happy to oblige.

"Passed," he answered. "I find it offers less interruption in conversation."

"Oh, good point," Tate replied. She patted him on the shoulder and went down the list of passed hors d'oeuvres options picking out her favorites. Tate looked over at Brooks when she was finished. She didn't really need it, but Brooks knew she was trying to include him by waiting for his approval. He nodded.

The rest of the meeting went pretty much the same until it came time for the dinner options. Brooks watched as Tate's hand fell heavy over the menu. She stared blankly at the list in front of her.

He leaned forward and rested his hand on her forearm. "Are you okay?" he asked.

Tate pulled herself back up and shifted her weight from the table to her feet. She blinked several times to erase the tears that had started to settle in her eyes.

"Oh, yes, I'm fine. Got a little sidetracked, that's all."

Tate shook all the memories that the French cuisine was stirring up out of her mind and regained her focus. She picked out her favorites and once again turned to get Brooks' approval.

He nodded, still keeping a careful eye on her. Though Brooks was still worried, he found it hard not to notice how Tate took charge. He found her dominance rather sexy. She didn't need a man in that room with her. She didn't need anyone in that room with her, but he was glad that if anyone was going to be here, it was him.

"I think that's it," Tate said. "If you could draw up a final proposal, I'll get back to you with any changes."

The chef nodded and reached out to shake her hand. That was Brooks' cue. He stood up and leaned in to shake his hand as well before the chef said goodbye to both of them and left the room. Tate scribbled a few notes into her planner before slipping it back into her bag. When she was done, she looked over at Brooks and drew a check mark in the air with her hand.

"Another thing off the list," she said. "Thanks for your help."

"Me?" Brooks said. "Come on now, you killed that meeting. You didn't need me here."

"Yes, I did," Tate assured him. "It's always nice to have a second opinion."

"Well, I'm glad I could give it," Brooks said. "You sure everything's all right?"

"Yes, absolutely. It's been a long few days."

"Okay," Brooks surrendered. "What's next on your list?"

"Lots of phone calls. I have to confirm final numbers for table and chair rentals, time of drop off to the Gateway Garden room, and all that good stuff. Nothing you need to worry about," she said.

Brooks wasn't worried. He could tell from day one that Delaney had made the right choice. Even if he wasn't longing for more time with the girl in the coffee shop, he could see it in the designs on her tablet, the details she went over with him, and the sparkle that never left her eye when she checked another item off her digital list.

"How about you?" Tate asked. "Any big plans for the rest of the day?"

"I'll be working late tonight. I have somewhere to go before I head in and lots to do when I get there."

"Oh," Tate said.

He could tell by the way her voice fell that she wanted to know more. He probably could've told her, but he kind of liked the way she squirmed at the mystery. His eyes followed her hands. Her fingers brushed her slightly sun-kissed hair behind one ear and then the other. She did that a lot, especially at Primrose May the day he walked up to her. Today, though, Tate's curls were missing. Each strand had been meticulously straightened, less unruly than usual. Brooks liked Tate's hair straight, but he missed the curls. The way each one unraveled differently than the next gave the illusion that maybe she didn't always have it all together. It brought her down to his level a little. Today, however, her hair fit every other aspect of who Tate Montgomery really was, and he liked that she was showing it off to the world.

Brooks had to admit, the perfectly refined woman standing in front of him was intimidating and quite possibly way out of his league.

"I guess I should let you go then," Tate said once the two of them were outside the restaurant.

"I have to head over that way a few blocks." Brooks pointed. "I pass the Tube station on the way. I can walk with you."

"Oh, no, that's okay," Tate said. "My friend and I are actually meeting for lunch, so I'm going to head down toward Charing Cross. Thank you though. Have a good day."

"Yeah, you too," Brooks said. The expression on his face fell as he watched her walk away. The smile Tate wore while twirling around the lamppost had been a tease for him. It was like a two-part episode of a TV series where part one ended on a cliff-hanger and the words "To be continued..." flashed across the screen. He didn't want it to be over yet. He didn't want to wait for another episode; he wanted this one to continue. He knew it was over, though, when he could no longer see her through the sea of suits between them. That was when he turned in the opposite direction.

On his way, he thought about how in the short amount of time he'd known Tate, he'd learned a few things about himself. The first one was that maybe he didn't want to be single anymore. He liked having someone to look forward to seeing. Even if today was part of his job, the extra pep in his step the entire way to Primrose May was proof that Tate's company was affecting him. The other thing he'd learned was that his contentment grew in the moments he saw Tate smile. When he was the reason she was smiling, it felt even better. He felt his pulse quicken, and it was if his whole body was smiling along with her.

Brooks was throbbing with happiness when he pulled the door open to the suit store for his fitting. Garett and Vera's wedding was leaning more toward British tradition, so, instead of a tux, Brooks would be wearing what was called a "morning suit."

"Good morning." A dapperly dressed man met Brooks at the front of the store.

"Good morning," Brooks replied. "I'm here to pick out a morning suit." Brooks pulled his cell phone from his pocket and scrolled through to Garrett's last text with all the details of what he needed.

"Wonderful! You're getting married, yes?" the gentleman asked.

Brooks waved his hand in front of him. "No, no, not me—my brother. I'm the best man."

"Well then, let's get you over here, and we'll get some measurements."

Brooks walked over to the mirror-lined wall. He unbuttoned his jacket and let his arms fall out while he waited for the gentleman to return. Brooks had bought his first suit in London over a decade ago, for his first company holiday party. He got away with wearing that suit for several years before his jacket started to struggle around his muscles. There were two suits currently hanging in his closet, but they didn't match the look Vera was going for, so he was about to add one more. In his line of business, a guy could never have too many suits.

"Okay, are you ready?" The gentleman had a tape measure clutched in his right hand.

Brooks nodded and turned towards the mirror. He lifted his shoulders back and felt the cold metal end of the tape against the back of his neck first. He relaxed his arms for the next measurement and then raised them.

"You're all set. Let me pull out a few with the look you're going for." The gentleman patted Brooks on his shoulder. He disappeared for a minute and returned with an arm full of jackets and slacks.

It didn't take long before Brooks was standing in the suit he'd be wearing on Garrett's wedding day. It was navy, the main color Vera had chosen for her big day. Coattails hung from the back of the jacket, which covered up a speckled gray vest with pants to match. Brooks tugged at the front of the jacket as he admired himself in the mirror before confirming the look.

Garrett had impeccable timing. Brooks' phone started to ring as he was checking out, and he answered right before it went to voicemail.

"Hey, buddy," Brooks said.

"Hey! How'd it go with the suit today?"

"I'm walking out now. I've got it in my hands. It's purple, and I decided to go with a bright pink vest and tie." Brooks knew Garrett well enough to know that right about now, his grip would be growing stronger on his cell phone. His nose was probably crumpled up as he rolled his eyes.

"You're hilarious."

Brooks thought it was funny. It would've been funnier if Vera had heard it, but Garrett's reaction was enough reward.

"I'm playing with you. I've got a full navy suit with matching tie and a gray vest, as requested by Her Majesty."

"Awesome! Does a wedding date come with the suit?"

It was Brooks' turn to roll his eyes and strengthen his grip on the phone, but there was clearly something in his hesitation that brought hope to Garrett's voice.

"Wait...does it?"

"No. I mean, there's this girl, but..." His voice faded.

"But what?" Garrett's voice grew louder.

"You know the Ball of Hope, the one you and Vera are coming down for in a couple of weeks?"

Garrett made a noise of recognition.

"Well, I've been working with the event planner and she's... she's so many things. She's talented, put together, gorgeous, and she's a spitfire, that's for sure. She makes me laugh, and she challenges my way of thinking, and—"

"And you like her," Garrett interrupted like a five-year-old on a school playground.

There was a glow across Brooks' face at the sound of those words. "Yes, I like her."

"How about her? Does she like you?"

Brooks wasn't sure how to answer that. Tate's unyielding personality when they'd first met was softening. She had grabbed his hand on their way to Cecil Court. Her vulnerability to share the book with her that sparked the *Starry Night in Paris* theme seemed as if maybe she was letting him in a bit, but he could tell there were still a few layers to chisel away if he was really going to get through to her.

"I'm working on it." That was the most honest response he could give.

Brooks hung up the phone with his younger brother and, with the weight of his suit hanging over his shoulder, headed to the bus stop that would take him home. He asked himself Garrett's question again, and while he sat in the open air on the top of the bus, he thought about his short journey so far with Tate and wondered if maybe it could be true. Maybe Tate was falling for him too.

~13~

After leaving the west coast, Tate had come to appreciate those rare spring days when summer came early, though she knew it would quickly dissipate and the coolness of spring would hit London again. The extra warmth of the morning hit her face as she sat outside on her balcony. Dawn had not yet awoken most of Notting Hill, which meant Tate could enjoy the quiet sounds of chirping in the distance while she sipped coffee from her mug. Her bare feet were propped up on the wicker chair she'd pulled from the other side of her tiny patio table. Below, she admired the trees lining the side courtyard. She saw hints of color trying to peek through their abandoned branches. Soon, the cherry blossoms Tate had become so fond of would be in full bloom.

In a few hours, Tate was meeting Brooks once again to taste-test tartlets, éclairs, and croissants, and hopefully to finalize the dessert bar menu, but before that, she wanted to get a run in. It had been an hour or so since she started trying to convince herself to get dressed, but she was too comfortable to move. The steam from her coffee had stopped rising, and the coolness was now seeping through her mug. Tate reached over to the table beside her and flipped her cell phone for the time.

"All right, Tate," she urged. "Time to get going."

She slid her bare feet into her slippers and headed back into her flat to get ready.

*

Tate could feel the weight of her ponytail and the burn in her calves rising. She had done a full circle around the outskirts of Kensington Gardens and was now making her way back through. In less than two miles, she would be at her door, but for the past three, she had run with her body fighting her the entire time. She finally succumbed to the discomfort and slowed her pace, turning into Kensington Gardens with a leisurely stride. There were droves of people on the sidewalk as she ran around the pond, and she was feeling much better by the time the gate came into view on the other side of the park. Her calves were no longer screaming, so, with one heavy inhale, she started to pick up her pace again.

It was only a mile now, and she'd be home free, walking up the stairs to a nice warm shower. But as she rounded the corner onto Bayswater Road, a different kind of heat came splashing over her.

"Rubbish," Tate heard a voice say as she stood motionless. She was still processing what was happening. Once she did, the warmth climbed to her face. *Brooks would love this*, she thought, horrified she was now standing in his shoes. She was guilty this time of being the one to run into an innocent hand holding a fresh cup of coffee.

"Oh, my gosh," Tate said. She gazed at the man's blue button-up, which seemed to have escaped the wrath of flying coffee. There were a few noticeable spots on his khakis, but no sign of it on the jacket he was holding. Most of the coffee had thankfully ended up on the sidewalk. The rest was now on Tate's black cotton pants.

"I am so sorry." That was all Tate could say. She waited for the man to raise his voice at her, but he didn't. Instead, he readjusted his thick-framed glasses over his brown eyes and started to laugh. Tate soon followed, but she wasn't sure if it was because she found the current situation humorous or the fact she now stood where Brooks once did, and she certainly hadn't been as forgiving.

"I'd offer to buy you another one," she said, "but…" She waved her hands over her pocketless outfit.

"It's all right," the man said. He wasn't as tall as Brooks, but Tate still had to strain her neck to see his face. She was surprised to find him smiling. "Would I be too forward if I asked to buy you one?"

"Me?" Tate pulled her hand to her chest. She could feel the sweat lingering on her forehead. Her breath was still heavy, and she tried not to look down to bring attention to the wet streak saturating her bra line.

The man nodded. Using the faint reflection in his glasses, Tate tried to smooth any strays that had come undone in her ponytail, but it was hopeless. She was a mess. Aside from her hair and beads of sweat, there were now spots of coffee splashed along her thighs. The smile that still covered his face didn't seem to judge.

"Yeah, I could use a drink." Tate smiled.

There was a small café inside the park. Tate always stopped there on the days she came to the park for leisure. She'd bring a book, grab a coffee, and find a bench to relax on. She'd always gone by herself, but this man's curious eyes lured her in.

"Very well," he said. "I'm Jasper, by the way."

Tate smiled at the way he said his name, pronouncing the "er" as "ah" as in most words over here in the UK. Her hands were still sticky from the coffee. She wiped them one more time on her pants before taking his hand.

"Nice to meet you," she said. "I'm Tate." And with that, the two of them walked in stride over to the line at the café.

Tate's body was still on fire as they came to the front of the café line, so she opted for an iced chai instead of coffee, and Jasper ordered a refill of what was now left on Bayswater Road. The park was quieter than usual, so they sought out one of the many empty tables in front of the café.

Tate's foot tapped a steady melody on the leg of the bench once she sat down. She took a long sip from her straw and watched over Jasper's shoulder as two shaggy dogs chased their tennis balls and frisbees. One of them overestimated the distance as their owner let the ball leave their grasp. The dog jumped too soon, and instead, the ball ran into the dog's chest and knocked it to the ground. Tate laughed, and Jasper followed her gaze behind him.

"A lovely lad, isn't he?" Jasper asked.

"Seems like it," Tate said.

"Do you have one?"

"Oh, no," she said. Jasper's expression fell. "I mean, I would love one. My family had dogs growing up, but it's hard here, with a small space and a crazy schedule. How about you?"

"I do," he said. "A French bulldog. Her name is Willow."

He was a dog person. That made Tate smile. She always thought people who loved dogs were special. To love a dog, you had to be patient. Only those who were extremely caring, understanding, and kind genuinely cared for a dog. They had to forgive quickly and hear the words gone unspoken. Tate thought that if someone could love a dog that much, they would be rewarded with the greatest gift: unconditional love.

"I love the name," Tate said. "My family dog growing up was a Lab. His name was Winston."

"That's very clever," Jasper said.

The way he said "clever" gave Tate room for pause. She swore she saw his eyes roll at the mention of her dog's name, but before she could investigate too much, their attention was drawn back to the dog who was now wildly barking at the ball that attacked him.

Tate watched Jasper as he laughed, tossing his head back every time. His boisterous laugh echoed. She didn't mind that it could be heard by all those around them. She observed him in silence as the chai in her glass slowly began to disappear with each sip. His boldness intrigued her.

Jasper. Now, that's clever, she thought as she watched him reset his glasses that had fallen from the top of his nose. There was an air of mystery to him. Walking around mid-morning in a clean, pressed button-up. Most would be sitting behind their office desks by now. Tate imagined if she hadn't run into him, he'd be hopping the bus to Square Mile, or perhaps he was on his way to catch the Tube to Canary Wharf, where he'd spend the day in his glass-encased office. That was assuming he lived here, near Kensington Gardens. She still had a bit to learn about the stranger sitting across from her—a task she was excited to check off her to-do list.

"So where is it you were heading before I pulled you onto a detour?" Tate asked.

"To work, I suppose," Jasper said. "I work in accounting over in the City."

A sense of righteousness smeared across Tate's face. Her instincts didn't disappoint. Accounting wasn't quite what she had in mind when she'd pictured that corner office though. His broad stature and clean-shaven look had her thinking something more along the lines of lawyer or stockbroker. But she was right about the location at least. Square Mile was most often referred to those who lived in London as "the City."

"How about you? With that accent, I don't fancy you're from around here," he said.

"I'm a long way from home," Tate said. "I grew up in Seattle, the far west of the American coast."

"I imagine it's quite different over there."

"To an extent, yes," Tate replied. "A quick flight in Seattle would take you to the beaches of California. Here, it's anywhere from cute cafés in France to the mountains of Switzerland. The weather though—I didn't escape that." She looked up at the gray covered sky. The thick clouds were now hiding the sun that came peeking over her balcony only a couple hours before. Instead of despair, she always found comfort in London's fast-changing weather patterns. Sometimes, it was so similar to home she thought she might leave her flat on a Sunday morning and find herself stepping out into the Fremont Market. That had been one of her favorite things to do with her mom and Grace back in Seattle.

"Do you travel often?" he asked. "I actually just returned from holiday. Went to Amsterdam."

"Ah, a place I haven't been. I don't travel as much as I'd like."

Jasper went on to tell Tate about his "holiday," which, Tate had learned back when she was living in France, was not a celebration as in the US holidays, but simply a vacation. That was one thing Tate loved about being over here. There was plenty more holiday time than back in America.

She listened intently as Jasper talked about walking along the canal, stopping at local breweries, and expanding his horizons by exploring museums. Tate was so intrigued that she completely lost track of time. A hint of light flashed from the table, and she looked down at her phone. It was the calendar alert.

Tate ripped the phone from the table. "Oh, gosh!" she yelled, jumping to her feet. "I am so sorry, I have to go."

Jasper quickly jumped to meet her on her side of the table. "Can I see you again? Tomorrow night, maybe?"

Tate's heart was thumping. Was he asking her on a date? He certainly was, and maybe a month ago she would've been happy to oblige, but right now seemed like the worst time. Her plate was filling up, and her obviously complicated feelings for Brooks were clouding her mind daily. Then, it hit her: the distraction she was looking for. The one she so desperately needed to keep Brooks at arm's length. It was right in front of her! Suddenly, the timing seemed perfect.

"I'd like that." She smiled. A twinge of guilt grew in her stomach, but Tate tried to ignore it. She really did want to get to know Jasper more, but she hated that in the midst of typing her number into his phone, she saw Brooks' fingers doing the same the night they'd typed her number into his phone.

She tried to push that vision from her head because, unlike Brooks, Jasper came with no complications. Tate could breathe easy knowing this kind of distraction wouldn't cost her career. Once her number was safely saved, she handed Jasper's phone back to him.

"I'll text you then," he said.

"Sounds like a plan." Tate waved at him before turning back toward the gate. Her hand was still holding tight to what was left of her iced chai. A smile rose on her face, but while she sped up her pace to get home, she wasn't sure if it was because of the text she would be waiting on from Jasper or because, in a very short time from now, she'd once again be in the presence of Brooks.

~14~

Leicester Square seemed to be a regular stop for Tate these days. She squeezed through the Underground crowd and emerged back onto the streets of London. The afternoon bustle of workers aboveground was no different than any other day of the week. They swarmed around Tate as she made her way to Soho. She always knew she was getting close once the Palace Theater came into view. The giant stature of the redbrick building welcomed her to Soho. Tate followed the narrow alleyways to the black awning of the French bakery and pulled the wooden doors open to head inside.

"Hey!" Brooks stood from a table in the back corner.

"Sorry I'm late," Tate said.

He stepped over to pull the chair out for her. "No worries. They're still getting everything together. Did you want something to drink?"

"Water is fine for me," she said. Her hand wrapped around the cold glass waiting in front of her. She took a quick sip and then unzipped her jacket before throwing it over the back of the chair. Tate took in Brooks as he sat across from her. This was as casual as she'd ever seen him. A long sleeve gray shirt and jeans replaced the suit jacket he normally wore. *Gray looks good on you*, Tate thought. She loved the way it brought out the blue in his eyes.

"No coffee? Are you feeling okay?" Brooks laughed.

"You know me so well already." Tate smiled.

"You're a hard person to forget."

Tate pulled the glass of water to her lips so Brooks couldn't see her reaction and turned toward the window before the rosiness of her cheeks gave it away. Those words reeled inside of her, but Tate refused to let it be noticed. As much as he was trying, she couldn't give in. There was too much at stake. So, once the craving for more started to fade, she took a deep breath and turned back around.

"So what are we indulging in today?" Tate asked.

"Oh, you just wait. I still can't believe you've never been here before." Brooks waved over to the counter.

A dark-haired woman arrived at their table with two trays in her hands. Her blue apron hugged her tightly as she placed the trays on the table in front of them.

"Bonjour! Bienvenue à l'amour de la pâtisserie." *Hello! Welcome to Pastry Love.*

Tate was surprised at how quickly her understanding of French returned. She wasn't fluent, but she knew enough to get by. Not that she had a need lately. She hadn't visited France very often since she left. Never, actually. She had no desire to return out of fear it would only bring back the memories she longed to forget. For the time being, though, at least her years in the city of love were not futile.

"Merci! Les desserts semblent délicieux." *Thank you! The desserts look delicious.* Tate wasn't lying. Everything in front of her looked delightful.

"Ah, vous parlez français?" *Ah, do you speak French?*

"Un peu." *A little.* Tate held her fingers up for measure.

In her best English, the dark-haired woman explained all that was on the dessert tray. Tate picked up pieces here and there as she pointed to each piece. There was a raspberry tart topped with a blueberry reduction, coconut almond macarons, a blackberry mousse souffle, and mini chocolate éclairs. The éclairs,

Tate didn't discover through her words but from the familiar sight of them sitting in front of her. She had spent many nights wallowing in front of the TV with a box of them on her lap deep in the Bastille neighborhood of Paris. She could feel the pit growing in her stomach. Her eyes were fixated on those tiny chocolate-covered pastries. Suddenly, the woman's voice withered away, and the sound of Tate's own breath began to suffocate her. She placed her hand against her chest and fell heavy against the back of the chair.

"Tate?" Brooks' voice was muted. "Tate, are you okay?" He pulled his chair around to sit next to her. His hand was now resting on her shoulder.

Tate didn't look at him. Her stare burned into the éclairs as Brooks continued to say her name. After he asked, "Tate, are you okay?" a few more times, her breathing slowed. Brooks was still at her side, his fingers massaging her shoulder as she came to.

"Yeah, I'm okay," Tate finally replied.

"Here, take a sip." He slid her glass of water closer.

"Thanks."

"Tate, talk to me," Brooks said. His voice was somber.

"I'm fine, really," she lied.

"You just had a panic attack over a tray of French pastries," Brooks said. "You're not okay, Tate—so, tell me, what is bothering you?"

Tate had dodged that question plenty of times over the past few weeks. Falling back into the corner of the café while she designed the photo booth backdrop, eyes watering while she looked over a menu full of her favorite French cuisine, and now this. A tray full of chocolate éclairs had reduced her to the lowest Brooks had seen her, and she could tell by his furrowed brows that he wasn't buying the "I'm fine" speech any longer. So Tate turned her chair to face him and inhaled a deep dose of courage before she began.

"It's not *what's* bothering me," she said, "it's *who*."

Brooks readjusted himself and gripped the bottom of his seat.

"Remember my heart that I followed over here from Seattle? His name is Cameron. I met him at a bar one night in college. We were friends for a while and only started getting serious after I graduated. After graduation, we were inseparable. It only made sense, when he was offered a job in Paris, that I go with him. I'd given four years of my life to him by that point. We survived a whole year with an ocean between us, and once I was finally able to fly over, I settled in with him in this adorable second-story flat in Paris overlooking a cobblestone courtyard."

The memory was vivid as Tate let Brooks in on what had eventually brought her from Seattle to Paris. She talked about the details of her charming new home.

"There was a cast-iron railing on our Juliet balcony. That extra little space made our new home not seem so little. Gosh, was it tiny. With the two of us in there, we barely had room to move, but we didn't care. We had each other, and we did everything together…until we didn't."

The first year was everything Tate had hoped it would be. They'd explored all of Paris together and went out almost every night to try a new restaurant. Cameron had made friends at work whom they'd grab drinks with often.

"Then, things just changed," Tate said. "I wish I could tell you when or how, but I can't because I don't even know. A part of me thinks he met someone else, but I don't know how he would. When he wasn't with me, he was working. I don't know how he would've found the time. One day, he was there, and the next, he was carrying the last box of his things out the door. I asked him once if there was someone else. He didn't really answer. He rolled his eyes and walked away from me. Suddenly, it went from him and me and this adventurous life in Paris, to me, all alone, in a city I barely knew."

"Wow." It was Brooks' turn to fall heavily back into his chair. "I'm really sorry."

"Éclairs were my favorite form of comfort food when I was packing up to move to London. I guess these beauties just took me back there."

"Those damn éclairs," Brooks said, reaching for one. "We've gotta get rid of these suckers."

Tate watched as he brought his hand closer to his mouth. He paused for a moment to flash a sly smile and then shoved the whole thing in his mouth.

"Oh, that is good," he mumbled, barely swallowing the first one before he shoved a second into his mouth.

"Don't choke!" Tate couldn't help but laugh at his chipmunk-esque cheeks.

"I bet you've never had an éclair like this before. Come on, try one." Brooks grabbed another from the tray and circled it around in front of her. "Come on, you know you want it."

Tate surrendered. She opened her mouth and let Brooks slide the evil chocolate pastry inside. She had forgotten how good these damn things were. Tate savored the burst of cream as it exploded through the pastry.

"Good, right?" Brooks asked.

"Delicious!" she said once the éclair was gone.

"Now, how about we move on to the tartlets?"

Without even realizing it, Brooks had erased all of the sadness from Tate's mind. She was no longer back in Paris turning the lock for the final time on the door to an empty flat. No—she was right here in this French café with a tray full of desserts ready for tasting. A smile grew on her face as she reached for a whipped cream-topped strawberry tartlet. She leaned in and felt her leg slightly brush against the side of Brooks'. For a second, she was tempted to jerk it away, but she didn't. Instead, Tate let it lean there against him while she took a bite. With her mouth full, she looked over to find Brooks doing the same. Then, she looked over at the last mini éclair resting on the tray in front of them and smiled. After two long years, it had taken only seconds to erase the pain. Thanks to Brooks and his clever thinking, Tate would never look at another éclair the same.

~15~

Tate and Brooks came stumbling out of the French café on a sugar high. Both of them were still laughing from the mouthful of éclairs they'd inhaled. Brooks took Tate's continuous laughter as a sign. He was hopeful he had washed away any remnants of sadness those pastries brought.

"I am stuffed," Tate said. "I ate enough sweets to keep me full for a week."

"That's how I feel every time I come here," Brooks said. "So what's on your agenda for the rest of the day?"

"Actually, I was about to head to the art gallery near the square. There are a few artists who've reached out about displaying their paintings at the event, and I want to look at some of their work."

"Oh." Brooks rubbed a hand across the back of his head. "That sounds like fun."

The crowded alley pushed the two closer as they walked side by side. The square was about a stone's throw away in the same direction. It was a last-minute idea Tate had decided on when she was on the Tube that morning. She had received an email response from the gallery, and since it was so close, it made sense. The event already had half a dozen artists confirmed, but as far as wall art went, Tate had only secured real-life photography. She wanted a couple of paintings in the mix.

"I'm looking forward to it," she said. "I've chatted with a few who have pieces on display there. They've already done some French-style paintings and have no problem with creating one that can be done by the event. They would be exclusive, one-of-a-kind pieces!"

Brooks loved the way Tate's eyes lit up as she spoke. Her hands flailed around in front of her. *She always talks with her hands when she's excited,* Brooks thought underneath his smile. She turned to look at him for a second, and with her hands still thrashing, she accidentally nailed a woman's purse as she passed.

"Oh, my gosh, I'm so sorry," Tate said to the woman. She was only met with a nasty glare. Tate folded her hands together in front of her and joined in with Brooks' amusement. "Oops," she shrugged. "Anyway, how about you? Are you headed back to work?"

"Yeah, I suppose I should. Unless…maybe you might need a second opinion?" Brooks said.

Tate looked up, and she could see it in his eyes. He was pleading for her to agree. She stared into them a little longer, the sun's reflection glistening in them. The light hit the paleness of his eyes just right, so various hues of blues appeared like stained glass. Why did he have to make saying no so hard?

"Would you like to come with me?" Tate asked.

"Well, if you insist."

Tate shook her head and shoved him to the other side of the cobblestone. Tripping over his feet, he caught his balance on a lamppost before giving her a wink. How could she not laugh? He always knew the right things to say and when to say them. It drove her crazy in a way she knew it shouldn't, but Tate couldn't help it.

Brooks picked up his pace and ran to catch up, following her lead to the art gallery in the square.

"These paintings are unreal," Brooks said, staring at an abstract acrylic painting of snow-covered mountains.

"Look at this one," Tate said. She pointed to an incredibly detailed painting of a young woman. Her head was resting on her hands, and a single loose curl sat upon her shoulders. The rest of her curls were pulled back behind her, exposing the freckles on her face.

Brooks leaned over Tate's shoulder. He examined the painting before taking a few steps to the side to get a look from a different angle. Brooks was a bit of a history buff. He dove into books and museums every chance he got. The Tower of London fascinated him. Art had never been something he'd paid too close attention to, but today was different. These paintings were captivating enough to pull his eyes away from Tate—a task that had become almost impossible since he met her.

"Such incredible talent," he said. "I don't even know how you choose."

"Well, the good news is, I don't have to," Tate said. She took a step back and crouched down to sit on the long white bench beside the painting of the young woman.

In her notebook, Brooks watched her jot down a few notes.

"I can use them both. I think both of their styles will be perfect for what I'm thinking."

"What do you have brewing in that head of yours?" Brooks asked.

"I want them to paint the parts of Paris that everyone dreams of, but only few really get to experience firsthand. I want them to tell the story of a first kiss in front of the Eiffel Tower, sipping espresso outside a café while the sun sets, and passing a stranger who turns into your forever as they walk the Champs-Elysées."

As Tate shared what she envisioned with Brooks, she felt the heat rise inside her. She had always adored how Paris was the city of love. She remembered overhearing conversations from tourists when she lived there. It was usually their first time visiting, and immediately, they fell in love and had to come back. Tate had done a lot of research on Paris while waiting for her visa to be approved. The intrigue from photos was nothing compared to what she saw when she first stepped foot outside of Charles de Gaulle. It was so much more. That was why it was so important to her that the paintings unveiled a piece of art showcasing what Paris truly was: the place that made you believe dreams were never too far out of reach.

Tate was so busy scribbling things down in her notebook that she didn't notice Brooks had come to sit beside her. When she felt his arm brush up against hers, she looked up. Through the strand of hair that had fallen across her face, her eyes locked onto his. Tate's heart started racing as she followed his hand. His fingertips subtly swept across her temple to tuck her auburn hair back behind her ear.

"You really are amazing," he said. "I hope you know that."

Brooks watched as Tate shied away from his glance, but he could still see her smile as his fingers traced the hollow of her cheek before falling back onto his lap. What a double-edged sword he had been handed. He wasn't looking, but there she was, this amazingly passionate woman. Every word she spoke left him spellbound. When he was with her, he was never close enough, he could never get enough, yet he had to stay reserved. Sitting there on that bench, Brooks wanted nothing more than to pull her into him and feel her lips against his. Her intelligent way of looking at life worked him up more than the night she'd met him on the top step of the Lanesborough in that tight-fitting dress. He clenched his fists hard to fight the urge.

"Thank you," Tate said. "That means a lot. This event means a lot to me, so thank you."

"No need to thank me," Brooks said. "You're doing a great job. Our clients are going to be blown away, I can tell already."

Tate placed her hand on his shoulder. She squeezed her fingers around it in gratitude, making Brooks clench his fists even harder. He didn't want this moment to pass, but he knew that if it didn't soon, Tate would be able to see what she was doing to him.

"Speaking of clients…" Brooks pushed himself off the bench and faced the wall of paintings. "Do you remember Aaron?"

Tate nodded. How could anyone forget Aaron?

"His company is hosting a speaking engagement you might enjoy. It's over in Canary Wharf, but it's all about marketing your brand and standing out in the age of imposters."

"Oh, that sounds awesome," Tate said.

"I still need a plus-one if you're interested," Brooks said.

"I'd love to."

Brooks loved that she didn't hesitate.

"When is it?"

"Tomorrow night. I can pick you up around six if you'd like?" Brooks turned back around in time to see Tate's expression drop. He'd thought he had her. Not in a triumphant way—she wasn't a prize. He just wanted more time outside of the event planning to show her that this wasn't a phase they were going through. They could grab a drink beforehand, and he would ask her questions to get to know more about her. With the event quickly approaching, he needed every moment he could get with her. He wanted to prove she didn't need to build walls with him around, but he could tell by the look on her face that he wasn't going to get the answer he was hoping for.

~16~

Of all the days Brooks could have invited her out, it had to be tomorrow. Tate's social life wasn't anything to write home about. Every now and then, she'd meet Genevieve for yoga or a cocktail. Some days, she'd sneak into her favorite clothes shop in Notting Hill and chat with Theresa, one of the employees who lived in a flat above the boutique. They were close in age, and Theresa had moved to London from Australia only a year before Tate.

That was the extent of what Tate would consider "going out," but now, she had *real* plans. She was going on a date with an Englishman. He seemed sophisticated and successful—both words she could use to describe Brooks. She would also use "sexy" and "intimidating." Jasper wasn't quite those two things yet, but during their conversation over coffee, he had struck her interest, and best of all, he was safe.

Brooks was still standing in front of Tate waiting for an answer. Her lips fumbled as she tried to find the words to explain her unavailability, but, before she could, she was interrupted by the sound of her phone. She looked down to find Jasper's name lighting up her screen. *What impeccable timing he has*, Tate thought. She swiped her finger across it to read.

Jasper: *How does six o'clock work for you tomorrow? I have a nice little place in mind.*

Cameron used to say that to her when they were dating, even back in Seattle. That was where she'd learned her and Cameron's idea of a "nice little place" was drastically different. The first couple of times it happened, she'd pulled out her favorite dress from her closet and scrolled through her shoe collection to find a pair that matched. (Tate had scaled her collection down quite a bit since. Closet space in Europe was slim to none compared to her last apartment in Seattle.) Cameron would always compliment her on her outfit, but he never warned her that she'd be out of place. After maybe three nights of walking into a sports bar or fast-food joint near the water, she stopped trying so hard. Not that she minded the places Cameron chose, but a heads-up that formal attire wasn't required would've been nice. Tate wondered what Jasper's idea of a "nice little place" would be.

She didn't reply to find out. Not then, anyway. Instead, she jumped up from the bench to distance herself from the questioning look on Brooks' face. With her back to him, she finally answered.

"I can't tomorrow night. I have plans."

"Plans, huh?" Brooks used his sarcasm to hide his disappointment. He didn't know his invitation would end up blowing up in his face. "Like, a date?" he asked.

"Kind of." Tate turned back to look at him. "Yeah, I guess that's what you could call it."

"Oh," he said.

Tate cringed at the pained expression that was so vivid across his face. Why had she told him the truth? Why didn't she just lie to him? Any other answer would've allowed her to avoid the uncomfortable position she'd now put herself in.

It wasn't until she let her confession slip there in the art gallery that she finally saw it. Yes, Brooks had used his sense of humor to flirt with her, but his feelings weren't a joke. In the bookstore, she had reveled in the way he aroused her while pinned between two bookshelves. She couldn't help but laugh when he'd shoved one too many éclairs in his mouth earlier that day. It was true, Tate loved being around Brooks, but she couldn't give in to his charm; she had to keep this professional. The last thing she planned to do was hurt him. Bearing the thought of that was hard.

"If I didn't, though," she said, trying to soften the blow, "I would've loved to have gone with you. Next time, maybe?"

"Next time for sure," he said.

Tate was relieved Brooks didn't pry any further. She'd figured even during his disappointment, he would find a way to make light of the situation and gain more info, but he didn't. He didn't ask what her plans were or who they were with. He only turned himself away and walked over to the other side of the gallery to admire another piece of artwork hanging on the wall. She took that time to pull up Jasper's message once again.

Tate: *Six o'clock works perfectly.*

Tate hit the "send" button, and with it came a wave of guilt. Was she doing this for all the wrong reasons? She only had to wait about twenty-four hours to find out.

~17~

It had been a while since Tate last went out on a date. Her legs barely carried her to the bus stop. Jasper had offered to pick her up, but in true Tate fashion, she'd politely declined. She preferred not to be picked up on a first date. In case of any mishaps, Tate wanted to know she had an out. She also thought it was best to avoid an awkward silence that may occur in a car with two people who barely knew each other.

On the ride to meet Jasper, nausea began to set in. She thought it was partly nerves but also the fact the look on Brooks' face still haunted her. Tate wondered what he was doing right now even though she'd tried to push him from her mind. She had to give this date a chance. Tonight would be a clear indicator of where her heart was.

She was starting to feel extremely weak when the bus pulled up to the stop where she needed to get off. Thankfully, she had a few blocks of walking to try and calm herself down. The fresh air felt good against her skin. She took it slow down Southampton Street, letting her stomach settle. Though, as she walked along the multiple storefront windows beside her, she noticed some of the color had drained from her face.

"Get it together, Tate," she told herself repeatedly.

Luckily, everyone who scurried by seemed otherwise occupied. No one seemed to notice she was having a conversation with herself, although the multitude of window planter boxes stuffed with greenery that she passed may have gotten an earful. Tate glanced down at the directions on her phone as she walked by a sea of red umbrellas secured above tables on various restaurant patios. The blue dot was only a few feet in front of her. That would make her seven minutes late, which was five minutes more than what she told Jasper in her last text.

She passed a red telephone booth and a row of parked bikes along the sidewalk as the blue dot grew closer. A few more steps, and she was finally standing on it.

Tate looked up and took in the delicious smell of her childhood from the burger place in front of her. Burgers were her family's meal of choice every Friday night growing up in Seattle. That was no exaggeration. Growing up with two working parents, they never faltered in declaring every Friday night family night. On Fridays, Tate, along with her mom, dad, and Grace, would head out to explore the city. They always started with dinner. Even with so many restaurants in Seattle, it was never hard to choose. For years, they went to the local burger joint a few miles down the road. Even their orders never changed; all four of them would get a cheeseburger. Tate's dad liked his medium rare and everyone else medium-well. Tate's order had extra pickles, and Grace's had no tomato.

Tate stood there on Southampton Street laughing as she remembered how Grace would always tattle on her for stealing an extra onion ring or how, when they were younger, Tate's mom would make sure the girls ate at least half their cheeseburger before she let them have a mozzarella stick. Tate would try to sneak a fry or two off her dad's plate and dab it in the leftover ketchup that fell from her burger. She still wondered if he ever noticed, or if he was only pretending to let her get away with it.

After a minute of reminiscing, Tate realized the address in her phone wasn't the burger place, but the restaurant next door. She exhaled a sigh of relief. With the dark marble columns standing on each side of the wooden entry doors, she knew her black jumpsuit and matching heels would blend right in.

Her finger was just about to close out the directions on her phone when the chime of a text came through. It was already past six—Brooks had to have known she'd be on her date already. Tate's stomach jerked as if someone had punched her. She was tempted to open it and see what he had to say, but the whole idea of tonight was to let him go. What could he possibly want? He should be on his way to Canary Wharf by now. *Hit the button, Tate*, she thought. *Hit the darn button*. Her finger rested on the side of her phone as she tried to get ahold of her muscles to push it.

She finally hit it, and the screen went black. Before she could feel guilty, she shoved her phone into her purse and wrapped her hand around the thick handle of the restaurant door to head inside.

"Welcome." A young girl with blonde hair pulled back in a low ponytail greeted Tate inside.

"I'm a little late," she said. "Reservation for Jasper."

"Jasper, yes!" the young girl said. "Right this way, please."

They maneuvered through a sea of tables, and Tate watched the chefs in action behind the majestic marble top of the open kitchen that encompassed most of the room. Jasper must have seen them coming while Tate was distracted by the quick and precise movement of each knife stroke because he was already waving at her when she arrived. He didn't stand though. Instead, he sat comfortably in his chair. Tate had to bend down for a friendly hug.

"Are you okay?" he asked.

"I am, thank you," she said. The new stubble on his chin was rough against her cheek as she pulled away from him. That overshadowed her annoyance he hadn't stood to greet her.

Once she let go, Tate pulled off her jacket and wrapped it around her chair. Jasper thanked the young girl by her name, Aurora, then he reached over to fill Tate's water glass from the pitcher in the middle of their table. *That's better*, Tate thought. She observed him as he set the water down. His arms didn't fill out his shirt the way that Brooks' did. Jasper was by no means out of shape, but his slender build left him room to breathe without his chest pressing against the buttons as if they would pop at any minute.

"Have you been here before?" Tate asked. She couldn't remember the last time she went to a restaurant and left knowing the hostess's name.

"For a few lunch meetings, yes, but never for dinner," he said.

"It looks lovely." Tate put her water glass down and looked around the room, admiring the mix of colors and textures throughout.

"I like it because the menu changes regularly. It's all local," Jasper said.

"Amazing! I knew I liked you." She brushed her hair behind her ears. That was what she did when she was nervous. It was the number one reason she left it down. It looked more natural to comb your finger behind your ear than to fidget with a ponytail. How awkward would she look twirling her hair in circles?

She reached again for her water glass and took a three-second sip. Grace had taught her that. She told Tate, if she was ever out in a situation where she'd run out of things to say or needed to change the conversation, to grab her water, take a sip, and count to three. It was enough time to collect her thoughts, but not long enough that it would seem weird. She'd done it quite often at client lunches and even at the Lanesborough during dinner with Brooks. Grace's trick had a one-hundred percent success rate. Tonight included.

"So tell me more about your travels," Tate said. "Where else have you gone this past year besides Amsterdam?"

"Lots of quick trips to the coast, but I mostly frequent Italy for their wineries and Edinburgh for the scenery."

"I've always wanted to go to Scotland," Tate said. "It's on my list."

Jasper reached into his pocket and started to push a few buttons on his phone. They were five minutes into the date, and he was already committing a faux pas. Tate always put her phone in her purse when she was out with someone; it helped her to not be tempted to look at it. These days, it was easy to answer a quick email for work, but Tate also found it rude when the person sitting across from her found whatever was on their phone more interesting than her.

"Here we go," Jasper said after a few more swipes of his phone. "This was my last trip to Edinburgh." He turned his phone toward Tate.

She leaned over her plate to get a closer look at the stunning views of Edinburgh Castle. Then, he flipped again to show a photo of him standing in the forefront overlooking the city. It was amazing how vivid the Balmoral clock tower was from afar.

Once Jasper had flipped through a few more photos, she'd forgiven him for his faux pas. With each one, he'd dive into a story, and he only paused once for the waiter to take their drinks orders.

"I'm so jealous," Tate said, swiping to the final photo of Jasper walking along Princes Street.

"I'll go again before year's end for sure," he said. "I'd welcome the company, especially someone as beautiful as you."

Tate could feel herself blushing and was thankful when the waiter returned with her wine. When he was done pouring her glass of pinot, she wrapped her fingers around the stem and lifted it toward Jasper.

"To good company," Tate said, tapping the tip of his beer glass.

If only the date had ended there. If only she had walked out after that toast. Maybe she should've ordered a margarita instead of wine. The tequila may have helped a little, but she didn't have tequila, and even her third glass of wine wasn't drowning out what became Jasper's nonstop talk about himself. Her intrigue for his adventures turned mundane once Tate realized he didn't care much about who the good company was, only that he had someone to talk about himself with.

He was so engrossed in talking about his climb to the top of Mount Kilimanjaro and the time he pet a kangaroo in Australia that he never asked Tate one thing about herself. The only time she tried to get a word in was when Jasper started talking about his trip to New York City. Tate tried to make a joke out of how un-American she felt because she'd never been to the Big Apple. She tried to talk about the summers she spent in San Diego, where her grandparents had retired to.

"We would spend hours at the San Diego zoo," Tate said. "I remember playing hide-and-seek with the polar bears." She found herself laughing out loud at her five-year-old self. "Do you know what it's like to play hide-and-seek with a polar bear? I never won." She looked over to see that Jasper wasn't laughing with her. *Take a three second sip*, Tate thought. *Save yourself.* While she counted each sip of wine, Jasper used the polar bears to take back the conversation.

"Did you know, the bear is the official symbol of Madrid? My grandparents have a place there." By "place," Jasper meant a posh penthouse, one they let him use every now and then, most of the time when he was on break from university and they were back at their row home in London.

It was like he was trying to one-up her, which wasn't hard. Tate knew she lived a rather simple life, but she wasn't ashamed of it. She didn't grow up with the opportunity to fuel up a private jet and go island-hopping, but she had gotten to escape north to Port Townsend and do some hiking at Mount Rainer National Park. When her dad wanted to go big, he'd take the whole family skiing in Breckinridge or across the border to whale-watch near Vancouver.

Tate loved those memories, but they seemed futile as she sat at that table. Breckinridge wasn't the Swiss Alps, and Vancouver didn't hold a candle to Iceland. Jasper actually referred to both as lackluster in comparison. Who even used a word like lackluster? What the hell was going on? This could not be the same guy she met in the park. *He loved dogs!* Tate thought as she half-listened to his mumbling. *Dog people are not supposed to be self-absorbed.* She drifted off with that in her head, wondering if maybe she was wrong. Now she thought about it, maybe there was an inkling of red tape during their coffee in the park. A small one, but it was there in the roll of his eyes when she mentioned her family Labrador. Now, she knew she wasn't seeing things.

"Could you excuse me for one second?" Tate said. The waiter had come to clear their final course of dishes. Tate reached down and grabbed her purse, then slipped out of her chair to find the bathroom. She walked hastily down a dimly lit hallway, pushed open the door, and leaned heavily against her hands on the counter. Her purse rested between them as she glared at her reflection with slow and steady breaths.

"It's almost over," she reassured herself as she stood staring into the mirror. She'd feel better after she ran some powder over her face. Her hands searched around in her purse. Before she found her compact, Tate swiped her hand across her phone. Brooks' text message was still waiting for her. She tried to argue, but the letdown of tonight had weakened her fight. Tate pulled the phone from her purse and opened the text.

Brooks: *Have fun tonight. Wish you were here.*

As if the punch to her stomach when she first received the text hadn't delivered enough of a blow, this one delivered enough force for a knockout. Tate knew that couldn't have been easy to send. It was another show of Brooks' maturity and compassion, but man, did it hit hard.

Tate returned to the table right as the check came. She thought she could breathe a sigh of relief. She even tried to play nice and banter with Jasper about who would pay. She immediately regretted it.

"How about you make it up to me?" Jasper said. "I've got this...you can get dessert?" He slid his credit card under the receipt.

Tate forced a smile. She didn't want dessert. This past hour had been dreadful enough. She wanted to get out of there. It was times like these she wished she was more like her sister. Grace wasn't afraid to excuse herself to the bathroom during a date and never return. There were even times Tate would answer a call from her only to hear on the other end, "Oh, my gosh, are you serious? I'll be right there!" After the first couple of times, Tate started to catch on. *Be more like your sister, Tate,* her voice screamed inside, but she failed miserably.

"Sure," Tate said. "I'll get dessert."

One of Tate's favorite places was around the corner. It was close, and it was take-out, which meant she could hopefully get rid of Jasper sooner. Genevieve had introduced Tate to Sweet Cakes not long after they met. She remembered Genevieve cursing the abundance of cheesecake options for the extra weight she carried around her hips, but she had convinced Tate it was worth every calorie. It surprised her that a native like Jasper had never been.

"The cheesecake cookie dough slice is my favorite," she said. The two of them were now standing in front of the counter. "The blueberry crumble comes in a close second."

"I think you had me at cookie dough," Jasper said.

"You won't be disappointed."

Jasper smiled, and, for a second, Tate thought that maybe they had turned a corner. She ordered two of the cookie dough slices while Jasper loaded up on napkins. The two of them sat on the open bench outside. Tate took a small bite. Crumbs fell onto her lap, and she could feel the chocolate sauce sticking to the side of her lip. In hindsight, it probably wasn't the best choice for a first date, but with the way this one was going, the crumbling of the cake seemed fitting.

Tate watched as Jasper took his first bite. "What do you think?" she asked.

Jasper took a minute to swallow. "It's rather bland," he said. "There's a place down in Chelsea I fancy quite a bit more."

Tate's patience had been wearing thin all night, but this was the final straw. Not only had he spent the night interrupting her and making her feel inferior, but he couldn't even try to appease her when it came to her choice of dessert. Heck, she hadn't even wanted to take him there. Her favorite dessert place was now tainted by a self-centered, egotistical jerk.

Tate sat stiffly on the bench next to him thinking about when she had taken Brooks to Cecil Court. Now, here she was, letting someone else in on the secret of her favorite places, but the feeling inside of her was nothing like that day. That day in the bookstore, the beat of her heart had been so loud she thought it would deafen those around her. All she felt now was heat—her fury at Jasper's disapproval and lack of gratitude.

She looked over at Jasper as he jabbed his fork into the crumbling piece of cake resting in his opposite hand. This night had ended long before they sat down on this blue bench, but Tate was ready to go home. She was done.

"Hey, Jasper," Tate said, rising from the blue bench. "I'm not feeling very well. If you don't mind, I think I'm going to call it a night." Those weren't the words Tate really wanted to use. She wanted to tell Jasper how she thought he was bland and shove her dessert right in his face, but she was classy enough to hold back.

"Oh, all right." Jasper leaned forward to pull himself up off the bench. "Which bus will you be taking? I can walk you there."

"No, it's okay. I think I just need some good fresh air on the way. Thank you though." Tate's eyes grew heavy, and her stature sank as she took in the delicious smell of a warm cookie. Sadly, her appetite had crumbled. She stepped over and dropped the dessert into the garbage.

"Can I give you a hug?" Jasper stepped toward her.

The corners of Tate's eyes drooped even more as she leaned into him. It seemed as if there was some good in Jasper, but the rude remarks overshadowed what little he had shown that night.

"We'll talk soon."

"Sure." Tate forced a smile, hoping it would hide her lie. She had no desire to see Jasper again. She gave a quick wave and then dusted off her hands before spinning back around into the crowded street.

Tate shook her head the entire way to the bus stop. Her fingers exploded her anger via text to Genevieve, who responded immediately. She told Tate not to go home and that she would meet her out for a cocktail. The story was too good for Genevieve not to hear in person, and even though she felt a little dizzy from three glasses of wine, Tate didn't mind the idea of another. Even though her fury was strong, Tate knew exactly what tonight was. It was karma. She had tried to play it safe. She had tried to take the easy way out, and it had blown up in her face. Tate had wanted a distraction, and boy, did she get one.

She was so put off that, to be honest, for the first time that night, she wasn't even thinking about Brooks Walker as she stood alone on the London street and his name once again popped up on her phone.

~18~

Brooks hated that he was sitting there alone. The entire way to Canary Warf, he had tried to think of an excuse not to show. He wasn't even planning on coming, but he had thought Tate would join him. This was more for her than him, but there he was, sitting at the end of the aisle as Aaron clapped for everyone's attention.

While Aaron introduced the speakers of the evening, Brooks wondered if Tate was already on her date. He felt a pit in his stomach as he thought about her getting ready for a night out with someone else. Not that the Lanesborough had been a date, but he couldn't help but hate the fact Tate would be dressing up like that specifically for someone who wasn't him. He wanted so badly for it to be him. So badly, he pulled his phone from his pocket and scrolled through. He didn't know what he wanted to do once he found her name, but he wasn't going to call her. Brooks wasn't *that* guy. He stared intently into his phone as Aaron's words softened.

He wasn't going to call her, but he wanted her to know he was thinking about her. That he only wanted the best for her, and maybe, while doing so, it would send the slightest hint that the best for her...was him. He pressed the message icon on his phone and typed something out before deleting it. He did that at least three more times before he settled on what he felt was the right thing to say. Before he lost the courage and deleted it again, he tapped the "send" button and watched as it floated underneath the last message between them.

Brooks didn't want to give any time for her disappointing silence to flow through him. He slid his phone back into his pocket, readjusted his tie, and looked up at the front of the room. The seminar had begun. Tate's date had begun. He glanced at the clock. Time had never moved so slowly for Brooks.

"Sixty more minutes," he whispered to himself. That little needle just had to tick around more than three thousand times before he would allow himself to check his phone again.

It was going to be a long sixty minutes.

*

Brooks was able to sneak out during the applause. He was now overlooking the water of the middle dock at Canary Wharf contemplating his next move. It was almost half past eight. Tate's date was surely in full swing. He hated the fact he was even thinking about it—Tate on a real date. The time he'd had to get to know her was making the thought of tonight awfully hard. He leaned up against the railing in front of him and wondered if she'd worn her hair up the way she did the night they went to dinner at the hotel. If so, she'd probably spend the night the same way she had then, brushing the one uncooperative strand out her eye after each sip of wine. Maybe she had worn it down. He pictured her sweeping strands of her pin-straight hair behind her ears. He gripped the railing tighter, picturing another guy's hand caressing hers from across the table. Would she let his hand lay against the small of her back as the two of them galivanted down the street?

That was it. That last image drew his blood to a jealous boil. He pushed away from the railing and swiftly shoved his way through the nighttime dinner crowd. This feeling of heat rising inside of him was unfamiliar. He'd never wanted to wrap his hands around anyone's throat before. He wished he'd asked more questions. He wished he knew where she was. Then, maybe he'd have someplace to go right now. He could sneak inside. She'd never see him, but he would see her and know right away if she was slipping through his fingers before he'd ever even had a chance. He had to know. Even if another phone call would display his pure desperation, he had to know what she was doing.

It started ringing before he even had the phone to his ear. One full ring, then two, and still no answer. By the time the third ring had gone by, Brooks was starting to doubt his decision. Her phone was probably deep down in her purse, the ringing softened by her lively laugh.

"She's on a date, you moron," he said as the final ring before voicemail sounded in his ear.

He heard the click. Her message would start any minute, giving him a few extra seconds to decide if he'd leave a message of his own. The sound of "hello" echoed in his ear, but when silence fell afterward, he realized it wasn't the voicemail he had heard.

She had answered.

Suddenly, Brooks' chest felt as if a boulder had plummeted into him. He scrambled to find something to say as she repeated the word again, this time with a question mark at the end.

"Hello?" Tate tried not to sound irritated as she spoke. She wasn't exactly irritated at Brooks; Jasper was the source of that. She was, however, kicking herself for picking up. She was supposed to be stronger than that. It wasn't even nine o'clock yet. A good date didn't end before nine o'clock. He couldn't find out. Her heels clicked along the cobblestone beneath her as she hurried toward the bar, where Genevieve was waiting.

"Tate?" Brooks asked, surprised.

"Yeah, it's me."

"Oh, hey." He tried not to sound too eager. "I was going to leave you a voicemail. I thought you had plans tonight." Brooks was buying himself time. He wanted her to pick up, but now, he was at a loss for what to say.

"I did." She hesitated and then started again. "I mean, I…I do. I just thought it might be important since you knew I had plans." Tate hadn't meant for that to come out as rude as it sounded.

The boulder that was already suffocating Brooks' chest fell heavier at her response. She did have plans. She had made them with someone else. That still hit him hard. There wasn't much left to do but try to salvage whatever bit of dignity he might have left.

"Yeah, sorry about that. Delaney asked if I could have the dessert bar menu ready to show her tomorrow. Could you forward that list you chose over to me? Not tonight, of course. Tomorrow morning will be fine." Brooks gripped at his forehead as the words came out.

The look on Tate's face intensified as she neared her final destination. They weren't set to meet about the event for another few days. She hated the thought of someone else showing Delaney something that wasn't ready, but Delaney was the boss. Tate knew better than to second-guess.

"Sure, I can get it over to you before the morning," she said.

When Tate arrived at the bar, Genevieve was already inside. She didn't want to talk too long with Brooks because then he might get suspicious, so she walked into the bar, and the noise that surrounded her hinted to him through the speakers.

"That would be great. Sorry again to have bothered you."

"It's fine. No worries."

Genevieve looked at her with questioning eyes as Tate scooted onto the bar stool next to her. She pointed at her phone and mouthed Brooks' name. If only Brooks could see what happened after that. He would've seen from the way Genevieve made a heart with her hands and danced it around in front of Tate's face that her date was over. Tate slapped Genevieve's hands away as Brooks said his final goodbye.

"Enjoy the rest of your evening. Goodnight, Tate."

"Goodnight, Brooks."

After she said his name, silence filled the line. Brooks was mortified, but at least he had been able to lie his way out of his reason for calling. He was fairly sure his story was convincing. Huge gasps of air filled his lungs as he was finally able to breathe, but the fire still roared inside of him at the thought he was going to be going home alone with only thoughts of Tate to fill his mind, while someone else had her in their arms.

~19~

Tate was barely coming to the next morning when the sudden explosion of texts lit up her phone. They were from Delaney, and those texts were the fiery follow-up to two previous missed calls. Had she seen the menu already? Did she disapprove? Tate knew she never should have sent those to Brooks with no explanation, especially at one in the morning just to prove a point.

Tate was curled up in bed by eleven. Genevieve had convinced her to have a second martini while she hounded Tate about her feelings for Brooks, but she'd stood her ground. She was still trying to sort out the mixture of fear and bliss that was rolling through her at the mere mention of Brooks' name. She liked him. Gosh, did she like him, but the night before was still weighing heavy on her. What would happen if she let him in and then it all came crashing down? She would lose him. She would get hurt again. She would fall apart, and she wasn't sure she could handle that again.

That was why she had set her alarm for one in the morning to wake herself up. She needed to send over the dessert menu before he arrived at work that morning. When he received it, he would see the time stamp and maybe think she was just coming home from her date. Maybe the thought of her being out all night with someone else would make him grit his teeth. It might also make him back off, which would help Tate immensely since her ability to fight him off was weakening.

Once the blur from her eyes disappeared, Tate shot her head up off her pillow and read through the texts. Delaney was summoning Tate into the office for an emergency meeting. *This is it. I'm getting fired.* That was all she could think as her hands ripped the covers from her warm body.

Thankfully, the curls were still hanging in her hair from the night before. She brushed some powder onto her face, swiped mascara over her lashes, and dabbed some gloss on her lips before searching through her closet for the first acceptable outfit. A silk beige skirt and an oversize cowl-neck sweater grabbed her eye, and once she was in them, she threw her giant purse over her shoulder and was out the door, hopping down the hallway with one shoe still in her hand.

Thirty minutes later, Tate was speed-walking into the lobby to get her badge and squeezing in past the closing elevator doors to the fifth floor. There wasn't even time to sink herself into one of the comfy looking chairs before Delaney whipped around the corner.

"Tate, thank you for coming so quickly!" She gestured for her to follow her down the familiar hallway.

This time, instead of the meeting room, Delaney guided Tate into her corner office. She'd never been in a corner office before. Tate looked around. The sun lit up the room through the floor to ceiling windows. They gave a faint view of the River Thames. Two leather chairs waited for Tate in front of Delaney's desk. *If I'm going to get fired,* she thought, *this is definitely the way to go.*

Tate slid into one of the leather chairs. She crossed her legs and pressed her hands down firmly on her knee in an attempt to keep her legs from shaking. Delaney sat silently opposite her, looking up as her office door swung open and Brooks appeared. The other leather chair was no longer for show.

Brooks looked so calm in his black blazer as he sat down beside her. Tate tried not to look over at him, afraid of the piercing look she'd shoot his way.

She was going to lose her job, and even though she didn't want to, she was blaming him.

"Thank you both for coming," Delaney said, leaning back in her chair.

This was it. Take took a deep breath and prepared to take the punches. She hoped she could retaliate whatever was about to be thrown at her. Surely, she could talk her way out of this. She was good at her job. This event was coming together nicely. She could add more tartlets and less éclairs or vice versa if that was what Delaney wanted. She just had to give her the chance.

"I have some exciting news," Delaney continued. "A friend of mine is offering to donate an exquisite painting for our charity event. It was created by a French painter of the River Seine, and it's a one of a kind."

Tate sat frozen in her chair. That was the big emergency? A wave of air streamed through her pursed lips. Her shoulders fell back against the leather chair as she smiled in Delaney's direction.

Delaney's hands were folded, waiting for a reaction.

"That's amazing!" Tate said. She didn't feel it warranted the flood of texts on her phone that morning, but it still would be a perfect addition to the event.

Delaney wasn't done though. There was more.

"It certainly is, but there is one small problem," she said.

Here it comes... The real reason Tate was thrust out of a much-needed sleep. Tate held her breath.

"The painting is rather large, and shipping it could cause extensive damage, so..." Delaney paused. She pulled her elbows to rest on her desk, and her chin conformed to the fold of her knuckles. "I'm going to need your help in getting it."

Tate shrugged her shoulders. It seemed like an easy request. "That's no problem at all," she said, looking at Brooks.

He nodded.

"Where is it?"

"It's in Paris," Delaney said.

"Paris..." Tate suddenly felt the weight of the emergency fall upon her shoulders. She melted even further into the back of the leather chair. Then, she looked over at Brooks. He was the only other person in this room who knew what Paris meant to her. She stared deep into his eyes in the hope he could save her. He'd done it before.

"Paris," he said, turning to Delaney. "I'd be happy to make the trip. I know Tate has a lot to do here..."

"No, no," Delaney interrupted. "I would feel much more comfortable if the two of you went together. It's large and fragile. I've already reserved two rooms at the Maison de Saint Michel. You leave tomorrow afternoon. I will handle anything here that needs attention. Tate, you let me know."

Tate swallowed hard, but the golf ball in her throat remained. She managed to sneak out a few words she thought were convincing enough. "Yes, absolutely. I have a few meetings I can push, but I'll email you the things that can't wait, and we will..."—she paused to once again look at Brooks—"head to Paris tomorrow afternoon."

"Wonderful! I am so excited about this!" Delaney shrieked.

Tate smiled, hoping it was enough to drown out the nervous breaths that had suddenly overtaken her. She watched as Delaney slid back her chair. She thanked both Brooks and Tate again before leaving them alone in her corner office.

"Are you okay?" Brooks asked.

Tate squinted through the windowpane watching all those who seemed to be carelessly strolling through the streets five stories below. She too wished that right now she could be down there, unearthed from this plan, which, in less than twenty-four hours, would take her back to the city where she had left her crumbled heart.

"Yeah."

Tate was lying, and Brooks knew it. There was a gloom filling her eyes he'd never seen before. He hated seeing her like this. Her hands were fidgeting in her lap. He wanted to calm her, but he wasn't sure what to say. Instead, he reached over and cupped his hands over hers. Almost immediately, he felt her trembling ease.

"She doesn't have to know," Brooks said. "I can go. I'm sure I can handle a painting myself."

Tate smiled. She appreciated his offer and the concern in his wide eyes, which were now staring straight into hers. It was a gesture she wished she could accept, but she knew better. This was her job; her one chance to show what she could do. She'd come in here today thinking she'd be leaving with the event ripped from her hands. That wasn't the case, and she was thankful for it. So, even though she welcomed Brooks' invitation, she was certain she would be seeing Paris in the very near future.

"I'm going," she said. She pulled one hand out from Brooks' grasp and placed it on top of his. "I'm going to stop by the florist on my way home and confirm a few things, but I'll be ready for tomorrow afternoon."

Brooks released his grip, and Tate pushed herself out of the chair.

"Okay," Brooks said. He adjusted his pale yellow tie before joining Tate in the hollowed opening of Delaney's office door. "I'll send a car to pick you up. I'll get all the details in place and let you know when to expect it."

"Sounds like a plan," she said. "I guess I will see you tomorrow."

"Yes," he said. "See you tomorrow."

Tate's legs were weak with each step she took down the hall. By the time she was in the elevator, she could barely hold herself. She pressed the button, thankful no one else was inside. Once the doors closed her in, she fell against the wall, letting the coldness of the metal catch her. She was going to Paris and, if that wasn't torturous enough, she was going to Paris with Brooks in tow. She could barely fight the urge to stay away from him the hour or two she saw him on most days. Now, she would be spending the night away with him in another city—and not just any city. They would be in Paris, the city known for love, and only a wall would be separating them.

Tate held strong until she took her final step onto the marble floor of the lobby. Once the wind hit her face, tears flowed. Why did Paris have to be so complicated? The intimate details of this event had consumed much of her over the past couple of weeks—so much so that even the Paris she was bringing to life wasn't as tangible as the one she'd left behind. She had been planning the event as if Paris was only an imaginary city in a captivating novel, but now... Now, she was about to be in the real Paris. It would not be long until Tate would be walking the same streets she'd once adored. She'd be taking in sights she'd shared with only one other person, and her heart would remember all the things Paris had taken from her. Soon, she would be face-to-face with the Paris that broke her, and she would be there with the man she so badly wanted to put her back together.

Tate was terrified. Her life felt like a volcano brewing. All of the heat was coming together at the epicenter of it all, and she had no idea if she could keep it at bay. Whether she wanted it to or not, that volcano would soon erupt, and it would either cause vast disruption or intense pleasure. All she could do was wait until that moment and find out which one it would be.

~20~

The train station was overly crowded when Tate pushed through the entrance. She was surprised at how little it had changed since her initial arrival from France two years ago. The abundance of light that shone through the glass of St. Pancras International bounced off the arched ceilings and ignited the exposed beams. Tate could feel the warmth on her face as she wheeled her suitcase through the open room.

Brooks had sent a car to arrive outside Tate's flat just after noon. She was surprised when the driver opened the door to the back seat that there was no one else inside. A few minutes later, a text from Brooks confirmed he would meet her at the station and exactly where he'd be waiting.

Tate stopped halfway in and scrounged through her purse for some coins to use for the restroom before she headed to the departure lounge where Brooks had said she would find him. She spotted him slouched in one of the chairs just outside the gates, leaning against his oversize luggage. His eyes were closed, and his head bobbed with each inhale. *He is so damn good-looking.* His tanned skin glistened with the sun shining in on his cheeks. His broad shoulders were covered with a white T-shirt that was so thin Tate didn't have to imagine what was underneath. She knew she would have to play it cool during the next twenty-four hours, but she had to admit, if there was anyone she wanted to be there with her to keep her sane from the memories Paris held, Brooks was the best choice.

"Good morning," she said once her shadow was covering him. His eyes flinched from the small poke of her finger to his bicep.

"Hey, you," he said. "You ready to go?"

"Ready as I'll ever be."

With that, Brooks reached into the front pocket of his duffel bag and pulled out both of their tickets. He examined them carefully before handing Tate the one with her name across the top. She followed Brooks' lead to the ticket scanners and then through security check. Once they were through to the departure lounge, Brooks pulled out a book and flipped it open to where the bookmark was hanging.

Where the Crawdads Sing were the words written in white across the cover. Tate had heard great things about that book, but with little time for reading these days, she hadn't had a chance to pick up a copy of her own.

"How are you liking that so far?" she asked.

"A mix of mystery and courtroom drama," Brooks said. "It's got me hooked. Even the romance pulls me in, and that's not typically my genre."

"Surprising," Tate said.

His eyes looked up from the words on the page. The muscles on Tate's face struggled to keep from smiling as he cocked his head toward her.

"What's that supposed to mean?" he asked.

"Well, it's just that you're such a smooth talker. You know, a real gentleman. I figured you got that from your fair share of romance novels."

"Are you mocking me?" He closed the book again and set it on his lap.

Tate's muscles had given in, and instead of the sneer she tried to hide, she was now laughing. She wasn't mocking him. He *was* a smooth talker, and when it came to being a gentleman—well, even before the train fell off the tracks, she had judged Jasper during their date because he hadn't done the things Brooks did. He didn't pull out her chair at dinner to seat her. He didn't ask her what she preferred on the wine list, and he never asked a single question that would hint at his inkling to get to know her.

She had felt bad initially for judging Jasper when she was pulling out her own chair. Not that it was necessarily wrong. This was the twenty-first century, and she was more than capable of seating herself. But when Brooks had pulled her chair out at The Lanesborough, it made her feel something she hadn't felt in a long time: special. Tate knew before she sat down that night with Jasper that he was in trouble. Even if he wasn't an egotistical jerk, he still needed to fill the shoes of Brooks Walker. Those were some pretty big shoes.

"Not mocking." Tate said, finally able to catch her breath. "I'm being serious. You seem like one of the good ones." She stopped mid-breath. She knew better than that and winced as soon as the words came out of her mouth. A heavy sense of guilt fell over her, but the smile on Brooks' face immediately erased any of her regret.

"Ms. Montgomery," Brooks said, leaning his shoulder into hers. "Are you hitting on me?"

"Oh, for real!" Tate pulled herself away and shoved her hand against his chest. The firmness underneath her palm immediately sparked an illicit thought: *Pull him closer.* The rush through her body was eager to submit. She leaned her hand harder into him, and this time, she really did push him away— but she did it slowly, savoring every moment the two of them were connected.

Tate followed her fingers with her eyes as they slid down each ripple of his carved abs before letting go. The arousal her thoughts ignited was taking over. She had to get out of there. She had to collect herself and stop the image of her hands caressing the bare skin underneath that T-shirt from filling her mind. Tate shook her head. She was letting her imagination get the best of her, and if she didn't stop, she would soon be melting into a puddle right there on the train station floor.

"I'm going to get some coffee," she said, pulling her hand from the armrest. Right now, it was the only thing separating the two of them. Tate was equally as thankful for it as she was resentful. She liked being near Brooks, but the temptation was becoming too much. "Do you want anything?" She stood from her chair and wrapped the strap of her purse over her shoulder.

"I'm good. You go ahead," he said.

So she did. She took the long way down the aisle before turning toward the café. With each step, she wondered if Brooks was watching her; studying her as much as she was him when she pressed her hand into his chest.

~21~

She was killing him. He could feel it. There was a sharp pain digging deep through the skin where his heart hid. He gripped the fabric of his jeans as she swayed away from him. Her steps were meticulous. She could've turned down two aisles by now, yet there she was, teasing him with each step she took, making sure he could see how those sea blue leggings accentuated every toned muscle of her calves, her thighs, and her backside.

Brooks let his head fall against the back of his chair once Tate was finally out of sight. Of course she had to do this to him in a heavily populated place. He closed his eyes and took a few deep breaths, trying to think of absolutely anything but Tate Montgomery. It took a little, but by the time Tate returned with her coffee, the blood flow had moved from one brazen area of his body and was now flowing evenly throughout. His heart was no longer endangered by the sharp blade of Tate's tantalizing knife.

"Are you okay?" Tate asked. She lowered herself back down into the seat next to him.

"Yup, never better." Brooks knew that wasn't going to be the case for long, so he grabbed the handle of his suitcase and used it to help him stand. "The train is boarding. You ready to get this show on the road?"

"You bet!"

Tate reached down to adjust a few things in her bag. While she struggled to zip it back up, her black V-neck revealed a shade of pink covering her chest. It caught Brooks' eye long enough for him to realize he was now staring at the crevice peeking out of her sports bra. He shot his glance away and turned quickly to start the walk to the train platform.

"Here, let me help you," Brooks said.

The two of them were now on the train. They stood in the aisle as Tate struggled. It was nothing that hadn't happened to her before. Tate had inherited her mother's petite frame. Heels helped her to overcome it on most days, but today, her decision to wear flats meant she could barely lift her bag over the lip of the luggage rack above them. Brooks' hands swept in between hers as he lifted the bag from her hand and set it directly above her seat.

"Thank you," she said.

"No problem," he replied. "Do you want the window seat?"

Tate looked up at the handsome man towering over her. It was another gentlemanly gesture. She loved the window seat, but Brooks had already done so much with sending a car and getting the tickets, she didn't want to be the one to choose.

"It doesn't matter to me." She shrugged.

Brooks smiled and waved his hand in the kind of way Tate quickly knew translated into "after you." He couldn't fool her.

With that shrug came a shimmer of hope in Tate's eyes that Brooks heard loud and clear. He liked that he could make her happy, even if it was over something as minuscule as offering up the window seat.

Brooks had always been a fan of the window seat. He and Garrett always fought over it on the plane when they lived in California—so much so that his parents started booking two seats together instead of trying to seat them in the same row. Garrett would sit with his mother, and Brooks with his dad. He never took his eyes off the window. He'd pretend he was the captain of a ship in a faraway galaxy. He'd make up villains as the flight went on. They'd fly through the air, and he'd jerk in his seat to knock them down.

That wasn't why Tate liked the window seat though. He knew that.

Tate actually didn't care much for the window seat on an airplane. It was harder to get up to pee. On the train, however, she loved it. There was so much to see, such as livestock grazing the hefty grass or women who enjoyed simplicity hanging clothes from the lines over their gardens. Tate's world was fast-paced; she was always running somewhere. She loved the idea of those picturesque scenes. Sometimes, she would even find herself escaping into one as the train roared by.

Here she was again, on the search for an alternate reality. This time, though, she wasn't sad or lonely; she was content. Her life was rolling out smoothly like the red carpet before an awards show. Hopefully, nothing was coming to stomp on her. She had dodged that bullet the day before, thinking her event career was about to come crashing down over a platter of petits fours. Tate couldn't hold in her humor about it all, and suddenly, a tiny squeak escaped her lips.

"You all right over there?" Brooks asked. He was now sitting down next to her. The pages of his book were opened once again to where the bookmark rested.

As Tate's laugh became louder, Brooks' curiosity grew with it. He leaned his elbow onto the table and closer to her.

"I'm sorry, yes," she finally said. "I'm fine. I was just thinking about Delaney's emergency meeting yesterday."

"What about it?"

"Well, I actually thought that when I showed up to her office, she was going to fire me."

"You, what? Why?"

"I thought she hated the dessert menu. I figured you showed it to her first thing and it was all wrong, and she texted me so she could let me go."

A wave of guilt rolled through Brooks' stomach. He had completely forgotten about his mortifying request until right then. It was still sitting in his inbox, unread. That morning after he asked, he had scrolled through his emails and saw Tate's name in black lettering. He saw the dessert menu subject line and placed his arrow to click on it but paused when he saw the timestamp. It read 1:22 a.m. He didn't even have to question why Tate would be sending it to him so late. He knew. She was getting home from her date. She probably hadn't undressed yet, and he hoped that when she did, she would be doing it alone. The late-night email already nailed defeat into his heart like a hammer; he couldn't bear the thought of someone else taking her to bed. So he never opened the email; he just left it there to torture himself.

"Oh, Tate," he said, "I'm really sorry."

"It's not your fault. Sometimes, I just let things get the best of me. You didn't tell me though, what did Delaney think of the dessert menu?"

The waves in Brooks' stomach had stopped rolling. They were now raging inside like rapids as he prepared his confession.

"No, it is my fault," he started. "Delaney didn't ask to see the dessert menu."

"Wait, what?" Tate's head turned in wonder as she waited for clarification.

"When I called you that night, it was because I was all up in my head. Look, I know this"—he wiggled his fingers between the two of them—"is maybe more one-sided than I'd like it to be. The idea of you out with someone else was driving me crazy, so I called thinking that if you didn't answer, I'd have my confirmation, but with the slight hope that if you did answer, maybe there was a still a chance. Except you did answer, and things were going well. I panicked, and that's the best excuse for calling I could come up with."

Tate fell back in her seat. Her stony face gave away her disappointment, but that was what she wanted Brooks to see. She wanted him to feel bad—for a minute, at least. Inside, though, her heart was pounding. Yes, that call had wreaked havoc on her morning, but the overall gesture was kind of sweet. It also made her feel better about slightly stretching the truth that night he called.

"I am so sorry, Tate," Brooks continued to plead. "Don't hate me."

Tate sat stoic for another minute. Then, when the train horn sounded, she decided it was time to even the score.

"I don't hate you," she said. "I actually have a tiny confession myself."

"You? What confession could you possibly have?" Brooks asked.

"When you texted me the other night, I was on my 'date,'"—she wasn't afraid to pull out the air quotes—"but later that night, when you called me, I was on my way to meet my friend Genevieve."

"Really?" Brooks' eyes widened as he leaned against the table. "Like, with your date?"

"Heavens, no." Tate rolled her eyes. "By that time, I'd faked a stomachache and pretended I needed to get home."

"It was that bad?"

"It definitely could have gone better," Tate said.

Brooks hung on to every word as Tate went into each dreadful detail. He couldn't help but wish he had actually shown up that night. Maybe then, he could've saved her. On the outside, his eyes showed concern, but internally, he was jumping around with as much excitement as a kid in a candy store.

"And it's not one-sided," Tate smiled. "It's just a little more complicated from my side."

Brooks' eyes widened as did the growing smile on his face. Tate didn't want to give him too much to hold on to. She nodded and slid her headphones into her ears before turning to look out the window. Brooks let his head fall against the headrest. With the smile still on his face, he closed his eyes. There was still a chance. Though she was fighting the clear chemistry that was building between them, there was one thing that gave him hope: she had lied to him. She had wanted him to think she was still out on her date because, just as he hoped, maybe she liked him a little bit more than she let on.

~22~

It was only a two-hour train ride into Paris. Brooks made it through just two chapters of his book. He slept the rest of the way. Every now and then, his head would drop onto Tate's shoulder, and when it did, she would grip her coffee tighter. Admittedly, on a few of the occasions his head landed on her, Tate gave in and tilted her head toward him until she felt the prickle of his hair on her cheek. She only stayed that way for a few seconds though. Before he was jerked awake by the movement of the train, Tate would pull herself back up and take a nice long sip of her coffee.

Brooks was still sleeping as the train passed through the Channel Tunnel. Tate sat with her headphones in and tried to ignore the fact the tunnel was underwater and not the kind of tunnel to try and hold your breath through. She and Grace used to do that in Seattle when they were little. They'd hold their breath, close their eyes, and make a wish. Sometimes, those wishes came true, but Tate was always skeptical if it was really the tunnel that turned her luck.

Thirty-five minutes after traveling under the sea, Tate was looking out at the French countryside. It wasn't long after that, they pulled into Gare du Nord station.

"Wake up, sleepyhead." Tate nudged Brooks once the train came to a stop.

Together, they followed the crowd out onto platform number five and headed into the concourse.

"So what exactly is our plan for today?" Tate asked. She had yet to see the itinerary. The two of them were standing still in the middle of the concourse while others swirled by them. There wasn't any direction Tate turned in which crowds of people weren't scurrying to their trains. It didn't surprise her. They were standing in the busiest station in Europe.

"It looks like we have dinner with Mr. Bastien at half past six," Brooks said.

Tate looked at her watch. It was almost four. The hotel was surely ready for them to check in.

"We're staying over near Le Jardin du Luxembourg," Brooks said in his best attempt at French accent. "That's only about a ten-minute cab ride."

"Great!" Tate smiled. "Let's do it." She reached down to grab her bag, but Brooks already had it in his grasp. He winked at her as dragged it alongside him, and although she wanted to protest, she let him take it and only nodded with a smile before spinning around to the doors that would lead them out onto the bustling streets of Paris.

Brooks was right—it didn't take them but fifteen minutes to fight their way through the traffic. Tate stared out the window the whole way, taking in all the sights. She'd never forgotten how beautiful Paris was; she had simply chosen not to reminisce about it. Now that she was here, though, it was hard not to fall back in love with the pristine architecture and café-lined streets. Everywhere she looked, people were deep in conversation, coffees in hand underneath café awnings. *Oh, Paris, I've missed you...* That was all Tate could think as the sights whisked by.

"How are you doing?" Brooks asked. "You know, being back here?"

"Surprisingly, I'm doing okay so far," Tate said.

"Good. We've got a lot to keep you distracted tonight too," Brooks said just as the taxi turned onto a familiar street

"I'm looking forward to it."

The Grande Maison de Saint Michel was one of many hotels adjacent to Luxembourg Gardens. It was a little bit of a hike from the flat Cameron and

Tate had shared, but on days she was feeling ambitious, Tate would walk there to enjoy the surroundings.

As they drove by, the nostalgia began to set in. There was Café de Sucre. She'd gone there almost every Saturday morning for her coffee. When the car turned onto the street of Tate's favorite boulangerie, she gasped. She had gone there weekly while living in Paris. She'd wake up early to make sure she was able to get her hands on their baguettes. If she arrived after ten any day of the week, they were always sold out. *Maybe I'll go there tomorrow morning,* she thought. *For old times' sake.*

The final turn led Tate and Brooks right to the entrance of their hotel. She let Brooks open the car door for her, but, this time, she grabbed her bag before Brooks could get ahold of it, then followed him up the stairs and into the lobby. There was a line of guests waiting, so Tate pulled out her phone. Her hands almost threw it to the floor when she saw a text lingering on her screen.

It was Jasper.

A deep sigh escaped her. She had forgotten where she was until a dark-haired man with a matching mustache turned around.

"Sorry," she whispered.

He nodded and turned back to the front desk.

"You all right?" Brooks asked. "You're kind of pale."

"Yes, I'm fine," Tate snapped. "That guy from the other night just sent me a text."

"Hmm." That was all Brooks could come up with.

Tate swiped her finger over her screen. She was annoyed, but she still wanted to see what he had to say. She was so agitated at seeing Jasper's name, she didn't notice Brooks peeking over her shoulder. His neck was stretched as far as it could go; he wanted to see what he was up against.

Jasper: *I hope you're feeling well. Would love to see you again. Fancy a drink?*

Seriously? Starting off on the wrong foot was an understatement. That night had felt more like a freaking tornado came ripping through. It was as if they had tripped and tumbled down a colossal flight of stairs, taking everything in their path with them. Tate appreciated the effort, but instead of asking her out again, she thought Jasper might have fared better if he'd given an apology.

Tate: *I'm feeling better, thank you. Out of town at the moment. I'll get back to you.*

She knew the text was too subtle to get her point across, but it would at least get Jasper off her back for long enough to form the right words. She had no desire to see him again.

Jasper: *Okay. Looking forward to it.*

Take shook her head as she read it. That text did not warrant any reply. She let it sit in her phone as she shoved it back into her pocket.

"All good?" Brooks asked.

"Fine." That was all Tate could muster without exploding.

Brooks smirked. He'd never seen her so riled-up before. The way her cheeks flushed and her lips puckered, he found it incredibly sexy.

"What?" Tate snapped.

"Nothing. Your personal life is none of my business," Brooks said.

"Well, yes, that's true, but as you can tell, it's not like my personal life is going very smoothly."

"No personal life?"

"None." Tate shot Brooks an intense glare. She knew what he was getting at, and there was no door opening for him. It had been locked since the day they met, but now, after Jasper, she'd flicked the deadbolt and thrown away the key. Men were her least concern right now.

"I see," Brooks said.

Even with him half a step ahead of her, she could still see that sly smile on his face. He reached a hand up to scratch his head in order to hide it, but he wasn't quick enough. Tate wanted to say something to confirm how serious she was, but she didn't have time.

"Bonsoir. Welcome to Saint Michel. How can I help you today?" A young man waved them over. His English was slightly hard to understand, but between the two of them, they grasped onto enough of his words to be able to get the keys to their room. "Rooms three-two-six and three-two-seven," he said, handing both keys to Brooks.

"Merci," Tate said. "Bonne journée." *Thank you. Have a nice day.*

Halfway down the hallway of the hotel's ground floor, Brooks commented on Tate's French. It was the second time she'd attempted to test her knowledge in front of him. Funny seeing as after she left Paris, she'd had no other reason to until now.

"Bonne journée," he said in a higher-pitched voice. It sounded nothing like Tate's, but she knew what he was doing.

"Hush," Tate said, letting the door to the stairwell close on Brooks' chest. She heard the thud followed by a scowl and couldn't hold in her laugh.

"I'm very impressed by you, that's all."

"Mhmm," Tate responded.

By the time Tate reached the top of the third flight of stairs, she was gasping for breath. Brooks wasn't far behind. She had never understood how she could run miles on end without barely breaking a sweat, but when it came to stairs, she felt as if she'd just hiked Mt. Everest. Tate tried to take in slow, deep breaths so Brooks wouldn't notice. If he did, he hid it well as he passed her.

Room three-two-six came first. Tate volunteered to take it. Both of them stopped outside, and Brooks handed her the key. Tate slid the key card into its slot, and when it turned green, she propped the door open and swung back around to face Brooks.

"All right, neighbor," he said, "how about we meet down at the lobby at six? The restaurant isn't too far from here."

"Six it is," Tate said.

"Okay then, I guess I'll see you later."

Tate nodded and pushed her way into the room. It was small, but everything she needed was in it. There was a tight squeeze between the dresser and the bed, but Tate made it through to place her bag on the chair next to the window. The curtains hid a gorgeous view of Luxembourg Gardens. When Tate slid them to the side of the glass, she was mesmerized by the color of the flowers starting to bloom. The trees were beginning to rebirth their leaves around the fountain. Gosh, how she loved that fountain. She used to sit on the bench beside it for hours. Sometimes, she'd bring a book, and other times, she'd just sit there in silence watching people as they walked by.

In the midst of admiring what was outside her room, she almost forgot about the room next door. Tate heard faint movement coming from the other side of the wall and tried to ignore it as she pulled her toiletries from her bag. The walls were thin. From the bathroom, she could hear the drawers open and close. She welcomed the distraction from the stream of water coming from the shower once she turned the handle. Her hair loosened from her ponytail and fell to her shoulders.

The noise next door stopped as she was slipping out of the pair of leggings she'd been snug in all day. Steam had filled the air, and Tate's reflection disappeared in the bathroom mirror. Now, all she was left with was herself, a hot shower, and thoughts of the guy next door.

~23~

Tate readjusted her dress as the hotel room door pushed open into the hallway. It was a couple minutes after six, and she was sure Brooks was already down in the lobby waiting. She slid into her heels as she hopped down the hall to meet the elevator. The yellow earrings from the Portobello Market were now dangling from each ear.

The line to the front desk was even longer than when they arrived that afternoon, but through the crowd, Tate spotted Brooks across the lobby. He was sitting at the bar in the lounge, his hand wrapped around a cocktail glass. His dress was much more formal than when she last left him by her hotel room door. The T-shirt she couldn't stop staring through had been replaced with a navy blue suit and brown dress shoes. Without even knowing, he had perfectly complemented her pale pink dress with the button-up shirt that sat underneath his jacket. If he was a stranger at the bar, she'd be sure to slide into the seat next to his. She'd order a drink and swirl her tiny black straw around in the glass, hoping he'd notice. He'd say hello, and she'd reciprocate with a faint smile. Only, Brooks wasn't a stranger. He was her client, and although she had given up on trying to pretend his good looks didn't soften her guard, she still had to remember there was a line she dared not cross. She was already teetering close to it as their flirtation grew more daring.

Even as she was walking into the lounge, Tate's desire for Brooks to see her newly bronzed skin intensified with each step she took. She was sure the sound of her heels would grab his attention, but he was concentrating hard on the bottom of his almost empty glass.

"Starting early, I see," she said. Her hand on his shoulder broke his concentration.

"Liquid courage," Brooks replied.

"Are you nervous?"

That was when he finally looked up. Their eyes met just as a loose curl fell from the bun Tate had worked so hard to secure with more than a dozen bobby pins. She smiled as if it was the first time she'd ever seen him. His jawline, which was usually hidden by stubble, was now smooth. His eyes were brighter against that navy blue, and Tate watched as they traced her from head to toe and back up again.

"You look..." He paused. His eyes were burrowing into her, but he didn't finish; he only turned back to the bar, raised his glass to his lips, and shot back the rest of whatever he'd been sipping on before Tate arrived. Then, he stood and reached out his hand to her.

"Ready?" he asked.

"Ready."

Tate took his hand and let him lead her out the door. Brooks was right: the restaurant was only a short walk from the hotel. When they arrived through the tall black gate, it hit Tate like a ton of bricks. She'd been here before. In fact, she'd been here many times before.

"Who are we meeting with?" she asked Brooks. She knew he had told her at the station, but she was too distracted by everything going on around them to fully absorb the information.

Brooks had to take out his phone again. He scrolled through Delaney's text until he came to the name. "Mr. Bastien," he said. "Pierre Bastien."

Pierre Bastien owned Château Lumière. Tate knew that because before she left Paris, Pierre was someone she had become quite fond of. She would've considered him a friend, but obviously not good enough of a friend to not know his last name when Brooks first mentioned it. Tate and Pierre hadn't spoken since they'd said goodbye the night before she left Paris. She remembered the way the tears fell from her eyes as she hugged him for the last time.

Tate stood back while Brooks went to the hostess stand to let the young girl know they were here to see Pierre. She disappeared into the restaurant to find him. The sound of Tate's pounding heart was so loud in her ears she could barely hear the violins playing in the corner. She placed her palm over her chest. It was throbbing, quick and steady, like a horse on a racetrack. Would he recognize her? That was her only thought before Brooks returned. Of course he would. Her hair may have been shorter and her eyes less puffy, but other than that, she hadn't changed much since the last time she sat right over there, at the corner table on this front patio.

She had always sat at that table. *They* had always sat at that table, Cameron and her. She stared over at it remembering all the times he had pulled out the chair for her. Then there was the night he'd sat silent and awkward across from her before tearing her life apart. There was a couple sitting there now. Tate thought they had to be in their mid-twenties. A bottle of wine sat chilling on the table between them. His hand was holding tightly onto hers. The way they laughed put Tate in such a trance she forgot all that was around her. Vaguely, she heard her name. The sound of it grew louder until Brooks' hand fell on her shoulder, pulling her back into reality.

"Tate," Brooks said, "where'd you go?"

"Huh?" But Tate didn't have time to answer. The hostess had reappeared, with Pierre following close behind. Tate tucked herself behind Brooks. She needed time to catch her breath. So many thoughts were flooding back into her mind. Her legs were getting weaker by the minute, so she had to grasp onto the back of Brooks' jacket to balance herself.

"Bonjour," Pierre said, reaching his hand out to Brooks. "Bienvenue au Château Lumière." *Welcome to Château Lumière.*

"Merci," Brooks said with a perfect roll of his tongue. "We are delighted to be here."

Brooks stepped aside so Pierre could see who he meant by "we." Tate was still holding tightly to his jacket as he started to introduce her, but once Pierre laid his eyes on Tate's olive skin and chestnut brown eyes, it was clear she needed no introduction. Pierre remembered. His dark eyes widened along with his lips as she stepped into his view.

"Ma bella?" Pierre took a step closer and cupped his hands around her face. "Ma bella! Est-ce vous?" *My beauty! Is that you?*

"C'est moi," Tate said. *It's me.* She tried to blink back the tears that were pooling in her eyes.

Pierre threw his arms around her and pulled her in tightly as he repeated "ma bella." Brooks' curious expression hung on his face as he shifted from side to side. Tate watched him from over Pierre's shoulder, but all she could do was shrug slightly while still in Pierre's grasp.

He pulled away, cupping his hands to her face one last time before he escorted the two of them inside. "Venez, venez," he said, waving for them to follow. *Come on, come on.*

Tate turned to Brooks as they walked side by side through the busy bistro. "You know him?" Tate lip-read his words clearly and mouthed back, "Long story."

Brooks nodded, but Tate knew the wide-eyed grin covering his face meant she had some explaining to do.

Pierre stopped in front of a two-person table by the fireplace. He ordered a bottle of the restaurant's finest white wine and called for a server to read the evening specials. Before he excused himself, he let them know he would return once dinner was over with the painting they had come here for. Then, he disappeared into the kitchen, leaving Brooks and Tate alone.

"Okay," Brooks said, leaning in. "Catch me up."

Where do I start? Tate thought. Pierre was one of the first people she met when she finally arrived in Paris. Cameron was working late, and she was still unpacking in the apartment. The day had gotten away from her, and her grumbling stomach reminded her she hadn't eaten all day. She was hungry and tired. Living by himself, Cameron didn't hit the supermarket too often, and the only things in the fridge were bottled beer, a jar of pasta sauce, and a couple of Cameron's leftover boxes from work lunches.

Tate had sighed as the fridge door closed and threw her disheveled hair into a bun before heading out to see what she could find. There was no destination in mind as she walked the streets that August night. She was so mesmerized by the sights around her that she didn't realize how far she'd walked, but when the peaceful sound of violins came flooding toward her, she was so glad she'd wandered off as far as she did. She followed the sounds and came upon the black iron gate.

The black iron gates were some of her favorite architectural pieces in Paris. There were some enclosing the courtyard of her and Cameron's flat. That was where Tate had first noticed them, but the longer she stayed in Paris, the more she spotted. That night, Tate pulled open the gate to Château Lumière and walked inside. The hostess said she could sit anywhere, so she sat at the closest table she could get to the violin, the one in the corner. She ordered a glass of chardonnay and a bowl of pasta—ironic, since she probably could've made that back in the flat. For two hours, Tate sat there enjoying the night sky and classical music. Pierre came out to check on her twice while she was there. That was something Tate loved about this city: the owners were so attentive.

"This was my favorite place to go when I lived here," Tate finally said. "I lived just a few miles down that way." She pointed through the fireplace, and Brooks' gaze followed as if he could see through it. "I never went out alone when I was in Seattle, but Paris made me brave. I'd come here on nights Cameron wasn't home, and this was always my top choice when he was home and I didn't feel like cooking."

"Tate, I am so sorry," Brooks said. He slid his hand across the table, grabbing onto hers. "I didn't even think... I should've told you where we were..." He struggled to finish any of his sentences.

"It's okay," Tate meant it. "How could you have known? The irony."

The waiter arrived just in time to pour Tate the glass of chardonnay she so desperately needed. *He remembered that too.* Tate smiled as she read the label on the bottle. The wine list at Château Lumière was never-ending, but that never seemed to matter to her. Cameron would joke each time they came that Paris had brought her out of her comfort zone, but not when it came to wine. When wine was involved, Tate was simple. Once she found a wine she liked, she was devoted wholeheartedly. Sometimes, Pierre would slip her a sample or two during dinner to try and broaden her horizons, but they never compared. Not to that chardonnay.

"Merci," Tate said. She raised her glass. *Thank you.*

"Cheers," Brooks said, tapping his against hers.

"Cheers."

Tate took a long, slow sip from her glass and took in all that was around her. She couldn't believe how little the bistro had changed. The lights were dimmed, the room illuminated with wall sconces and a mix of pillar and votive candles strewn across each table. She could see the flicker of their table votive shimmering in Brooks' eyes as he investigated the brown in hers. The weight of his hand was still heavy on top of hers in the middle of the table.

They said that sometimes, the past came back to haunt you, but for Tate, tonight, it felt different. Tonight, she felt as if she was slapping the past in the face; throwing a big "I told you so" at it as it surrounded her. Instead of feeling suffocated by the memories, Tate was surprisingly appeased by how far she'd come since the last time she set foot in this bistro. Her fingers wrapped around her glass for another sip. She leaned her head back and let the chardonnay slide down her throat, tipping the stem of her glass up like a big middle finger to the memories that might have still lingered inside.

~24~

Dinner was as mouthwatering as Tate remembered. She ordered the escargots as an appetizer and dangled them in front of Brooks' face.

He scrunched his nose, and his brows fell the closer Tate's hand came, but eventually, he gave in to that intoxicating laugh and let her slide that slimy looking thing onto his tongue. The rubbery texture made him wince, and Tate laughed so hard she snorted water from her nose. Brooks gritted his teeth until he was finally able to swallow.

"Well?" Tate said. Her laugh was still ongoing.

"Never again," Brooks replied. Then, he gulped down half his water.

The main course was much less adventurous. Brooks ordered the beef tartare, and Tate couldn't inhale her mushroom risotto fast enough. When they were finished, the waiter set down two bowls of coconut sorbet topped with pineapple and lime zest on the table. "Compliments of the chef," he said.

"I'm stuffed," Tate said once the waiter had left.

"The chef will be offended." Brooks dipped his spoon into the sorbet.

"All right," Tate said, "but whatever I can't finish, I'm making you eat for me."

Brooks took a bite and then laughed, but before she knew it, Tate was scraping the bottom of her bowl. The taste was so tantalizing she couldn't get enough of it. There was none left to share with Brooks once she set her spoon down.

Brooks could see the shimmer that still stuck to Tate's lips from her lip gloss. That was the first thing he'd noticed when she startled him in the lobby. He loved the way her lips shined when they parted. She patted her napkin against them, and Brooks couldn't help but wish it was his lips instead of that cloth. He was so drawn in he didn't notice Pierre walking up behind him.

"Bien?" he asked. *Good?*

"Tres bien!" Tate said. *Very good!*

In his hands, Pierre held a large cardboard box. It spanned about four feet in length. He set it gently on the floor and opened the top. The painting was a blur as he lifted it from the box already wrapped in its protective plastic. Tate squinted to get a better look. She could see a faraway shadow of the Eiffel Tower from a sailboat that was perched on the calm waves of the River Seine. It was exquisite even hidden behind layers of plastic.

"C'est parfait," Tate said. *It's perfect.* She had faith in Pierre and Delaney that the painting would be just what they needed to take the charity auction over-the-top.

Pierre handed the painting over to Brooks and thanked them both for coming. He refused to take any payment for dinner and insisted it was on him. Tate stood from her chair and reached in for one last hug.

"Au revoir, ma bella," he whispered in her ear. *Goodbye, my beauty.*

This time, Tate couldn't hold it in. A stream of wetness cascaded down her cheeks, but she quickly wiped it away before her grip loosened on Pierre.

"Au revoir, Pierre," she said.

He gave one last squeeze of her shoulders before she and Brooks made their way through the restaurant, back out into the stillness of the Paris air.

"Are you tired?" Brooks asked.

Tate was tired. She could feel the heaviness in her eyes after her second glass of wine. She would've had no problem crawling under the covers of her hotel bed and lying there for the rest of the night. If she did, she'd probably be out like a light in less than ten minutes. Saying yes, though, would mean saying goodbye to Brooks, and she wasn't ready to do that. Tate loved being around him, especially tonight. She wasn't ready to let him go yet.

"Not really," she lied.

"Do you want to grab a drink? I noticed an Irish pub across the street from the hotel," he said, pointing across from where they stood. "I can run the painting up and meet you there."

"That sounds good."

Brooks left Tate for the hotel, and she briskly walked across the street to the place he had pointed to. The wooden door to the pub was heavy. It took all of Tate's strength to get it to open, and when she did, she quickly came to the realization she was overdressed. No one else was trying to hide their petite frame with a pair of heels. She could feel the stares burrowing into her as she stood in the doorway. *It's not too late to turn around.* That's what she would usually say. *Nah. Let them stare.* Tate smiled as her heels clicked all the way to the bar.

"French 75, please."

The bartender slipped a coaster in front of her and grabbed a glass. It'd been a while since Tate had ordered that drink—the night Cameron had to practically carry her back to the flat after celebrating her birthday. Poor Camille and Gerard. That night was the last time Tate ever saw the two of them.

Cameron and Gerard had worked together. He and Camille had been dating for a few months at that point, and Tate and Cameron had met them out a few times before. She always enjoyed their company even though she sometimes felt judgment cast upon her. It felt good to be putting down roots in Paris and solidifying a *friend group*. That budding friendship quickly came to a halt, however, when Hurricane French 75 swept through the city that night. That was how Cameron referred to it after. He thought it was amusing, but Camille and Gerard did not. *Typical American.* That was what Cameron told Tate he'd heard Camille whisper under her breath as he slung Tate's arm over his shoulder. She'd leaned on him the whole way to the car. She couldn't remember much after that, only the bits and pieces Cameron filled in.

Tonight, Tate was back again, a typical American sitting at a bar, overdressed, with probably too much makeup on. She was okay with it. Back then, Tate had tried so hard to be what Cameron needed her to be that she'd hidden behind a façade. The night of her birthday, she'd used each glass of French 75 to erase the Seattle girl she had somehow become embarrassed of. She traded dance classes for yoga because that was the thing to do. Her midday pick-me-ups became green juices instead of sugar-filled blended coffees. Though she came to love yoga and the occasional green juice, there were days when she really had to force the old Tate not to come out. Her birthday night was one of them.

Not tonight though. Tonight, Tate just wanted to enjoy a drink at a bar with—

The door to the bar swung open. Brooks no longer had on his navy jacket. The top two buttons of his pink shirt were open. Tate gripped the edge of the bar as she got a glimpse of the bare complexion that was now peeking out. This more relaxed look Brooks wore was teasing the butterflies in Tate's stomach.

"Is the painting safe?" she joked.

Brooks pulled out the stool next to her. "I cleared the desk and laid it on there. Should sleep well for the night." He laughed and tapped the top of Tate's glass. "What's good?"

"French 75."

"I can't do champagne." He waved to the bartender. "Vodka tonic for me." He saw Tate flinch at his order. "What now?" His voice was high-pitched.

"Nothing!"

"I feel like you're always judging me," he said.

"I am not judging you," Tate laughed. "You just surprise me sometimes. When I think I have you all figured out, you go and order something like a vodka tonic."

"Okay, Ms. Montgomery…" He leaned over and rested his elbow onto the bar. "What kind of drink do you think Brooks Walker drinks?" He waited for her answer. His eyes were straining to stay in line with hers. He was too close to her. She would notice, but he so badly wanted to look down, to study her—every single part of her. Brooks wondered if she could tell; if that was the reason she was shuffling in her seat.

Tate finally broke her gaze from his and reached for her drink. "You strike me more as a bourbon guy. An old-fashioned, maybe, or a classic Manhattan with an orange twist, but I also don't think I'd be surprised if you could handle a scotch on the rocks. How am I doing?" Tate took a sip. Her lips pressed firmly on the rim of her champagne glass.

"Fine," Brooks said. "Mighty fine."

He wasn't wrong, but Brooks wasn't talking about the drinks, and Tate knew it. She knew because his eyes were no longer on hers. If any stranger in this bar looked at Tate the way Brooks was looking at her right now, she knew she would slap them silly, but not Brooks. Tate had been waiting for him to look at her in this way all night. That deadbolt was slowing becoming unlocked around her heart. Now, he was right where she wanted him: where she'd refused to let him go before, but where each sip of her French 75 was allowing him to sneak in.

Right when her inhibitions were about to give him what he'd been wanting for so long, Brooks snapped back to the gentleman Tate had always known he was. He cleared his throat, pushed back off the bar, and wrapped a death grip around his vodka tonic. Then, he changed the conversation completely.

"Have you been to this bar before?" he asked.

"Um..." Tate was shocked. Her body was still quivering. She leaned back in her chair and took a three-second sip of her champagne. "I haven't, actually."

"Well, good. We don't need you taking any more walks down memory lane."

"We sure don't," Tate said. Her shoulders sank. What in the hell had happened?

Tate tried not to think about it for the half hour the two of them sat in the pub. Brooks asked her a lot of questions about her time in Paris, but even as she answered, he never again looked in her direction. He would nod and sip his drink, his eyes staring intently at the frames lining the wood-paneled wall.

They held photos of famous celebrities shaking hands with the bar staff as they passed through.

Brooks took the final sip of his second vodka tonic and slid his glass to the end of the bar. That was Tate's cue she wouldn't be ordering a third round. Her heart had fallen and was now a pit in her stomach. It was happening—the one thing she had been trying to prevent between the two of them; the awkwardness that came like a teenager posing for an Instagram-worthy photo not knowing where to put their hands. Tate felt defeated but more disappointed in herself. She knew not to mix business with pleasure. She knew better. She thought hovering close to the line was dangerous enough, but tonight, she had stepped her toes on it, and now, she was stuck. She still had another whole day in Paris with Brooks, and there was still an event to plan with a guy who was no longer able to look her in the eye.

Brooks signed for the check, and they walked single file to the exit. When he opened the door, a flood of water came rolling in.

~25~

The rain was coming down so hard that none of the cars passing in the street could be seen. Brooks only knew they were coming by the sound of water that gushed up after they passed.

"Whoa!" He jumped back. "When did it start raining?"

All the two of them could do was laugh. Brooks wondered if this was his punishment. He thought the downpour was his karma for pushing the envelope with Tate. He had sat on that stool next to her tracing every bit of her pink dress. While she was describing the kind of whiskey drinker she thought he was, he was wondering what it would feel like to unzip the back of her dress and feel the bareness of her skin on his fingertips.

For that reason, Brooks made the first move. He stepped out under the covered overhang and watched the water splash up from the deep puddles on the street.

"We could stay for another drink," Tate suggested.

They could, but Brooks knew one more drink would get him into trouble. He was already struggling to keep his hands to himself.

"Here," Brooks said. He unbuttoned the rest of the buttons on his shirt. He had a T-shirt on underneath, and he didn't know the kind of mood white cotton put Tate in. "Put this over your head," he said.

"You sure?" she asked.

Brooks nodded.

Tate swung his shirt up over her head, and Brooks wrapped his hand around her elbow. He counted down from three and followed closely next to Tate as they splashed through the endless puddles. The rain was hitting hard against Brooks' face. His shirt was hugging his skin so tight he found it hard to breathe as they darted up the hotel steps into the lobby.

Brooks wiped the wetness from his face enough to see Tate standing next to him. His shirt hadn't helped her much; her hair clung to the side of her face, and streams of black flowed down to her chin.

"What?" Tate asked.

Brooks didn't say anything. Instead, he lifted his hand to swipe the wet strands behind her ears. Then, he took his fingertips and brushed away the black that was beginning to stain her cheeks.

"Thank you." Tate smiled.

Brooks couldn't believe that even with her whole body drenched and her hair and makeup disheveled, he still didn't want to take his eyes off her. He was hypnotized by the way droplets of water ran down her smooth complexion. She must've noticed his stare because it wasn't long until she was shaking the loose water from both arms. Tate handed Brooks his soaked button-up shirt, and they walked to the elevator.

Brooks stood on the farthest side of the elevator from where Tate was standing. Not that it was far—it was a tiny elevator—but he was in desperate need of the space. Before Paris, he had liked the playfulness flourishing between them. Yes, he would flirt with her and found himself stealing glances whenever he could, but the more time he spent with Tate, the more he wanted. Tonight had been exceptionally hard for him. He'd found himself more often than ever before wanting to take her hand, caress the small of her back, and feel her skin against his lips. Those were all things Tate had made absolutely clear were off-limits, and he respected her enough to oblige. Tonight, though, he had almost given in, and now, he was clinging to the space between them to make sure he didn't go against her wishes.

When the elevator doors opened, Brooks motioned to let Tate out first. Neither of them said a word until they stopped in front of Tate's door.

"I guess this is goodnight," she said.

Brooks swore he heard a twinge in her voice but wondered if it was his hopefulness playing tricks on him. He wasn't ready to watch her go.

"I had a lot of fun tonight," he said.

"Me too."

Silence fell over them. Tate brushed her hair behind her ears again, and Brooks shoved his hands deep into his pockets. Tate shuffled through her purse and pulled out her room key.

"I'll see you in the morning?"

"That, you will," Brooks said. He held up his hand in salute and watched as Tate slid her key into the door.

The light turned green, and she twisted the handle. She didn't look back as she pushed through it; she just let the door close behind her.

That wasn't what Brooks had in mind. That wasn't how he wanted the night to end. He stepped closer to her room and raised his fist. It. It lightly fell against the door, but not enough to make a noise. Brooks wanted to knock. He wanted her to open the door again so he could grab her and wrap her in his arms. He wanted to back her up against the wall, press himself against her, and finally feel what it was like to kiss her lips.

He lifted his fist but couldn't find the strength to bang it against the door. If only he knew Tate was on the other side of it, her back pressed up against it, wishing, just for tonight, he would forget about everything she'd said to him. Tonight, she didn't want to be off-limits—but Brooks couldn't read minds, nor could he see through walls. So, instead of giving in, he walked away. He opened the door to his hotel room and threw his rain-soaked shirt on the floor.

Brooks grabbed a towel from the rack in the bathroom and rubbed it over his head. He heard a bang on the other side of the wall and slid the towel down the back of his neck to listen. He heard a faint sound of running water. He leaned up against the wall and closed his eyes, envisioning Tate on the other side of that wall, slipping out of her dress. God, what he wouldn't give to see what was underneath... He pictured her wet curls falling to her neck as she swept her towel across every inch of her moist skin. The thought of it had his heart racing. It pounded as if he was standing front-row at a heavy metal concert.

"Screw this," he said.

He couldn't take it anymore. He tossed the towel in the sink, flung open the door to his room, and the next thing he knew, his fist was colliding with the only thing that separated Tate from being in his arms. He heard shuffling on the other side of the door, and for a second, he felt like an idiot. She was probably looking through the peephole praying for him to go away. He slid his fist back down to his side, but right before he was about to admit defeat, he heard the lock turn.

Tate's untamed curls appeared in the doorway. Her body was covered in a white robe. Brooks pushed the door open and stepped closer. He didn't wait for her to speak; he just took her face in his hands and let all of his tension escape with the breath between his lips as they pressed against hers.

Soon, he felt Tate's arms wrap around the dampness of his white shirt. Her body fell heavier against him. Brooks pulled away just far enough for Tate to whisper his name. Her eyes were still closed, the dampness of her cheek leaning against his.

"I know," he said, "but just in case I only get tonight, I needed to."

His hands slid off the back of her neck. He turned to walk away, but her hand tugged at his forearm. She pulled him around, closer to her, and brushed her fingers across his cheek. Tate's grip was firm against him as she pulled him in, each kiss received with less protest than the one before. The sound of pleasure escaped between Tate's lips right as the elevator at the end of the hallway pulled them apart.

Brooks held Tate firmly against him as they turned to watch a couple walk down the hallway toward them. No one said a word, but Brooks could feel the tension in their eyes. There he was, soaking wet, Tate covered in a robe that was coming undone in the middle of a hotel hallway.

Once they passed, Tate rested her head on his chest, and they both broke out in laughter. He felt the tip of her finger rubbing back and forth across the part of his chest uncovered by his collar. He pressed his lips firmly against her temple. He didn't want to let go, but he felt Tate loosen her grip on him. She pushed the door to her room back open and stepped aside.

Maybe Tate hadn't whispered his name in protest. Maybe she wanted him as badly as he wanted her. He stepped in a little closer. He had to know.

"Are you sure?" he asked.

Tate stepped even further back into the room. Brooks watched as she turned to face him and lowered herself onto the bed. She leaned back on her hands, her white robe falling slightly over her right shoulder.

Brooks let go of the door, and the last thing that hallway saw was Brooks leaning over her, Tate's head resting on his hand, and their lips meeting once again before she wrapped her hands around him and let him gently lay her down on the bed.

~26~

The next morning, Tate rolled over to find Brooks fast asleep in her bed. One hand rested on the pillow over his head, and the other across his bare chest. Tate had to admit she liked the idea Brooks was lying where there was usually an empty space. Normally, she'd sprawl out in the middle, but last night, she was content curling up into a ball against him. His arms had gripped her firmly until she slipped to the bathroom in the middle of the night. When she returned, he'd moved over to his side of the bed.

The curtains still hid the morning light when Tate slipped out from the under the sheets slowly, careful not to wake him. Her robe covered the nightstand next to her. She grabbed it and swung it around behind her. Her arms slipped through, and she wrapped the belt tightly to cover her bare skin before sneaking off to the bathroom. The mirror exposed every bit of last night's activities.

Her hair was a mess. She wasn't sure if it was the second or third time for her and Brooks when they'd taken their interlocked bodies to the shower. After they were done, Tate stood under the cool water to calm herself. Exhaustion set in sometime after one in the morning when she let her damp hair fall onto the pillow. Now, it sat like a lion's mane on her head. She pulled the wavy strands back into a bun and scrounged through her suitcase, pulling out a purple jumpsuit.

"Are you about to do the walk of shame from your own hotel room?" he asked, his voice still raspy from a solid night's sleep.

Brooks' voice startled Tate. She sprang up with her jumpsuit in hand and turned around. The man in her bed—untidy hair, minimal stubble around his lips—flashes her a sexy smile and flexes his biceps as he lifts his head from the pillow.

"I was going to pick us up some breakfast," Tate says.

She pulls her robe tighter around her as if Brooks hasn't already seen what's underneath.

"I guess we did work up quite an appetite," Brooks said. "Where did you want to go?"

"It's a secret."

Tate lifted her finger over her lips. There were still a few hours until checkout and Tate didn't want to leave Paris without making a stop at her favorite boulangerie. The roaring in her stomach also made it painstakingly obvious how many calories she'd burned the night before. She welcomed the carbs.

"A secret?" Brooks said. "I'm intrigued. Can I come with?"

Tate nodded and Brooks slipped his muscular physique out from under the covers. A pair of fitted boxers was the only thing now covering him.

"Give me ten minutes, and I'll come knocking," Brooks said as he slid his shirt over every ripple of his abs.

Tate's eyes locked on the button of Brooks' pants as he clasped them tightly. A grin appeared on his face when he caught Tate staring. Before last night, she'd probably have been embarrassed, but this time she rolled her eyes theatrically and bent back down to pull a strapless bra from her suitcase.

"You do that." Tate locked eyes with Brooks and he winked at her before showing himself the door.

Ten minutes later and Brooks was once again knocking on Tate's door.

"It's open!" she yelled.

Brooks pushed open the door as if he knew he belonged there. Tate was standing in front of the mirror twisting a hair tie around her curls. The purple jumpsuit she was wearing left her shoulders bare and wrapped in a bow around the back of her neck. It made him think of the night before when she was curled up against him in bed. There were a few times he woke up and kissed the bareness of her neck and shoulders. She'd flinch at his touch, but he was sure to be gentle enough not to wake her.

"Hey," Brooks said. Tate tugged at her ponytail. "You look very spring-ish today."

"Thank you?" Tate looked over at him with wondering eyes. She wasn't sure how to take that.

"I like it," he said. "So where are we going?"

"I told you, it's a secret." Tate squeezed past him to the door. "Let's go."

In the hallway, Brooks reached out for her hand, and she let him take it. She curled her fingers in his, and the two of them smiled like teenagers at their first school dance. The elevator button light disappeared, and once the doors opened to their floor, they both stepped inside.

There was no room for space between them, especially when it stopped on the third floor. A family of four stepped inside, and Tate pushed back into Brooks. She felt his fingers strum against her arms as the numbers on the wall ticked down.

Brooks was testing her. It was subtle, but just enough to see if he could draw a reaction. Tate didn't move, but from the chills on her arm where his fingers were stroking was all he needed to know he was wearing her down.

Tate knew Paris was only temporary. Her dream of being with Brooks was just that—a dream. Tate knew the real world would come back to play, but that wasn't until she stepped off the train in London. For now, she was going to enjoy the way he made her feel. If they were in London, she'd swat his hand away, but there were still a few hours left in Paris. So, instead, she stood still with her back against him and the warmth of his breath against her temple until they made it to the lobby floor. The rest of the way, Tate kept a teasing distance—enough that sometimes, her hand would graze against Brooks' as they walked along the sidewalk. She finally let him take it once they were in front of the boulangerie.

"Here we are!" Tate said. She stopped abruptly in the middle of a sea of people. Brooks had to swerve not to run her over.

Café Amélie was just as she remembered. The gold lettering above the teal awning and black trim around the windows made it hard to miss. Its French doors were ever-revolving with customers. A young girl was writing the daily specials on the window with a white marker. The specials changed daily, but Tate knew no matter what day she came, she could always find them on that window in perfectly written cursive.

"Remember those éclairs I used to stock up on?" Tate asked.

"The ones you used to muffle your sorrows?" Brooks asked.

She laughed but nodded at the truth in his question.

"They're from this place, huh?"

"Yup, only the best in the city. You ready?"

"Let's do it!" Brooks said. "We can't not try what Tate Montgomery says are the BEST goodies in all of Paris."

Tate's hands clapped together frivolously. She spun around to catch the door just as a man walked through it with a bag full of fresh baguettes. The aroma hung in the air as Tate walked in, and the sounds of her stomach reflected her intense craving.

Brooks' eyes widened as he took in the endless case of baked goods in front of him. He bent over to get a better look through the glass.

"I can't decide," Brooks said. He'd been eyeing everything on the trays, and they all looked so good. His eyes bounced from sweet to savory and then cream-filled, to frosting-topped. "There's too much to choose from."

"You know what the solution to that is, right?" Tate asked.

"No...what?"

"Order a little bit of everything," she said. "What do you like? Sweet, tart, plain?" She had sampled pretty much everything in that case over the time she'd lived in Paris. If she could get a good enough idea of his taste, she'd be able to find something for him.

"Chocolate is always good, but I kind of want to try something off the beaten path."

"Daring," Tate said. "I like it. I've got you."

Brooks squeezed Tate's shoulder, and she shot him one last smile before turning to inspect the remainder of the case. As the line shortened one by one, Tate's list of what she would order grew longer in her head. Some for her and some for Brooks and maybe even a little for the train ride home.

"Bonjour mademoiselle, comment puis-je vous aider?" *Hello miss, how can I help you?* The young man behind the cash register waited for Tate's response.

"Bonjour, je vais prendre deux croissants, deux pains au chocolat..." *Hello, I'm going to have two croissants, two pain au chocolat...* Tate paused, looking intently through the glass case. She couldn't decide between the macarons or the strawberry tarts. She ended up going with both.

Brooks had no idea what she was saying. He raised his eyebrows as she finished out the order. The cashier's fingers hurriedly pressed the keys in front of him. He must've caught all of it because once Tate was done, he nodded and got to bagging.

"Did you just buy the whole store?" Brooks asked. "We're going to need a whole other train seat for your pastries."

"Shut up." Tate jabbed her elbow into his side. "I had to make sure we have leftovers. Trust me, you're going to want leftovers."

"I trust you," he said. "Hey, do you want any coffee? I think I might hit up the place next door, wake myself up a little."

"Oh, yes! I would love some. A cappuccino for me, please."

"Cool, I'll go grab those. Meet you outside the front door?" Brooks asked.

"Will do. Thank you." Tate waved as he walked out. There was no denying that she loved what was happening right now. She had woken up with a smile, strolled off to a morning breakfast with a smile, and now, Brooks was off to buy her coffee. She couldn't have planned it better herself, and she was one heck of a planner.

Ah, if only she could carry this feeling with her back to London... But she knew better. If Delaney found out what had happened on her dime, her job might really be in jeopardy. Tate's smile turned to a frown as she thought more and more about it.

This was a business trip, and look what she had done. Sure, all work and no play may make for a boring life, but she had played all night long with Delaney's right-hand man. She was so torn. Damn her head and damn her heart. Yup, either way, she was damned. Suddenly, a sharpness stabbed her in the chest—a sharpness that was interrupted by the ruffling of the bags being placed in front of her.

"Mademoiselle?"

Tate jolted herself back around to find the young man staring at her. She could see the concern across his face. Her hands gripped the bags quickly as she yanked them off the counter. A "thank you" slipped through her lips again—in French, of course—before she headed out the door.

Brooks was nowhere to be found once Tate was back outside the café. She found an open space to wait near the windowsill and slid down to sit on the exposed brick. The stillness put Tate's focus back on her rumbling stomach, and the delicious smell of the bread and pastries from the bags wasn't helping. She could totally scarf down a croissant before Brooks returned with her coffee. *He wouldn't even know.* That was what she was thinking when she slid her hand into the bag with the chocolate croissants.

She was so close to heaven. Her hands were about to pull out the long-awaited pastry when the sound of her name startled her. At first, she thought it was Brooks. *Damn!* she thought. *Caught red-handed.* Then, she heard it again, and this time, she knew it wasn't Brooks calling her name.

"Tate?" the voice said. "Is that you?"

Tate's hand froze inside the bag. The croissant fell back to its original place at the bottom, and her eyes locked on the pavement in front of her. That voice wasn't deep enough to be Brooks, but it was familiar—too familiar. It couldn't be.

She looked up.

It could be, and it was.

"Cameron." Taste swallowed hard as every muscle in her body fought to pull her up from that redbrick wall. "Hi."

His hair was shorter than Tate remembered it. His curls usually flapped in the wind, but not anymore. It looked darker too; the color almost matched his almond-shaped eyes. Tate could see his lips quiver as he tried not to smile, but he failed. She wished he hadn't; she had always liked his smile. Even then, in the aftermath of heartache, it pulled her down memory lane. Tate didn't make it far down the road, though, before noticing something that pulled her to a sudden stop. His hand was intertwined with another's.

He wasn't alone.

I knew it! Tate prayed her eyes wouldn't give away what she was thinking as she stared at the woman's scarlet hair blowing in the wind. Her red lipstick matched it perfectly. Her pursed lips tried to hide her displeasure at Tate's presence, but it wasn't working—Tate could tell by the way her eyes fixated on her black boots that she'd rather be anywhere but standing in front of her.

That was fine with Tate. She did not need to see her eyes. She did not need an introduction. She knew right away it was Camille's hand wrapped tightly in Cameron's. All along, she had wondered if there was someone else, and now she had her answer. Cameron didn't have to go out to find anyone because Camille had been there the whole time. As the realization hit Tate, she wished she could summon the pelting raindrops from the night before to wash her away from this agony.

"How are you?" he asked.

Tate wasn't oblivious to the way Cameron released his grip from Camille's or the death glare Camille shot him once he did. Tate was sure he hadn't noticed though because he was looking straight in her direction with curiosity in his eyes. Two years ago, when Tate had walked out of that apartment down the street, Cameron didn't know where she was going. Everything she owned was shoved into her rental car until it was full to the brim, and although she had been lucky enough to find a temporary place in London's Camden neighborhood and she had a part-time job lined up with Rosewood Events,

Cameron knew nothing of it. A part of her wondered if he feared this very moment every day, not knowing she had left Paris.

"I'm doing fine."

He didn't deserve any more than that, and, thankfully, Tate didn't have any time to offer up anything else. Cameron's lips moved once again to speak, but he was interrupted when Brooks appeared from behind him holding two cups in his hands—one of which, he released from his grasp once Tate held it firmly in hers.

"Thank you." Tate smiled at him.

"Of course," Brooks said. Then, he turned toward Cameron and reached out his free hand. "Hello. Brooks Walker."

"Hi."

That was all Cameron had to say. He didn't offer up his name, but he made sure Brooks noticed his cold stare. Camille was now standing with her arms folded over her chest. Her eyes rolled to the sky.

"Brooks," Tate said, cutting the silence like a knife, "*this*...is Cameron." She paused for a moment, but she made sure not to leave out Cameron's guest. "And this is Camille." She emphasized her name, but Camille still refused any acknowledgment.

Tate coughed at the dryness that had entered her throat and looked over at Brooks. He gave her a subtle nod, and she was relieved he remembered who Cameron was. She didn't want to be in this alone.

"It's nice to meet you," Brooks said. "Thanks for keeping my girl company."

His arm reached behind Tate and rested on her hip. She managed a smile but was so caught off-guard by Brooks' quick thinking that she couldn't form a response.

"It's no problem," Cameron said hastily.

"It was nice to meet you—both of you—but, babe, I think we should probably go." He glanced at his watch. "We've got a train to catch."

"Absolutely," Tate said. "We have to get home...to the dog. Our dog. Right, hon?"

"Yes...Scooby," Brooks said.

Tate's lips pressed together as hard as they could in order to keep her laughter inside. She wasn't the only one. The emerging dimple on Brooks' face was proof he was struggling too. Cameron didn't deserve the satisfaction of knowing this was a façade; that there was no "our house" or "our dog," but the daggers his eyes shot at Brooks confirmed they were both playing their parts quite well.

"It was nice to see you," Tate said. She didn't even bother to look at Camille; she only gave Cameron one last wave before Brooks swung her around in the direction of the hotel. His arm was now slung over her shoulders as they walked away. She leaned into him. "Scooby?" she asked.

"What? You put me on the spot," Brooks said. "That was the first name that came to mind. Besides, you're the one who gave us a house and a dog in less than three minutes."

"I know…I panicked," Tate said. "Do you think he bought it?"

Brooks looked behind him. "Hook, line, and sinker. You know the only thing you could've done differently?

"What?" Tate looked up at him.

"You should've called me Leo. It sounds much sexier—more personal."

Brooks leaned in closer and wrapped his arms around Tate. He kissed the top of her head and smiled at her sarcastic laugh. A sense of pleasure stormed through him—partly because he was happy to come to Tate's rescue, but, let's face it, also because he had been waiting since day one to refer to Tate as *his* girl, and right now he really felt like she was.

"Oh no," Tate said. "We're not going there."

"Where?"

"Me, calling you Leo and getting *personal*."

Brooks appreciated her air quotes. "I think we already got *personal*." He mimicked her.

"That may be true, but we're still in event planning. That means Brooks Walker is in and Leo…is…out." She crawled her fingers up his chest and pressed the tip of her pointer finger against his nose.

Brooks let that last comment slide. He continued to hold onto Tate while they walked back to the hotel and her lack of resistance was assurance that he was getting closer. The house and the dog may have been a ploy to remove them from a bad situation, but, he had to admit, he liked the way it sounded. He liked the flat he lived in, but the more time he spent around Tate, the more he thought about where he was in his life. The idea of a house in the country was growing more appealing to him, especially if Tate would be there to help him fill it.

Tate couldn't help but feel a sense of victory walking away from Cameron. He hated holding hands when they were dating. He always said that was too much PDA and preferred to keep the affection behind closed doors. Maybe Camille insisted it was something they had to do. She seemed like the type of person who was adamant on having things her way, but even if she had won the hand-holding game, that day, it was clear Cameron seeing Tate with someone else had irked him.

Not that this was a game. Tate always hated when people said that about love. She never believed it was true. If love was a game, that meant that someone always had the upper hand, and, in her mind, that was not how love was supposed to be. There wasn't a winner and loser, not in real love. In real love, both sides won. In the way Tate saw love, there was no opponent, only a teammate who would go to battle for you but never against you.

Tate looked up at Brooks wondering what was going on in that mind of his as he blankly stared off into the distance. She hadn't realized until then that he'd covered his eyes with a pair of thick-framed sunglasses, and with his broad shoulders straight back, he looked taller. She had always thought Brooks' confidence was striking, but as the two of them walked down the busy streets of Paris with their hotel in view, something looked different about him. Brooks Walker was valiant and assertive. Both of those traits covered him like a suit of armor; like a warrior who had just come out of a battle. A battle that, perhaps unknowingly, he had fought for her. When they took the final turn to the hotel, Tate's words flooded her mind again.

In real love, you don't have an opponent, only a teammate who will go to battle for you, but never against you...

~27~

It was a whirlwind afternoon before Tate and Brooks headed back to London. After they left Camille and Cameron, the two of them sat outside on the patio of the hotel. Tate sipped on her cappuccino while Brooks savored at least one of everything she had ordered from the bakery. There wasn't one thing he didn't like, and by the time he'd finished the bite of his chocolate croissant, he fully agreed with Tate. He wanted leftovers.

Those leftovers were now sitting atop the luggage rack next to Tate's bag on the train. The painting was on the seat across from them, and Brooks' hand was resting on Tate's knee as the horn sounded and the train began to pull out of the Paris station.

"Big day for you today," Brooks said.

Tate was staring out into the darkness of the tunnel, but she turned back to look at him. "It sure was."

"How do you feel about it?" Brooks asked, furrowing his brow as he waited for her to respond.

"I feel like I finally have closure. I know now that there was someone else. It stings a little that it was her, but I needed it."

"Wait—you knew that girl?"

Tate nodded with a tight-lipped smile. "Yup. She used to date one of Cameron's colleagues. We all went out a few times together. I wouldn't say we were friends. Cordial was more like it, but I didn't hate her."

"How about now? Do you hate her?"

Tate thought about his question. It would be in her rights to hate Camille. Her soft curls of red locks were the reason Cameron left her. Her first answer was yes, but then she thought about where she was now. She was on her way back to London from Paris with a painting for an event she was planning. Her very own event company was making a name for itself. Tate wasn't sure this was a step she would've been comfortable taking here in Paris. That was reason enough to change her answer.

"No, I don't hate her. I don't necessarily wish her well, but I don't hate her."

"Good." Brooks patted her knee.

"You know, I feel like we always talk about me and my relationship problems. What about you?"

Brooks jutted out his bottom lip. "What about me?"

"Do you have any 'woe is me' stories to share?"

Mya immediately came to mind. She was the only girl who had really made Brooks feel what it might be like to have your heart ripped from your chest. It was hard on him when she packed up her things from the bottom drawer of his dresser. It had taken a lot of strength for him, a guy who feared commitment, to offer up that drawer. He still remembered the way her eyes lit up when he pulled it open that night to show her, he was serious. She'd looked down at first with narrowed eyes into an empty drawer. "It's for you," he remembered saying. She had squealed and thrown her arms around him. For Mya and Brooks, an empty drawer meant so much more, but in the end, that gesture wasn't enough.

"I've got one," Brooks finally answered. Tate leaned in closer. "Her name is Mya. We dated less than a year, but she meant a lot to me during that time."

"What happened?" Tate could see the emptiness reflected in Brooks' eyes. A twinge of guilt shot through her for having even brought it up. "I'm sorry, that's none of my business."

"No, no, it's okay. I don't mind. Mya was successful. She's a pediatric nurse, and being that she had it all together, she was ready for the next step. She wanted kids and a place out in the country, somewhere like Farnham. I just wasn't ready for an hour's commute into London, and, honestly, kids were nowhere on my radar then. We had long conversations about it every night the last week we were together. She cried a lot, and all I could do was hold her."

Brooks thought back to the final night with Mya. She finished working at the hospital, and, like any other night, she had hopped on the bus to his flat and let herself in with the key he'd given her. Garrett was still at work. It was only the two of them. She wouldn't sit down.

"I could see the pool of water building in her eyes, and I knew. That was it," Brooks said. There wasn't anything I could say to change her mind. My honesty only hurt her more."

Mya had stuffed everything from that bottom drawer into her shoulder bag the same night. She kissed Brooks goodbye softly on his cheek and placed her key back on the counter. He'd waited at the top of the stairs, hoping she would turn around, but she never did.

Tate's bottom lip quivered. She placed her hand on top of his. She had been so focused on herself this past couple of weeks she hadn't even stopped to think that maybe she wasn't the only one. Now, she knew. Brooks had felt heartbreak too.

"I'm sorry." That was all Tate could muster.

"It's okay. It seems like ages ago at this point. Everything happens for a reason, right?"

Tate nodded. That was what she believed. She didn't want to pry any further; Brooks had shared enough for one day, but his story made her think. She wanted kids, at least two. Having grown up with a sister, Tate thought it was important to have a built-in best friend in a sibling. She wouldn't be giving up her Notting Hill flat anytime soon, but a house in the country sounded nice down the road.

The past twenty-four hours in Paris had been magical for Tate. Most of it was unplanned, but she wouldn't trade any of it. Her conscience weighed on her as the train pulled into London with Brooks still holding her hand. She liked him...a lot. She liked kissing him, talking to him, and being near him. After listening to his story about Mya, some of her fears had been put to rest, but there was still one that lingered.

Brooks was her client. This event would be a huge turning point in her career. Delaney could not find out about what had happened in Paris. It would be the end for Tate. She knew that, so she held onto Brooks' hand for as long as she could, and when the screeching of the breaks signaled their return to London, she left everything that had happened in Paris behind.

~28~

It was a struggle once Tate was back in London. She found herself picturing the night she stood in that hallway, half-wrapped in her robe, with Brooks' hands around her waist. While she was sitting on the stool at her kitchen island the next morning with a half-eaten baguette in her hand, her lips started to tingle. Like a movie, she watched as Brooks leaned in and press his lips against hers. She'd rewind each time he pulled away. It was a vision Tate replayed until she finally realized she'd let the baguette fall and the jam that once covered it had slowly slipped off onto her lap.

Pull yourself together Tate. She scolded. Thankfully, she was able to do so long enough to meet Genevieve for lunch. If there was anyone who could help her untangle everything she was feeling, it would be her. They were meeting at their favorite juicery in Chelsea, and after the overconsumption of carbs and alcohol, Tate was looking forward to a nice meal full of greens.

The bus stopped at Hobury Street, and Tate followed the sidewalk to a fork in the road. The world of spinach and kale was straight ahead through the double doors of the juice bar. Genevieve was sitting at their usual table by the window. The sill was lined with bright blue planters filled with herbs.

Genevieve stood from the table, and Tate laughed at the way her long ponytail danced as she waved over at her. Large pink glasses framed her face. It was too early for Tate to be as put together as Genevieve was in her high-waisted royal blue pants. A large bow at the waist tucked in a tight white bodysuit. Tate was lucky she was even able to slip into the jeans she was wearing. She'd spent the past twenty-four hours hauled up in her flat in sweats and oversize sweaters, knee-deep in planning mode. Genevieve threw her arms around Tate once she was within reach and squeezed her so hard, she couldn't even find the space to breathe.

"So tell me all about it!" Genevieve clapped. She had been longing for this moment since Tate first told her she'd be heading to Paris with Brooks. As they walked up to the counter to order, she eagerly waited for the story to begin. "Don't leave out any details."

The story started out relatively uneventful as Tate talked about reliving the details of her past. Then, she came to the nightcap at the bar, and Genevieve leaned in closer. The straw to her cucumber and aloe concoction was flattened by her lips.

"I think I completely escaped into a different world," Tate said, referencing the moment Brooks had walked into the bar across from the hotel. "It was like he wasn't the big company executive or my client. He was just a guy in a bar who made me feel...alive again."

"And, I imagine, not so uptight?" Genevieve asked.

"I'm not uptight!"

"Oh, come on, Tate. As amazing as you are, you have a hard time stepping off the straight and narrow sometimes."

"I stepped off it that night."

"No, you bloody didn't!" Genevieve's voice was high-pitched. She slapped her hands over her mouth to muffle her screams. "So you're together now, yeah?"

"No, we're not together. It was one night." Tate jerked her gaze to the ceiling and covered her face with her hands. As they slid back down to her chin, she sighed. "It was an amazing one though."

"What are you waiting for then?"

"It's complicated," Tate said. "Look where the last rash decision I made got me."

Genevieve slid her straw out from her mouth and shot straight up in her chair. She took in a few heavy inhales and then rested her hands on the table. There was a fierce look in her eyes that made Tate's stomach churn. She knew what was coming. Over the past year that she'd known Genevieve, Tate had been the brunt of her pep talks. This was how she prepared to lay into her. Tate took one long sip of her kale smoothie and leaned back waiting.

"Yes, Tate, look where it got you. That crazy detour you took brought you here, to London. You're now living in a flat most would kill for. You've worked for an esteemed event planning company, and now, you work for no one but yourself. Not to mention, it brought you to me, and I think most would say that's worthy enough."

Tate laughed, but she knew Genevieve wasn't finished yet.

"You took a risk, and maybe it didn't turn out the way you planned it, but that doesn't mean it didn't lead you to exactly where you're supposed to be. Maybe even to have met the guy you're meant to be with."

"And what if it doesn't work out?"

"Then it doesn't work out," Genevieve said. "Don't you think the two of you are professional enough to figure out how to handle it if it doesn't?"

"I don't know," Tate said.

She and Brooks had gotten to know each other quite well over these past few weeks, and she wanted to believe Genevieve was right, but she had to wonder, did you ever really know someone? Did you ever know how they'd react in a situation until they were put into it?

"Look, I can't tell you what to do or how to feel," Genevieve said. "I can tell you, though, that there's something different about you today, and I don't think it's the glow from that smoothie. That feeling inside that bar, the desire to be underneath him, why would you want to walk away from that? Don't punish yourself for your past. You don't deserve that, and quite frankly, neither does the guy who's clearly falling head over heels for you."

"Ugh!" That was all that came out of Tate's mouth before her head fell into her hands.

Genevieve patted the top of her ponytail, and they both laughed.

Ironically, just as Tate and Genevieve were wrapping up their conversation about Brooks, a text from Delaney came through. With only one week left until the big day, it was time to meet and nail down any last-minute details. As Tate slurped up the last few drops of her smoothie, she was confident in the way the event was coming along. She figured she would be in and out of Delaney's office with no hiccups, but this was Tate Montgomery, and what would her life be if not for any hiccups?

~29~

Tate's strides were powerful as she walked into the building over in Westminster. She had tied up pretty much every loose end, and the ends she hadn't tied would have a neat little bow on top of them by the weekend—which, she would be sure to let Delaney know, was perfect timing for an event that was now eight days away.

The fifth floor no longer intimidated her. When she stepped off the elevator, she glided over to the lobby chair and fell blissfully into it. She even scooped up a magazine and flipped through a dozen or so pages before a whistle came from down the hallway.

Tate slammed the magazine into her lap as she looked up to find Brooks peering out from behind the wall. He was back in his business attire. She wasn't quite sure yet which Brooks she liked the most: the casual jeans-wearing Brooks who swept her in for a night of pleasure, or the well-dressed Brooks who teased every inch of her with his off-limits grin. She didn't have time to decide. He yanked his head toward the hallway, and Tate obliged.

Brooks' hand pressed up against Tate's back as soon as she was close enough for him to reach. Once she felt it, she gave him a quick "not here" message with her eyes and dropped back behind him. It'd been two days since they left Paris, and they had been texting back and forth since. Tate had ignored his texts until her talk with Genevieve, but afterward, she felt a bit more confident that maybe this could work out.

There was a mix of business talk in the texts, but most of them were heavily flirtatious. Tate had even sent a few photos. None too risqué—she knew better than to send those through the digital waves. She sent one of her legs peeking out of the bath, and another with her lips puckered as she lay in bed.

This was the first time they'd been together since, and of course, it had to be for a meeting with Delaney. The churning in her stomach was a mix of complete nervousness for this meeting and her desire to wrap her arms around Brooks' neck and lean in for a kiss. Clearly, he was thinking the latter when the two of them sat down in those leather chairs in Delaney's office. He scooted toward her and brushed his fingers along the nape of her neck.

"Stop it," Tate snapped. Her tone was sprightly at first, but when Brooks tried again, it became stern.

"What? She's not even here yet," he whispered.

"She could walk in at any minute."

Tate slapped Brooks' hand away again, and this time, he knew she wasn't kidding. He let out a disheartened sigh and moved his chair back to where he originally found it.

"Good afternoon. So sorry I'm late!" Delaney walked briskly into the room about fifteen minutes after Tate and Brooks sat down. "I hear all went well in Paris." Delaney looked in Tate's direction.

She felt heat rising to her cheeks at the mention of it, but quickly realized that even though she hadn't seen Brooks in two days, Delaney had. The tight grasp she had on the arms of her chair loosened when she realized it was Brooks who'd delivered the news to her and it was strictly about the painting.

"Yes, yes, it did," Tate said. "The painting is gorgeous, isn't it?"

"Exquisite," Delaney said. "Now, let's get down to business. Do we have the final guest count confirmed? Is the head of Optima going to be able to make it? He was our top donor last year."

With a flick of her wrist, Tate opened her notebook and scrolled through the list she had printed for this very reason.

"We are looking at about five-hundred or so right now. There's still about twenty who haven't RSVP'd, and I reached out to them this morning. Rupert will be in attendance. He's bringing his wife Ariella this year."

"Wonderful!" Delaney slapped her hands lightly on her desk. "Catering, photographer, music… Are we set?"

"Yup! I'll be arriving four hours before the doors open to show all rentals where to go and to help the musicians set up. Appetizers start at six, and dinner promptly at seven."

"Tate, you are an angel."

She probably wouldn't go that far, but Tate appreciated the compliment. She also appreciated the nod from Brooks' direction. His opinion had become something she greatly admired and respected, possibly even more than Delaney's at this point. She knew he was fielding a lot of Delaney's questions about the event, and Delaney's high praise was coming mostly from what he'd been telling her.

"Okay then, if that's all," Delaney said. She stood from her chair and reached her hand in Tate's direction. Tate stood too and met her grasp from across the desk before Delaney did what she did best. She excused herself off to another meeting and disappeared from her office. That left Tate and Brooks standing there, just the two of them, alone. It was a moment Brooks had been waiting for since he left Tate at the train station.

He never thought it was going to be that hard. His arms had wrapped around her outside of the station. He'd closed his eyes and taken in the sweet floral scent of her hair. Their suitcases sat beside them as they waited for separate cars to take them to their respective homes. When his pulled up, he was pleased Tate let him pull her in for a long, slow kiss. He'd thought coming back to London would put a halt on the progress the two of them were making in their romantic relationship. Brooks thought Tate's fear would get the best of her, but as he took her bottom lip into his mouth one last time before they pulled apart, a sense of hope surged through him. The texts that followed the kiss only exhilarated him even more than the night in Tate's hotel room, but it would be short-lived.

"Alone at last," Brooks said. He slithered his hands around her waist.

At first, Tate didn't struggle. She let him clasp his fingers behind her back, but when he leaned down for a kiss, her hands fell heavily against his chest. They pressed hard against it, hindering his lips from coming any closer.

"Brooks, seriously."

Tate walked to the glass windows. She hated how badly she wanted him, but she also hated his ignorance right now. They were in Delaney Donovan's office was not the time to try and play tonsil hockey.

She felt Brocks' hands slide around her from the opposite direction. Her back pressed firmly against his chest, the wetness of his lips against her temple. Suddenly, her pulse was racing, and the sound of her heart muffled every single cry that told her to make him stop. Tate let him turn her toward him. She let his lips trace her forehead down to her nose. She even welcomed them as they pressed heavily on her lips. She gripped his chest with her hands, trying so hard to ignore the cries. She squeezed harder, taking him in until she couldn't anymore. She pushed him away and squirmed out of his grasp.

"What's wrong?" Brooks asked. He tried to grab her hand, but she pulled it away.

"This!" she whispered with a hiss. "This is wrong. I knew better."

"What does that even mean?"

"If I do this right, this event can be a huge stepping-stone for me."

"And you will. You're doing an amazing job." Brooks stepped closer. He grabbed both of her hands and tried to move his head to catch her gaze.

Tate hated this. She hated all of it. She wanted his hands on her body, his heart in her hand, but this was not a big screen movie. She wasn't guaranteed a happily ever after. The only thing she could control was her career. That would be here even if Brooks decided to walk away like Cameron did, and even if he didn't, it'd only been two days and it was already complicating things.

"Tate look at me." He pulled her in closer. "This isn't just some fling for me. Ever since that day in the coffee shop, I haven't been able to stop thinking about you. Paris only made me fall for you even more. You make me want that house in the country. I wasn't ready then, but I'm ready now because I've found you. I would give you every drawer in my dresser if you would give me the chance. We are good together—don't you see that?"

Tate turned her head away from him. "I'm just starting to get back on my feet again. I can't make stupid mistakes like this."

Brooks' jaw fell open. His head bowed to the floor. Tate's words cut through him like a knife. He had poured his heart out to her, and she may as well have pulled it from his chest, thrown it on the ground, and stomped on it. Brooks' hands let Tate's slip out of them. He clenched them into fists as he looked back up at her.

"Oh, I'm sorry. I didn't realize that's what I am to you." He shook his head and stepped away from her, back to the table to gather his things.

Tate's chest felt as if she'd been used as a punching bag while she watched him fumble to stuff papers into his briefcase. Then, he closed his laptop and shoved that inside too. His movements were sharp. The clasp of the briefcase as he closed it pierced through her ears. He swung it off the table and turned toward the door.

"Brooks, wait..." Tate pleaded with him as she tried to hold back tears. That did not come out the way she'd meant it. This was her fault. She'd given in. She'd let it go too far, but that was because she wanted it too. She wouldn't take back that night in Paris for anything. She just needed...

She really didn't know what she needed. She needed him to stay as much as she needed him to leave. She needed to kiss him as much as she needed to let him go. She was confused. Her heart was racing, and her mind was running at the pace of a marathon winner. It was all too much too soon, and she just needed time.

"I think we're done here," Brooks said, staring at the door. Tate wanted so badly to see his face, but he was too far in front of her now. "We've tied up all the loose ends. I think we can call it a night. Of course, if you need anything before, you can call me, but I don't think there's any reason to meet again before Saturday, do you?"

She wanted to walk over to him, but instead, she blinked back the tears that were starting to wash into her eyes and said nothing. That was the only answer he needed.

"Okay then," Brooks said. "Goodbye, Tate."

He paused in the doorway. Tate supposed it was to give her a chance.

Brooks wanted to be wrong, but the continued silence only confirmed that what Tate had said was true. He was a mistake, and he would walk out of there that day thinking no different.

Tate knew if she said anything at all, he would hear it. The way her voice would start to shake would draw him back in. Being the man she knew he was, he'd pull her into him and hold her so tight she'd never want him to let go. Tate knew she couldn't do that to him right now. This was his moment. This time, he was taking a stand. He needed this, and whether she wanted to or not, this time, she needed to let him go.

~30~

The sweat was damp on Tate's forehead as she rolled up her yoga mat. Sixty minutes of hot yoga was exactly what she needed. She hadn't spoken to Brooks in two days, and the children's gala was only a few days away.

She'd been drowning in floral arrangements that morning when all hell broke loose. She got a call from the caterer frantically apologizing for how he'd had to change the menu. The fresh cabbage he'd planned on picking up from a local farm had not fared well for the season. Tate tried to calm his nerves by going over other options. The two of them settled on Kohlrabi, which he was able to get from a neighboring farm.

After that, the furniture rental company called to change the delivery and setup time...twice. Her patience was wearing thin. The florist must've noticed the tightness in Tate's fists as they finished talking about where the peonies and daffodils would go because she put together a tiny bouquet of daffodils for her to take home.

Tate's yoga mat was hanging off her shoulder as she pushed open the door to leave the yoga studio. She was rummaging through her purse wondering how many fires had ignited in the hour she was deep in her vinyasa flow. Delaney's name was the only thing on her screen once she found it. Tate froze in stride as others brushed by her. She wasn't sure if she should exhale in relief that it was only one missed call or flinch that Delaney's name was on her phone at all.

This was one of the reasons Tate loved event planning. It was stressful, no doubt, but it was never boring. She loved having her hands in all the moving pieces, taking the worry off everyone else and, in the end, getting to be there to see each piece fit perfectly together like a puzzle. She reminded herself of that very reason as she hit the call button on her phone. It rang twice before Delaney answered, and Tate welcomed the contentment she could hear in her voice.

"Hello, Tate!" Delaney said. "Thanks for getting back to me so quickly."

"Of course! What can I do for you?"

"So, slight change of plans for Saturday."

Tate had started to weave her way through the onset of Londoners coming her way before she heard the words "change of plan." With that, she leaned back into the white brick wall beside her. She was confident the wall was sturdy enough to catch whatever catastrophic information Delaney was about to throw her way.

"Our publicity team has secured a few press interviews, which are very important for this ball. They'd like to come in prior to the event to grab some photos and do some reporting from the space. Please tell me it's feasible for setup to be done by three instead of five."

A smile smeared across Tate's face once Delaney was done. Did she not have enough faith in her? If so, she would've known Tate had already planned to have the complete setup done by 3:30 p.m. anyway. Pushing it up another thirty minutes, though challenging in some aspects, wouldn't be the end of the world. With the furniture delivery arriving earlier than she'd originally planned, she relaxed further against the white brick before giving her answer.

"I don't think that'll be a problem at all. Will someone be there to meet the reporters when they arrive?"

"Absolutely," Delaney said. "Brooks will be there around half past two along with our head of publicity, Jillian."

"Wonderful," Tate gritted.

"Thank you again, so much. I'll let Jillian know. You have a wonderful day."

"I will, Delaney. You as well."

There were a few delivery boxes waiting upon Tate's return to her flat. As if her home wasn't small enough already, the favor boxes and décor were starting to outstay their welcome. If she kept booking events like this, she'd need an office space much quicker than she planned.

She unlocked her door and flung it open before bending down to pick up the boxes. There were two stacks of boxes by her glass door to the balcony. Both of them were taller than she was, so she started a third pile next to them. Her phone rang as she turned on the shower. *It can wait*, she thought as she stepped through the steam into the rainfall. She closed her eyes and let the water beat onto her skin. She just wanted a few minutes of quiet. She was running crazy lately, but her mind was winning the race. It was constantly filled with thoughts. So many, Tate would toss from one side of her bed to the other for hours at night. She hadn't needed an alarm these past few days. The sun was sleeping in later than she was.

When the water started to run cold, Tate surrendered. She wrapped herself in a towel and peeked over at her phone to see who had called. She gasped with excitement. This call didn't have anything to do with work; it was her mother. She hit the redial button. It was awfully early in Seattle, but Tate's mom was an early riser, and sometimes, she liked to get her phone conversations in before Tate's dad woke up. Tate appreciated their mother/daughter phone calls. Especially that afternoon.

"Hi, sweetie!" Tate's mom shrieked. "I feel like I haven't heard your voice in so long."

She wasn't exaggerating. In the scramble for this event, Tate had only spoken with her mother on the phone twice in the past few weeks. They texted regularly, but before Tate was hired by Delaney, they'd had at least weekly, if not biweekly, phone dates.

"I know, I'm so sorry. That charity ball I told you about is on Saturday, and it's full steam ahead."

"How exciting! I'm so proud of you."

"Thanks, Mom."

Tate had yet to tell her mom about Brooks. She was a little nervous to say it out loud. There hadn't been a guy of substance since Cameron. Their heart-to-hearts about love over the past two years had consisted of Tate's mom reassuring her she needed to "trust in the timing" because "when it comes around, you'll know." It would've been nice if her mom had warned her it could've possibly come in the form of Brooks Walker. Then, Tate could've at least prepared herself. Her mom must've heard the confusion in her voice because she stopped mid-conversation about life in Seattle.

"Honey, are you all right?" she asked.

Tate took a deep breath. Her mother had always seen right through her. When she was five, she stole Grace's lollipop as they left the doctor's office. She insisted it was hers even though she had already eaten the one the doctor gave her. It took all of two minutes in the car for her mom to break her. She handed the lollipop right back to Grace.

Tate was sixteen the first time she snuck out of the house. It wasn't for anything scandalous, but it was past her curfew. She and some friends went to the local diner for milkshakes. She thought she was home free as she snuck up the stairs and crawled into bed with no movement from her parent's room. She had to confess the next morning, though, after her mom woke up to find the front door unlocked. Even with almost five thousand miles between them, Tate was comforted by the fact she had her mom to lean on.

"I met a guy," Tate said. "He's successful. He's funny. I laugh so hard when I'm with him..."

"But..." Oh, how Tate's mom could read her like a book.

"He's my client. I land this insanely huge event that could make or break my career, and I fall for my client."

"Well, the event is over Saturday though, right? You wait a few days, and then you're in the clear."

"That sounds all hunky-dory, Mom, but his boss holds events all year round. What if she hires me for more?"

"Then at least you know you'll be working with someone you know and trust."

"You're not helping!"

"What do you mean, I'm not helping?" her mom asked. "Realistically, out of all the events you might land in a year, how many would be with *this guy* as your client? Is it enough to sacrifice your happiness? I want you to be successful, honey, but I also want you to be happy, and I am confident I raised a girl who can balance both."

Tate hadn't really thought of it that way. She was too focused on how big of an event this was for her. Realistically, her mom was right. If Tate had three events a month, three dozen events a year, maybe a handful would come from Delaney, and there wasn't even a guarantee she would always hire her or that it would be Brooks' clients she'd be throwing an event for.

"It's just...I've sacrificed a lot to be here, Mom. I don't want to make a stupid decision again and lose everything."

"Oh, honey...is that what this is about? Listen, to be blunt, Cameron is a jerk."

Tate smiled. Her mom never swore. She was always so prim and proper, but she could always tell the moments she really wanted to, and she knew "jerk" was not the word she really wanted to use. Tate almost interrupted to tell her mom how she ran into him in Paris, but that was a story for another time.

"He sure is," she said instead.

"Not everyone is like Cameron, and, honestly, if this doesn't work out, you move on. You at least have to try."

"I think it might be too late. I messed up, Mom. I messed up bad."

In that moment, she was glad she and her mother had no secrets. Tate had never been afraid to talk about boys, sex, or any other truly uncomfortable thing parents tried to talk to their kids about.

"I slept with him and then, basically, after he confessed his feelings to me, told him it was all a mistake. It came out all wrong. I didn't mean it like that, but I hurt him." Tate's voice started to shake.

"Sweetheart, you have to remember, life is a long road. There are going to be bumps and wrong turns. The important thing is to make sure you take in the scenery. Snap your photos and hold them tight once you get to the end of the road. If you found some good scenery, why keep your eyes closed? Go make it right. Tell him how you feel before it's too late."

Tate smiled. "You're the best, Mom!"

She hung up the phone with her mom a bit more hopeful about Brooks. They had been on a pretty great ride so far. Brooks was a nice piece of scenery, and maybe it wouldn't be all so bad to enjoy it while it was in front of her. She knew what she had to do. She had to talk to Brooks. She had to be as honest with him as he was with her—but not yet. All of what she had to say was jumbled. She needed to make sure it all came out how she wanted it to. She grabbed a notebook from the top of her beechwood coffee table and spent the rest of the afternoon out on her patio writing down every word. When she was done, she read it again and smiled. She had written a letter to Brooks telling him exactly how she felt. All that was left was for her to find the courage to say out loud everything she scribbled down.

~31~

Tate was beyond grateful to have somewhat of an inner circle here in London. Her time at Rosewood Events certainly had its perks when it came to glamour. There were some events where an all-black button-up and pants just weren't enough. For the Ball of Hope, Tate wanted to blend into the background but in a way that still emanated the elegance of what she planned to turn the Gateway Garden into. Since she didn't have any high-class couture in her closet, she called upon her favorite evening dress rental store.

"Hello, Tate!" Madelyn screeched. She held the door open for Tate to walk in.

It'd been a while since Tate needed an excuse to rent cocktail attire. The last time was the final event she worked at Rosewood. Madelyn had picked out a silver halter dress. It hung right above the floor with Tate's heels on. The mesh overlay added a bit of character. Today, though, she wanted something with a little less flare. She was looking for something simple that would still shout "I'm in charge." She told Madelyn that on the phone and knew that when she arrived, there would be a rack of dresses waiting for her to try on.

"You're running your own company now, yeah?" Madelyn pulled back the drape to the private sitting area she had reserved for Tate.

"Yes. I started it a few months back. So far, so good."

"Isn't that wonderful!"

Tate knew the drill. She tossed her purse onto the plush blue chair and slipped off her shoes. Her jeans came next, and then she tugged at the loose white sweater until she was standing there exposed in her nude intimates.

"All right, let's try this one first."

Madelyn pulled a black jumpsuit off the rack. The sleeves were short but ruffled around the shoulders. Tate stepped into it, but the bottom half was too long for her petite frame. She'd have to wear pretty high heels to keep it from dragging on the floor, and that wasn't going to work if she had to hustle from one place to another.

Next was a long-sleeved wrap dress. It fit snug over every inch of her, but in the mirror, Tate felt as if she looked like she was heading to a funeral. She also feared she'd be looking down all night making sure the wrap hadn't come loose enough to expose her lady bits.

Three more dresses got the boot before Tate slipped into a one-shoulder mermaid cut gown. The sleeve ruffled at the shoulder like the jumpsuit she'd tried on first. She wiggled back and forth on the platform. It was comfortable. There was no restriction.

"Do a little spin," Madelyn said. "See about the back."

Tate did a little one-eighty so her backside was facing the mirror. She peered over her shoulder. It was mostly open back. The material came up just past her tailbone. Tate spun back around and did her normal event planner test. She bent down to the floor, then reached up over her head. First slowly, then she picked up the pace. She stepped off the platform and jogged around on the carpet.

"Yes, yes!" Madelyn clapped. "Beautiful! It's just beautiful! What do you think?"

Tate stepped back up onto the platform and stared into the mirror one more time. Her hands stroked over her hips. She'd been dressing up a lot these past few weeks. While she stared at the way this dress accentuated her marginal hips, she thought about the dress she wore to the Lanesborough and the way

Brooks' mouth dropped open when he looked up at her. Then, the night in Paris, when he finally took his eyes off his drink. They'd grown wide as he traced her from head to toe. She loved the way this dress looked on her, but, as she did one final twirl, she thought mostly about how much she loved that Brooks would love this dress on her. The fact that Brooks crossed her mind while standing on that platform solidified one thing for her.

Tate Montgomery wanted to enjoy the scenery. She wanted to enjoy every bit of it. She had found her co-pilot; her shotgun rider. Her mother had opened her eyes. There was no longer a doubt in her mind about what she wanted. The letter that said it all was still tucked between the pages of Tate's notebook on the coffee table, but she knew, while she stared at herself in the mirror, those words needed to find their way to Brooks sooner rather than later.

"I think we've found the one."

Tate smiled. "Yes, I think I did."

Sure, this dress was perfect for the charity ball, but when she spoke those words out loud, she knew she wasn't just talking about her outfit.

~32~

Brooks was relieved that Garrett and Vera were coming into London for the weekend. He couldn't think of anything that would calm his nerves tomorrow night better than having the two of them at the Ball of Hope. Even the glass of whiskey he held in his hands wasn't easing the tension he felt about seeing Tate.

He pictured her walking through the double doors of the ballroom. She'd most likely try to blend in with the evening's dress code. That meant he'd have to find some way not to notice the way her sun-kissed skin moved underneath whatever she wore. It would most likely accentuate all of his favorite parts of her, and he hated the idea that only his eyes would be able to trace them. Most of all, he hated knowing that it was most likely going to be more awkward tomorrow night than it had been all week. Brooks hadn't seen Tate since he walked out of Delaney's office. She had texted him a few times to see if he could reach out to a couple of his clients who had yet to respond to their invites. Then, there was the one text he received late last night. He was already in bed, but of course, when he saw her name, he couldn't resist the urge.

Tate: *Brooks?*

That was all she sent. He laid there watching the three little dots underneath it disappear and then reappear for at least a couple of minutes before anything else flashed across the screen.

Tate: *Are you awake?*

He checked the time again. It was half past midnight. Normally, he would've been, but the less time he was awake, the less time he had to think about Tate. He hated that they were arguing. Walking out of Delaney's office was unlike him. Usually, he was one to finish what he started, but the look in her eyes that day washed a heavy sense of defeat over him. He was at a loss for words. They had returned from an amazing night in Paris, and when he stepped off the train in London, he was hopeful he had finally convinced Tate that what they had was worth figuring out. Tate didn't feel the same way though. She had no problem pushing him away in that room. She seemed fine with him not being a part of her world.

Brooks: *Yeah, I'm awake. What's up?*

He had waited another minute after her question came through before he answered. His eyes once again fixated on the three dots hovering underneath his question as he waited for Tate's response. When they stopped with no words appearing on the screen, he felt a twinge in his chest where his heart was beating. What was it that she could possibly want after midnight? When the three dots reappeared, Brooks held onto the hope that maybe she had changed her mind; that the silence of the night had reignited her feelings, and she could no longer stand being away from him. That hope was short-lived.

Tate: *Do you think Rupert & Ariella should sit at table eight with the board members or table eleven with Delaney and her posse?*

Seating assignments? Seriously? That was what she needed from him right now? He rolled over and released a loud grunt into his pillow before texting back.

Brooks: *Board members. Delaney won't be sitting half the time anyway. He'll have better conversation there.*

She replied simply with: *Thank you!*

He hated that she'd used an exclamation point as if everything between the two of them was normal. She was all about the professionalism though, so, instead of letting it jab into him, he responded with a smiley face, then tossed and turned for the rest of the night.

Now, here he was, alone in his flat, holding tight to his second glass of whiskey. It would be the last of the night as he knew how important tomorrow was. He savored it slowly while he waited for Garrett and Vera to arrive.

Garrett texted from the street that they were there and were looking for a place to park. Brooks threw back the last drop in his glass and headed down to wait for them.

"Hey there, handsome, how you doing?"

He turned toward the voice yelling his way. Oh, how he missed Vera and her playful personality. Garrett had really hit the jackpot with that one. She was pulling at the pieces of long black hair that covered her face thanks to the gusts of winds flowing between the buildings.

"Hey, future Mrs." Brooks said. "It's been a long time!"

Vera threw her arms around Brooks' neck. Over her shoulder, he saw Garrett. Both of his hands were full of luggage. The two of them were only here for the weekend, but from the mountain of bags in his hands, you would've thought it was more like a couple of weeks.

"A little help here?" Garrett panted. He finally caught up to Vera. Brooks couldn't help but laugh before he pulled a few of the weighted bags from his grasp.

"Did you stuff your whole wardrobe into these bags?" he asked Vera.

"I couldn't decide what to wear," she said. "This is my first big, fancy event. I needed to have options."

"Speaking of big, fancy events," Brooks said, opening the door for the two of them. "How'd wedding dress shopping go?"

Brooks still couldn't believe that in a few more months, his little brother was going to be a married man. He was beyond happy for him even though he knew he'd probably be attending alone. Vera would never let him live it down either.

"Splendid! I fell in love with one right off the rack. It's hanging nicely in Mum's closet."

"Yeah, she teases me every time we go over there," Garrett said. "Then she gives me a hard time for pretending to sneak up and take a look."

"You can't see it before the big day, Garett!" Vera yelled over her shoulder.

Brooks set down the luggage on the bed in his guest room. He regretted sometimes that he had made the larger room his master. The bathroom may be smaller, but the view from the guest room was so much better. His looked across to the redbrick of the building next door. This room looked out over the city block. He'd thought about switching rooms sometimes, but the idea seemed like too much work, so, instead, he'd sneak in some nights when the streets were all lit up and just stare out at the world moving beneath him.

"Are you hungry?" Brooks asked.

"Starving!" Vera patted her stomach. "I kind of had my heart set on that Thai place you took us to last time. What do you think?"

Brooks smiled. "I think I can make that happen."

Vera squealed. Garrett unzipped the lone suitcase that belonged to him, and Brooks pulled out his cell phone to make a reservation. He watched his brother and his fiancée intently while the phone rang in his ear. Vera squeezed Garrett's arm playfully as she helped him to pick out something to wear. Her head leaned against his shoulder as she scrounged through the clothes he'd brought. Garrett's hand swept across her waist.

Mixed emotions ran through Brooks as he stood there watching. He loved seeing the two of them so happy but felt bad that a part of him bred a bit of jealousy for what they had. Usually, Brooks wasn't bothered by their relationship, and he always laughed off the jabs the two of them gave him about his social life. This time was different though. This time, he wanted what they had. He wanted someone to tell him he could not wear that shirt because it was wrinkled. He wanted someone sitting in the passenger seat of his car on a long drive to visit his family. He didn't want that with just anyone though. He wanted Tate.

For the first time, Brooks was starting to understand the void in his life.

There was finally an answer from the restaurant on the other end of the line. Brooks let out a sigh of relief. He no longer wanted to think about how the only thing that ever truly mattered to him was slipping through his fingers and he was powerless in stopping it.

~33~

Garrett and Vera decided they wanted to paint the town after chowing down at Vera's favorite Thai restaurant. Brooks took them to a couple of different bars on the way back to his flat. He stuck to his guns on his alcohol intake and only ended up drinking about a quarter of the beer Garrett placed in front of him at the last bar stop. Now, the three of them were sitting snug on the only couch in his living room.

Garrett was fast asleep—Brooks could tell by the heavy breathing coming from the other side of Vera. It was so loud he'd had to turn up the volume on the television a couple of times to drown it out. Even then, he wasn't really paying attention. His blank stare was unchanged even during the parts where Vera couldn't help but let out a rowdy laugh. His silence must've been deafening for her as she sat in the middle of the two brothers, both absent in their own worlds.

"There's something on your mind tonight, yeah?" Vera turned her folded-up body toward Brooks. His head was leaning heavily against his fist. He gave no reaction until Vera made a fist of her own and jabbed it into his thigh.

"Ow! What was that for?" Brooks yelped.

"I'll tell ya what that was for. All night, you've been a million miles away. What's in that head of yours?" Vera tapped her finger to the side of Brooks' head.

He sighed in surrender as he lifted himself up from the couch. Brooks may have been avoiding it, but this conversation was sure going to require some whiskey. He held the bottle up for Vera, but she shook her head. She'd never been much of a liquor drinker, though she could drink anyone under the table when it came to a stout. Brooks flicked his finger to pop the top off and poured himself a glass.

"It's about that girl, isn't it? The one you told Garrett about?"

Brooks didn't answer. The only thing his lips did was pucker up to take a sip of his malt beverage. Vera must have taken the quiet as a yes because her eyes lit up. She was always rooting for Brooks when it came to his love life and had asked from the beginning how someone as handsome, charming, and loyal as Brooks hadn't been snatched up already. It seemed the more she got to know him, the more she adored him. They'd become close over the past couple of years.

The two of them seemed to be the only ones who could handle late nights when it came to family gatherings. Over the holidays, they'd sit up while everyone else was fast asleep playing cards, watching movies, or indulging on leftover pie. Vera always had to know the details, and eventually, she became the one Brooks confided in. Tonight was no different.

"What's her name?" Vera asked.

"Tate," Brooks said. He was now back on the couch beside Vera, his legs crossed toward her as he said Tate's name again. "She's the planner in charge of tomorrow's event."

"Tate," Vera repeated. "Tell me about her."

Brooks didn't even know where to start. There was so much to say about what he was feeling. He was angry and frustrated one minute, and then lonely and longing for Tate the next. He was so drawn to her fearless nature when it came to her work. Whenever he was around her, he got lost in the intellect of her words.

"A girl with brains," Vera interrupted. "She sounds lovely."

"She is, and don't get me wrong," Brooks laughed, "she's gorgeous too." He couldn't help but remember the emotion that came across Tate's face when she'd held the éclair in the bakery. "I don't think her heart's as brave as her mind though. She holds back. I know she's been hurt, but I hate being put in that box, you know? No matter what I say, I can't get through to her."

Vera rested her hand on Brooks' shoulder. His tired eyes were once again staring through the television's now still screen.

"Have you told her how you felt? Genuinely expressed your feelings?"

"She shut me down."

"I'm sorry. But sometimes, good things take time. Maybe she needs a little more. Don't be sad, mate. You're quite a catch. I'm sure she'll come around. Will we be meeting her tomorrow?"

Brooks saw the hopeful look in Vera's eyes only grow wider as he nodded. She reached over and pulled him in for a hug. Her hand gently patted against his back. Vera had always known what to say to bring a sense of calm to Brooks. He was thankful she was going to be there tomorrow night; he could use all the encouragement he could get. There was no telling how seeing Tate was going to go, but hopefully he could get some time with her. Time, perhaps, to reiterate his feelings for her.

Tate was like a hurricane. He hadn't seen her coming, but she'd swept through and torn down all his insecurities about commitment. Even if he wanted to run for cover, he couldn't. She was already there, inside of him, consuming everything he owned. His heart, his soul—they were all hers now, and only she could decide whether to save or destroy them.

~34~

Tate chose the earliest pickup time for the van rental on the morning of the ball. She had never been more thankful for Genevieve as the two of them shoved everything in the back. By the time everything had been unloaded into the Gateway Garden room, it was almost eleven. By half past twelve, the furniture was set, and the Paris café backdrop was all pieced together in the back of the room. Now, all she needed were the linens and table settings so she could set the favors. That was proving to be a bit harder than she thought.

Tate's watch vibrated, and an unknown number flashed across her wrist. She ran over to her purse and yanked out her phone before the call went to voicemail.

"Hello?" All Tate could hear was static on the other end of the line. "Hello?" she said again. This time, someone answered.

"Ms. Montgomery?" The voice was deep and muffled through the phone.

"This is her," Tate said.

The delivery van carrying the linens and place settings was stuck somewhere en route. Their arrival time was going to be delayed. Tate could feel the heat rising inside of her at the thought of a delay, but as the man on the phone tried to explain the situation to her, anger suddenly turned to heaving bouts of laughter.

"I'm sorry," she said. "Did you say you're going to be delayed because of spilled milk?"

"Yes, ma'am," the driver said. "It seems the latches of two trucks came unhinged, and the milk bottles flew out the back. There's milk everywhere."

"Spilled milk?" Tate was struggling to hold in her amusement. "That's great. How late are we talking?"

"About forty-five minutes, ma'am."

Tate knew she'd have to jump in and lend an extra pair of hands to make sure setup was done on time, but it was still possible. She thanked the driver for the update and burst out laughing once the call ended.

"What on earth?" Genevieve asked.

"Our linens are running late because of a milk spill on the motorway."

The concept may have not been so amusing, but, in retrospect, Tate needed something to calm her nerves and keep her levelheaded as she continued to smooth out the bumps. Genevieve was now echoing Tate's laughter. They were so entertained by the thought of milk on the motorway that both of them had tears streaming down their faces.

"Look," Genevieve said, "we're both crying over spilled milk."

And that they were. They cried for another ten minutes at least before they both were able to pull themselves together.

Tate had planned on doing the auction table last, but since there was nothing else they could do without the linens, the two of them started on that instead. They set the French-inspired jewelry, pottery, and antiques across the tables and displayed each of the paintings on easels. The painting from Pierre was framed in the middle of two artists Tate had discovered at the London gallery.

The driver of the van carrying the linens had impeccable timing. Tate's phone rang again as she set down the final clipboard on the auction table. She had Genevieve meet him outside the loading dock, and within minutes, they were unloading the linens onto each table. Tate and Genevieve set up the place settings to move things along. Tate was also pretty particular when it came to how she wanted them, so she figured if she did it, it would save some time on having to fix anything once the staff was done.

"We're so close!" Genevieve said. The black-and-white layers on top of the linens illuminated the room perfectly.

Tate wrapped her arm around Genevieve's shoulder as they admired their work. "So far, so good," she said.

Now came the part she'd been waiting for. All of the black wire-frame birdcages had been unboxed and were patiently waiting in the front of the room. Genevieve ran over, grabbed as many as she could balance in her hands, and set them down at each place setting. She'd run back for another round, and Tate would follow behind her with the packages of stacked macarons to place inside of them.

"Tate, you hit the jackpot with these," Genevieve said.

They both stood back admiring all five-hundred-and-something birdcages sprinkled atop the rectangular tables that lined the middle of the Gateway Garden. Tate spun around to take everything in. Scattered down the middle of the rows of tables were tall white vases stuffed with bare branches, crystal garlands, and peonies. String lights hung perfectly above the tables, embodying the stars on a clear night in Paris. Tate's favorite element, though, had to be the café backdrop that was going to be used for the night's photobooth. They had even brought in a bike with a front basket that the florist filled with the brightest sunflowers.

"It's even better than I envisioned," Tate said.

She looked down at her watch. It was just gone half past two. That gave her about a half hour to finish up the final details. What she needed, though, wasn't more time to prepare the room, but more time to prepare her heart, because Brooks would be walking through that door any minute.

~35~

That extra glass of whiskey luckily didn't leave Brooks feeling any aftermath as he rolled out of bed on Saturday. He flipped open the blinds and let a dark shadow into his room. The sun was nowhere in sight, but at least the streets were dry.

It wasn't quite ten o'clock when Brooks pulled off the T-shirt he'd slept in. Until he stepped into the calm stream of water, Tate had been distant from his mind. Now his house was quiet, thoughts of her were beating through him like a drum.

He wasn't ready to see her today. That was a lie. The hours had been fleeting with each day that passed, and it was agony. The problem was, he knew today, he would have to smile and shake her hand like everyone else in the room. He didn't want to be like everyone else in the room, but he was going to do it for her. That was what she wanted, and tonight was her night. This type of event, for Brooks, ran like clockwork. He would tighten his tie, shake a few hands, nod politely during conversations, and then say goodnight.

Tate, on the other hand... He knew she'd be examining every bite of every appetizer and hurrying along the catering crew if they ran even a minute behind. She'd be lurking in every corner in the hope of overhearing even just one "How great is this event?" She needed it so desperately, and he was going to give that to her.

There was still time before Brooks had to button himself up in tonight's suit, and he knew Garrett and Vera would be sleeping for a while. Back in Reading, their usual nighttime routine had them in bed before ten each night, so crawling in a little after midnight was daunting for them.

After his shower, Brooks strutted to the kitchen in only his boxers and examined the nearly bare shelves in the fridge. There was a liter of milk, some sandwich meat, butter, and half a carton of eggs. Last time Garrett and Vera were in town, he set off the smoke alarm trying to make omelets. In an attempt not to relive that same experience, he pulled himself into a pair of jeans, threw on a clean shirt, stroked his fingers through his still-damp hair, and decided on taking a quick trek to the bakery down the street.

If Brooks ever did move out to a house in the country, this was one of the things he would miss the most. He loved the liveliness that hit him as soon as he walked out the door. "Good morning, Brooks," rang out from his neighbors leaning out over their tiny balconies. He waved up at them before turning the corner to the coffee shop he had taken Tate to. Just like that day, the line spread through the front patio. He shook off the thought of her walking up to him in Paris with that bright smile as he passed his favorite delicatessen, a launderette, and a couple of vintage clothes shops before stepping under the awning to the bakery.

"Good morning!" The voice was just the cheer he needed as he walked up to the counter. "Are you okay?" The smile that spread across the elderly woman's face was contagious. Brooks couldn't help but reciprocate.

"Doing fine this gray morning. You?" he asked.

"I'm lovely, thank you. Another day on this beautiful earth."

Brooks' smile grew as she peered over the register. She was barely tall enough to be seen over it. The gray curls in her hair added an extra couple of inches.

"Do you fancy a cuppa today?"

"You know, I think I'm going to stick to my regular," Brooks said. "I'll take a flat white."

"Delightful! Anything else?" the woman asked.

"Give me a dozen of your best bakery items. Whatever you fancy, I'll take it."

"You have that much faith in me?" she asked.

"I've got to put it somewhere these days."

The woman must have noticed the distress in his response. She tilted her head to look up at him. He noticed right away the concern in her eyes before she waved her hands over the bakery goods behind the counter. Faith, he usually carried around on a silver platter. There was never a reason not to. There were a handful of times in his life when it fell. The most haunting was when his family arrived a few minutes too late to the hospital to say goodbye to his grandmother. They had flown all night. It took three planes to get them in, but it wasn't enough. That had been a low blow.

His mother, though, he remembered how stoic she was standing in the waiting room. No tears fell from her eyes; she only smiled. When Brooks had asked why, she simply responded with, "Grandma's with the angels now." Brooks' mother didn't see it as the time she would never get back; she saw it as a time of reprieve for her mother, who was no longer shackled by the dementia that had stolen her years before. Kimberly always saw the silver lining, the "another day on this beautiful earth" mindset, just as the woman standing across from him did.

These past few days, Brooks had found himself balancing faith precariously on that platter. He'd been tripping at the thought of being so close to what he never knew he wanted, only to have it yanked away from him. In those moments, his faith would waiver close to the edge, but before it fell, he'd catch his footing and straighten it up again. It hadn't been easy, but that morning in that bakery, Brooks watched the woman gather his baked goods into a white box and exhaled his sorrow. He'd needed that woman today. Almost as much as his stomach was aching for those baked goods, his soul was searching for the silver lining.

~36~

Brooks tapped the breaks in front of the hotel valet just after 2:30 p.m. He had borrowed Garrett's car because it was there, and he didn't feel like waiting out the Tube that afternoon. He threw the car in park and admired the perfection of his tie knot in the rearview mirror. It was something his dad had taught him to do when he was thirteen. Brooks had been in his bedroom tugging at the lopsided knot over his white collared shirt. The homecoming dance was less than an hour away, and Cynthia Anders would be there waiting for him. He'd asked her the week before to be his date and had a white corsage downstairs to slip on her wrist.

"What's the matter, Leo?" his dad asked when he walked into the bedroom. Even Brooks' family used his middle name frequently.

"This stupid tie," he said. He yanked it up over his head and threw it on the floor.

"Now, now." Brooks could see his dad even now reaching down to pick up the tie and draping it back over his shoulder. He stood behind him and gripped one side of the tie with each hand. "Criss cross, wrap around, throw it back, then pull it down."

Brooks said that poem every time he stood in front of the mirror, and today was no different. The result, after he finished, was his charcoal tie perfectly centered between the collar of his maroon shirt. He slung his jacket over his shoulder and grabbed the ticket from the valet before leaping up the stairs. Jillian had texted him twice already demanding his whereabouts. He wasn't even five minutes late, and, truthfully, it didn't matter if he was because she was the one who'd be doing all the talking. Brooks was only there to lend moral support and occasionally whisper answers to the questions she didn't know.

He cringed when he arrived at the ballroom door. A part of him knew Tate would be on the other side of it, but mostly, he hated that Jillian's wrath fell heavy on his shoulders. Brooks had been working with her for about three years now, so he was well-equipped to handle it, but that didn't mean he had to like it.

Brooks' grip was firm on the door handle as he swung it open. His eyes first drifted to the magnificent transformation of the room he'd only been able to see in bits and pieces until now. He couldn't believe this was the same room he'd walked into with Delaney when they first secured the space. The arches and columns were stunning, but his overall impression had been that the space was cold. It was such a large space, he thought it would be impossible to fill it up enough to feel intimate, but he had been wrong.

The long tables were positioned in two lines all the way down the center of the room. An aisle had been left open between them so guests could pull out their chivari chairs with black bows and scoot up in front of... What were they scooting up in front of? He stepped closer to eye the birdcages neatly stacked with his favorite: macarons. He wondered how anyone even thought of doing something like that, but he wasn't surprised. From the short time he'd known Tate, he knew her imagination held far more enchantment than she let on. It was the kind that turned a hollow room into a fairytale. Brooks placed his fingertip atop the birdcage in admiration. He was so enthralled by the detail, it took him a minute to realize someone had walked up behind him.

"Earth to Brooks."

He knew that voice. The soft, pleasing tone was all too familiar to him. Brooks turned around to see Tate staring at him. Her lopsided ponytail hid the curls from her face. He always loved when she wore her hair up. It made her lips glimmer brighter from her lip gloss, and her eyes always seemed to be a deeper color brown when her hair wasn't falling across them.

"Hey, you!" He thought he'd have to force the excitement in his voice, but it spilled from his tongue with ease. Even with the tension between the two of them running high, she still made any bad day better.

It felt like the ground was moving underneath Tate once she and Brooks were standing face-to-face, but it was only her right leg violently shaking. She pressed her hand against it to try and keep it still, but it was no use. She'd noticed him as soon as he walked in, but his eyes were so fixated on what she now realized were the birdcages, he hadn't seen her nervous wave.

He saw her now though. She was without any makeup, her hair was a mess, and she had snagged her jeans on one of the tables as she walked by. There was a hole just under the back pocket to prove it. She was almost embarrassed to look directly at him, having no idea this was the look Brooks preferred the most.

Brooks had woken up that morning in Paris about an hour or so before she did. He'd lay there watching her for a good fifteen minutes before he fell back to sleep. The curtains were closed, and he'd already turned off the lamp by the bed that was still on when he came to. The room was dark, but somehow, he still had a clear view of the peaceful look on her face. She was sleeping soundly. He could hear a quiet breath escape as her chest fell. Her eyes were free of the color she'd been wearing before the rain washed it away. He liked it that way. He watched the naturalness of her lashes as they fluttered while he stroked his hand through her hair.

Brooks couldn't help but notice her lashes were the same way now. He noticed something new though: there were freckles painted on the tip of her nose. He would've stared at them forever if time let him, but, thanks to Jillian, his time was short-lived.

"There you are, Brooks! We're all over here." She pointed to the table near the auction items. Brooks followed her finger to see the cameras. They were waiting on tripods, and the crew surrounded them.

"Yup," Brooks said. "I'll be right over."

Jillian shot him a callous glare but obliged and turned away from him.

"Everything looks amazing. You've really done a number on this place." He took Tate's hand in his, surprised when she didn't retract.

"Thank you," Tate said. "I couldn't have done it without you." Their time together passed through her mind like a highlight reel. She felt the stiffness in her shoulders suddenly release as she said those words, but it seemed Brooks wasn't going to take any of tonight's hard work away from her

"This was all you." He squeezed her hand. "It's good to see you." He couldn't help himself. He pulled her hand in closer to him and wrapped his arms around Tate. He felt her surrender against him.

"It's good to see you too," she said.

Tate knew that Brooks was being summoned by the tapping of Jillian's heel. It echoed from across the room. There wasn't going to be any time to talk to him before the event, so, sadly, she'd have to wait until after.

" You'd better get over there before that woman throws her pitchfork at you."

"Haha!" Tate had always loved the sound of Brooks' laugh. "She's harmless, but you wouldn't know it just by looking at her. I'll see you later?"

"That you will."

Tate pulled her arms from around Brooks and rested them back against her still shaking legs. He waved at her, patted the birdcage one more time with a wink, and headed over to Jillian.

Genevieve had almost made it over in time to squeeze herself into the situation. She pouted when she met Tate in the center of the aisle after Brooks was already gone.

"Is that him?" She nudged the side of Tate's ribs.

"Shh," Tate hissed.

"It is, isn't it?" Genevieve joked. "He is gorgeous. That jacket is quite snug over all those muscles"

"Okay...okay," Tate said. She wrapped her arm around Genevieve's shoulder and staggered toward the door that would lead them into the lobby. "We should probably get ourselves ready. All is set in here for now."

Tate had rented a hotel room for the night. She thought it was the least she could do for Genevieve after all the help she was giving her. It also made it convenient to only have to take the elevator up a few floors to change into her gala look. That way, if anything went wrong or Delaney called with last-minute tasks, she could run downstairs and be there before anything unraveled.

"I can't wait for your Cinderella moment!" Genevieve squealed as he wrapped her arms around Tate.

The two of them were still moving toward the door. Brooks was fully absorbed in conversation with someone from the camera crew, while Jillian spoke into the microphone. Tate broke her stare from the stubble on Brooks' jaw long enough to give a puzzled reaction.

"What Cinderella moment?"

"The one where you walk out in this,"—Genevieve made eyes at Tate's current attire—" and you walk in with your hair done and red lipstick on, rocking the mermaid silhouette. I am walking in first so I can see his reaction."

"That's it! You get—"

Tate didn't have to finish her sentence. She snapped her fingers, and Genevieve sped to the door. The both of them were laughing.

Tate had to admit, she liked the sound of being Cinderella for a night. She'd be walking into the biggest display of her talent anyone had ever seen, and every single one of those who walked inside too would be judging her on it. That thought hit her like a ton of bricks as she stepped into the elevator and launched into a full-blown panic attack.

~37~

Genevieve helped Tate lower herself down on the bed once they were in the hotel room. Tate followed Genevieve's lead every time she told her to breathe in and out. The slow, deep breaths seemed to help. Color was pumping back into her face, and her clammy hands were drying up.

"You okay?" Genevieve asked.

"What if everyone hates it?"

"Hates what?" Genevieve asked. "The party?"

Tate nodded.

"Tate, it looks absolutely amazing down there. Stop putting so much pressure on yourself. We've got this. You're not alone, remember?"

Tate looked up at the genuine pride beaming from Genevieve's eyes. She was right. Thank goodness she wasn't in this alone. Genevieve would be there by her side. Rosewood Events had also given her all the experience she needed to catch whatever may be thrown her way tonight. She could do this.

"Thank you," Tate said. She patted the top of Genevieve's hand. "Thank you for being here with me tonight. You have been such a huge help since I started this business. I don't know what I would do without you."

"I am always here for you. You're my best friend. You don't have to thank me, but you do have to get ready. Do you think you can stand up?"

Tate pulled up her hand to look at her watch. They had two hours before they'd have to leave again. She pushed herself up off the bed. Her knees wobbled a bit, but she steadied herself on Genevieve's shoulder.

"You can do this," Genevieve said. The smile on her face sent a surge of excitement through Tate, replacing any fear that once was.

Tate took the bathroom, and Genevieve the vanity out in the open space. It took about half an hour for Tate to curl every strand of her wavy brown hair. There was now a mound of curls resting on her shoulders, which Genevieve would help to somehow tame on the crown of her head. While she waited for Genevieve to finish her own hair, Tate started on her makeup. She was never much into makeup. Lip gloss and mascara were her go-to most days. She fumbled with the false eyelashes that stuck to her fingertips and decided against them. Instead, she swept a taupe shadow over her eyelid and accented with a deep purple.

The final touches of eyeliner and mascara were being finished when Genevieve walked in. Her hair was well past her shoulders now she'd straightened it, and it outlined her black halter neckline perfectly. Tate let out a laugh when Genevieve spun in a circle so she could get a look from all angles.

"Are you ready?" Genevieve asked. She was holding a cluster of bobby pins in her hand.

"I'm ready!"

Tate slouched down as Genevieve picked up strands of her hair and secured them high on her head. She felt as if she'd gained another couple of pounds by the time her hair was securely in place. Her head was heavy, but the curls sat perfectly snug. Even her usual flyaway hairs were tucked back. Tate didn't want to be messing with them once the party was underway. She'd knew she'd have much more to worry about.

"Perfect!" Genevieve clapped. "Now, let's get you into that dress."

Tate walked over to the wardrobe where she'd hung the dress when they first arrived for early check-in. She wrapped her hand around the zipper and tugged it open. The dress was as perfect as she remembered. Her bronzed legs slipped through the opening as she wiggled her way in. Once she slipped her right arm through the solo strap, Genevieve pulled the zipper up to Tate's midback and clasped the pearl necklace shut, letting it fall over her collarbone.

"How do I look?" Tate asked. It was her turn to spin around for Genevieve.

"Like you were born to do this," Genevieve said. "Seriously, you look amazing!"

The fear that drove through Tate only a couple hours earlier had subsided. Staring back at her reflection in the mirror, her eyes lit up. She rubbed her hands over the curves peeking out from underneath her dress. They were subtle, but they were there. Her lips were bold tonight. Red was not usually her color of choice, but she was inspired by the woman in the story from the bookstore. Before she stepped out onto the streets of Paris to peruse the bakery windows, she had swiped a strand of red lipstick across her lips. With that red lipstick on, all of her dreams had come true. There was no other night more perfect to emulate the woman in that story. All of Tate's dreams were coming true. Soon, she would be pushing open the large oak doors into the Gateway Garden room. The overhead lights would be lit like the stars under the open sky, peering in through the glass ceiling. Soon, everyone would be swept off to Paris, and it was Tate's hope that when the end of the night came, no one would want to leave.

However, only time would tell. Time that was quickly ticking away. Time that interrupted Tate's longing stare into the mirror.

It was almost five o'clock when her phone interrupted her. The musicians had arrived. That was her cue. She glided into a pair of black wedges, clipped her radio to the bra underneath her dress, and slipped the earpiece in her ear.

"I'll be on channel three," Tate said. She placed Genevieve's radio and headpiece on the bed next to her.

"Fantastic. I will be right behind you." With that, Tate swiped her clipboard off the entry table and headed out the door.

*

The musicians were unloading their cars at the loading dock. Security was already standing guard outside the doors when Tate snuck around to the back entrance. She had set up their space before she went to get ready. With an hour until the doors opened, they would have plenty of time to settle in.

Tate guided the musicians into the room. It was still free of guests. The cameras were now tucked into corners of the room—something she had discussed earlier with Delaney. She knew they needed to be there, but she didn't want them to be intrusive on the party. The camera crew was nowhere in sight, and neither were Jillian or Brooks. She had figured as much—they didn't need to be back until around half past five—but it still made Tate's heart flop at the thought of having to wait longer to see Brooks again.

She was feeling better about their interaction earlier. Brooks had seemed relaxed. The way his eyes gazed longingly into hers made her feel like he was less distraught about the two of them. Tate wanted to do a final walk through anyway, so she appreciated not having a distraction. She tapped her heels around the room making sure everything was in place. The place cards were set. Brooks would be on table six. She picked his place card up off the side of his wine glass and rubbed her finger over his name. Soon, he'd be back again.

Before Tate could a get chance to say a word to him, her heart would drop again—only, this time, in shock at what she saw when he walked through the door.

~38~

Brooks had always been thankful he got his time management skills from his mother. Though he was never early, never was he more than five minutes late. Garrett, on the other hand, followed in his father's footsteps. At five o'clock, he had just turned off the shower and was about to turn on the razor to soften his beard. If Brooks waited for him, there was no way he'd make it to the Ball of Hope on time.

"You guys go ahead. I can hop on the bus and meet you there," Garrett shouted.

"Are you sure?" Vera asked. She had accepted Garrett's tardiness at this point in their relationship. Normally, she would've waited for him, but she had been counting down the days for this soiree. She never had any reason to doll herself up in Reading. Maybe for a special evening out with Garrett, but even then, there was no endless supply of champagne or array of finger foods without a bill attached.

"I'm sure. Go enjoy yourself. I won't be far behind."

Vera shrugged and gave Brooks the go-ahead. He scribbled the address on the back of a half-ripped envelope so Garrett could find his way and then headed down to the street where the car was waiting. Vera stepped down the stairs slowly behind him, gripping the railing to steady herself in a pair of stilettos. Brooks watched the heavy concentration on her face as she eased down each step waiting for one wrong move to send her plunging to the ground. It took her some time, but she made it to him and the two of them were on their way.

At 5:25 p.m., Tate pushed open the doors to the Gateway Garden room. She wanted everyone who passed by to be able to get a glimpse. Layla and Prue, Tate's interns, had arrived and were with Genevieve by the auction tables. Their two-way radios were all set on channel three and there was nothing left to do now but wait—but not for very long.

It was exactly 5:30 p.m. when Genevieve's voice came through in Tate's ear. "Mother bird is landing," was all Tate needed to hear. She nodded at the musicians, and without hesitation, the strings began to exude the sounds of France. Tate swallowed hard and squeezed her hands together in front of her as she watched Delaney walk in through the door. She froze for a minute, her eyes gazing around the room.

"Oh my..." Delaney made prayer hands at the front of her chest. "Tate! Oh, Tate, this is exquisite. Well done, darling!" Delaney wrapped her arms around Tate's neck and alternated air kisses on each cheek.

It meant everything for Tate to receive Delaney's approval. After exhaling a heavy sigh, she gave her a tight squeeze. Those who had walked in with her smiled too as they admired the details. Some pointed out the string lights, and others noticed the café backdrop right away. They sped over to get a closer look while Tate walked Delaney over to observe the auction items.

"Could we pull these easels around to the front? I like how they're set up, but I don't want them to get lost in the crowd."

"That's not a problem," Tate said. "I can do that right now."

"Wonderful." Delaney glanced away when a voice called out for her over by the café backdrop. "Duty calls. Most guests will be arriving around six. Be sure to have the appetizers ready."

"Absolutely." Tate hugged Delaney one more time before excusing herself. When she was out of earshot, she squeezed the button on her radio wire.

"Genevieve, can you do an ETA check on the appetizers? Make sure they'll be ready for six o'clock sharp."

"Ten-four."

Tate couldn't help but let out a giggle. Genevieve had heard that on one of her crime show obsessions a few months back, and she'd been using it ever since.

Tate stepped around to the other side of the auction table to maneuver the easels to the front. She took the smaller paintings first, then she radioed for Genevieve's help on the big one. If two people needed to pick it up from Paris for it to arrive safely, she wasn't going to chance any hazards happening right before the event started.

"I hate to put it over here." The look of concern on Tate's face grew. "I know she wants it showcased, but what if someone bumps it or, heaven forbid, spills something on it?" She tapped her foot for a bit, letting her mind slip into deep thought. "I have an idea! Don't move!"

Genevieve shouted out another "ten-four" as Tate sprinted to the loading dock where the totes of supplies were stored. She pulled up the lid and started to sift through. Tate always had extra decor on hand. Even if she thought it wouldn't fit the vibe at the time, there were some events where she was thankful for it later. This was one of those times. At the very bottom was a large mason jar full of white rose petals. She snatched it and headed back to where Genevieve was standing.

"What are you going to do with those?" Genevieve asked.

Tate was celebrating her genius idea by waving the jar over her head and doing a little salsa step as she danced up to Genevieve. "We're going to move this over there." Tate pointed over to the side of the table. "That way, it'll still get traffic, but it won't be in danger."

"And the rose petals?"

"You'll see." Tate winked. "Just help me."

The two of them picked up the painting once again and rested it on the tabletop before grabbing the easel. This time, Genevieve joined in on Tate's dance of "a little to the left, a little to the right" until the easel was in the perfect spot. They set the painting gently in place, and Tate picked up the mason jar again.

"Okay, now we're going to sprinkle these in a circle around the easel. Close enough for people to see the details, but far enough away that they can't touch."

"So smart," Genevieve said.

"I know." Tate shrugged.

She sprinkled the last few flowers down to connect the circle on her side and slapped Genevieve a high-five when it was finished. There were about ten minutes until the appetizers would start their rounds, and people had started to make their way in. Tate headed over to stand next to the large white scroll-framed chalkboard at the entrance. She wanted to be there to help people find where they were supposed to go as they arrived. She wondered, as she shuffled her feet back and forth, where Brooks was. She assumed he'd be there by now, but she couldn't see him anywhere in the small crowd when she scanned the room.

A few dozen guests skimmed the list of names for their seats as six o'clock approached. Tate heard whispers from a few of them as they walked by. So far, there were no objections to the vision she had brought to life. Most people noticed the string lights first. "It's as if you're really gazing up at the stars," one person said.

Tate looked away from the door for a moment to queue the appetizers, and when she looked back, she stiffened at an unexpected sight. Further into the lobby, she saw Brooks walking toward her, but he wasn't alone. Next to him, with her arm wrapped through his, was a stunning woman with one side of her hair pulled back by a silver clip. The bottom of her yellow dress flapped with each step she took. Tate didn't recognize her as anyone from Brooks' office. It was possible she was a client, but if she was, what the hell was she doing hanging off his arm?

"Houston...can you hear me?" Layla's voice came through Tate's ear right as Brooks walked through the door. Tate knew she'd need to answer. Any sentence that began with "Houston" didn't bode well—that was the word Tate had told her team to use as an incognito way to report something was going wrong. She squeezed the headpiece to her ear and was about to answer when Brooks said her name.

"Tate," he said. "You cleaned up well."

This was not the Cinderella moment she was hoping for. Tate forced a smile as Houston soared into her ear again.

"Thank you. You both look lovely." She tried to stall long enough to figure out who it was standing next to Brooks.

"Tate, this is Vera," Brooks said. "Vera is—"

That was as far as Brooks was able to get when Tate apologetically excused herself. The third "Houston" rang in her ear. She took a few steps away from the door and hit her radio.

"Houston...go ahead," Tate said.

"We need you in the kitchen."

"On my way!"

Tate grabbed Genevieve on the way to the kitchen. She pointed over at the chalkboard.

"Who the bloody hell is that?" She too had noticed the woman in the yellow.

Tate shrugged, but she didn't have time to analyze. Genevieve headed over to the entry with a ruthless stare while Tate ran to the kitchen. A couple of runners were out with the appetizers, and they were flying off the plates like hotcakes. They'd surely run out before the hour was up, and the kitchen needed direction.

Tate pulled out her tablet and scrolled through the operating budget she and Delaney went over. Originally, it had been set for about seventy more people, so there was enough room to bump up the numbers. She gave them the go-ahead and then paused for a moment at the door to take a breath. She leaned her hand against the wall and let out a loud sigh before heading back into the room. It was filling up quickly, but even through the crowd, she could see Brooks. The lady in yellow was still close to his side, and they were both laughing.

Tate stepped around a group of people engaged in conversation to see if she could find out who the two of them were laughing with.

"Charlie!" Tate whispered sharply to herself. She suddenly felt a twang in her stomach as she thought back to that night at the Lanesborough and Charlie's boisterous laugh. That was the first time she'd found herself really fighting her feelings for Brooks. Now, after weeks of pushing him away, she was finally ready to give in.

Tonight had been the night she was going to tell him, but, as she watched Charlie with Brooks and the unknown woman, she could see their laughter growing, and a horrifying thought crossed her mind. Maybe she was too late.

~39~

Brooks was sitting at table six relishing in the last bite of his beef bourguignon. Garrett had made it to the gala right as dinner was being served. If he came any later, Brooks might have stolen his as a second round. The food was so good. He'd been trying to catch Tate's eye for the past half hour to let her know, but anytime she got close, she never looked in his direction. He hated that he wasn't able to introduce her properly to Vera, and he hoped Garrett could meet her as well.

Tate was busy. He knew that, but the couple of glances he caught her stealing seemed uneasy. He had thought they were turning a corner that afternoon when he hugged her. He'd fully expected her to step away, but, instead, she fell into him. Now, he felt like they were back at square one.

"Bro, I must say, you did good." Garrett pointed his fork at the table two down from theirs. Tate was standing over an older couple.

Brooks stared intently as she laughed with them in unison. How was it that she grew more beautiful each time he saw her? This time, it wasn't her legs teasing him; he watched the bare skin of her left shoulder twitch as she tossed her head back. He could hear the faint sounds of her stuttered laugh from where he sat, and a modest sense of jealousy washed over him. Brooks wanted to be the reason she was laughing. He wanted an excuse to get up, to whisper in her ear and watch the delight on her face, but he didn't have one. For the moment, he'd have to settle with enjoying her presence from two tables away.

"I haven't really done anything...yet," Brooks said. "I'm still trying to figure her out."

"But you like her, I can tell," Vera said. "You haven't taken your eyes off her all night. You've been gawking in every direction she's turned."

"You make me sound like a stalker," Brooks whispered in Vera's ear.

She swiped her hand across his shoulder. "No, no, I'm just saying, I think she's worth the effort. She seems very poised and put together."

Brooks couldn't agree more. He wrapped his arm around Vera's shoulder and pulled her into him. He had to admit, out of all of his family, Vera's opinion seemed to matter the most lately. When Garrett first introduced them, she had seemed shy. She'd held back the bubbly personality that was now apparent in everything she did. Vera had become the sister he never knew he wanted. Brooks confided in her about a lot more than Garrett probably knew, such as when he fell asleep on the couch last night. Vera had to hound him for a full episode of the show they were watching before he folded.

He'd kept their night in Paris between him and Tate, but he'd let the kiss outside of Tate's hotel room door slip. Brooks couldn't help it. The yearning he had for Tate was stronger than he'd ever felt for anyone. He'd felt sick for the past few days at the thought he'd lost her. He hated to think he was a mistake. But this afternoon, he thought maybe he still had a chance.

God, he hoped he was right.

Brooks watched her walk away. Her dress barely covered the part of her back where he'd rested his hand many times before. He was determined to talk to her before the night was over and was thankful that once dinner was done, he would finally get the chance.

There had been a small break from the live music during dinner, but the violins were back to playing, and some guests were using the open space as a dance floor. That was when Brooks saw his chance. Dessert wasn't coming out for another half hour, and the auction was well underway.

Tate was hiding back in the corner by the bar. He watched her eyes move promptly across the room. Brooks did the same.

A group of people huddled around the auction table, their hands swiftly moving the pen across the paper attached to the clipboards. Delaney was holding tight to a cocktail glass while chatting with a group of women in swanky dresses and diamond earrings. Brooks caught the stare of big man on campus, Aaron, and gave him a wave. The party was lively but calm. There didn't seem to be anything pulling Tate from Brooks' advance, so he walked over to her and reached out his hand.

"May I have this dance?"

Tate slowly turned her head to look at Brooks. She crossed her arms and gave him a smug look. Inside, she was restless. She'd been stealing glances at him all night. When he was deep in conversation, she'd watch him. He'd rub his fingers over the stubble on his jaw, and it would force her heart to start beating rapidly. There were a couple of times she found him whispering in the ear of the woman in yellow. Even then, she couldn't turn away. She would only let out a shy wince before Genevieve called in her ear, "Stop torturing yourself."

Her firmly crossed arms over her chest separated the two of them. Tate couldn't help but wonder about the woman in yellow. Where was she? Why wasn't Brooks dancing with *her*? Tate thought he had a lot of nerve to be standing there in front of her. She couldn't let that endearing smile pull her in.

"Where's your date?" she snapped.

"My date?" Brooks could see Tate's apprehension staring back at him. The glow he saw in her earlier was now masked. Her smile was tight-lipped, and he paused for a minute before wanting to kick himself for not realizing it earlier. He had walked in with Vera on his arm. They'd been having private discussions with each other all night. Mostly about Brooks' next move to win Tate back, but she didn't know that. Vera was a stranger to her. At the same time his stupidity flourished, so did his amusement. She was jealous, and he liked that.

Brooks would tell Tate who Vera was eventually, but, he had to admit, he liked watching her stir.

"She left me for the time being." Brooks pointed over at Vera. She too was lost in the sea of dancing bodies, swaying to the soothing sound of the violins. Her arms were gripped tight to Garrett's shoulders, and her engagement ring was impossible to miss, especially with the way the light hit the dance floor.

Tate had been so hot and bothered by her closeness to Brooks when they walked in that she hadn't even noticed. If she did, she wouldn't have spent the past two hours in a puddle of immense emotion.

"Hmm...serves you right anyway. The least you could've done was warn me."

"Right," Brooks said. He slipped his fingers around the tight grip Tate was still holding strong in front of her chest. "Because you've been so talkative lately."

"What are you doing?" Tate asked. She clenched her muscles as he clutched her hand, but she didn't try to yank it away. Her eyes shot over in Delaney's direction. She was still deep in conversation, which helped to ease her muscles.

"Come on...please?" Brooks begged.

Tate gave in. As angry as she wanted to be, she was also yearning to be close to him. She wanted to fall into him like she had that afternoon. She let him lead the way to the dance floor, but her eyes never left the yellow dress. Tate observed closely. The woman was awfully cozy with her current dance partner. His hands were slightly lower than friendly on her waist.

"Your date seems to be awfully chummy over there," Tate taunted.

Brooks spun Tate around once before pulling her into him. His hand slid softly above where her zipper stopped, and his palm pressed firmly against her delicate skin. Soon, the distance between them was obsolete, and Tate could feel the warmth of his breath on her cheek. He looked over at Vera and Garrett and tried to hide the smirk on his face by leaning in closer.

"It seems to be that way, huh?"

"That doesn't bother you?"

Right as Tate finished asking her question, Garrett spotted them on the dance floor. He tilted his head, and his lips met Vera's ear. He whispered something Brooks couldn't quite make out, but whatever it was had Vera's head jerking over in their direction. Her face lit up, and her dancing started to forcefully pull Garrett closer to Brooks and Tate.

"Well, hello there!" Vera squealed.

Tate's body was still tense as the two of them swayed on the dance floor. Her eyes wandered across the crowd, making sure she wasn't needed. During the one minute she'd pulled her eyes from Vera, suddenly, she was standing next to them. She wasn't sure whether she should run or hold tighter onto Brooks. All she knew was that her heart was beating steadily against Brooks' chest.

"Look at you and your two left feet," Brooks joked as he patted Garrett on the back.

"Are you going to introduce us to your friend?" Garret asked.

"Of course! Tate, I'd like you to meet Garrett and Vera. My brother...and his fiancée."

Brooks relished in Tate's pale complexion. She refused to turn her eyes to him. He watched her shoulders sink as a heave of air filled her lungs. Her hand that was holding tight to his let go. She covered her mouth as she cleared her throat and hid her embarrassment with a faint smile.

"It's very nice to meet you," she said. "Are you both enjoying yourselves?"

"We are! This party is wicked," Vera said.

"Oh, good," Tate replied. She continued to force a smile. She refused to let Brooks see how horrified she was at her assumption and was thankful when Vera gave her an escape.

"If you'll excuse me," Vera said, "I'm going to find the loo."

"Yes, of course," Tate said. "It was very nice to meet you both." She gave both Garrett and Vera a wave as they moved through the crowd.

Once they were gone, Tate turned her displeased look to Brooks, who still had a smug look on his face. He went to take her hand again, but before he could, she slapped it against his arm.

"You jerk," Tate said. She pushed herself away from him and stomped off the dance floor.

"What?" Brooks threw his arms in the air. He stood frozen that way until he realized Tate wasn't planning on coming back. Then, he jogged after her.

When he was within arm's length, Brooks gently grabbed at Tate's arm to make her stop. She didn't want to cause a scene, so she did. She made minimal eye contact with Brooks but forced a stiff smile in order to not draw attention to herself.

"Why did you let me think she was your date?" Tate's voice was soft but firm, and her arms were once again crossed tightly in front of her.

"I didn't! You assumed."

"And you did nothing to make me think otherwise."

At first, Brooks had been charmed at the thought of Tate being jealous of Vera. He liked to watch her squirm in his arms, but, now she had turned this around on him, she was making him look like the bad guy here. He was not the one who'd said he couldn't do this. Brooks wanted nothing more than to "do this" with Tate. She was the one who had pushed herself out of his arms. She was the one who had let him walk out that door. The way her eyes dug into him now had him slightly miffed, as they would say here in London, and he didn't like it. He didn't want to be frustrated with her.

"Why do you even care?" he whispered so no one else would overhear, but he made sure his words were firm. "You didn't want this, remember? I wanted you. I still want you, damn it, but you don't get to have it both ways. You're either in or you're out, so...which is it?"

"I can't do this right now." Tate's smile grew in order to mask the bubbling frustration. She ironed out her dress with the palms of her hands and started to walk away, but Brooks followed.

"Oh no, you don't get to walk away from this," he demanded. "Did you not tell me that this was a mistake?"

Tate stomped her feet together and calmly turned herself back around. "Those words were taken out of context." She took a quick glance through the room to make sure no one was staring before she started again. "You were never a mistake, and I'm sorry I made you think that. I was scared and under a lot of pressure, but I've been doing a lot of thinking this past week, and I actually came here tonight with the hope of..." Tate couldn't let herself finish. This was not how she wanted to tell Brooks how she felt. Not here, in the middle of a party, with voices echoing all around them. She smacked her lips closed before she let anything else slip out.

"With the hope of what?" Brooks asked.

"Not here, okay?" Brooks could see a sense of appeal in Tate's eyes as they grew wider. "I have to get back to work. I promise, we'll talk later."

"I can't wait until later." Brooks' voice was stern.

Tate reached over and squeezed Brooks' hand before leaving him. Hundreds of people were standing there in the same room as him, yet he had never felt more alone. He fell back into the wall, longing for the feel of Tate's body back against his. He clenched his fists as her hot and cold demeanor rushed through him. The two of them, they were so good together. The way this event was going was proof of that. He knew she saw it too. It was in the way she leaned toward him at the bar that night in Paris. Outside her hotel room, she had looked adoringly into his eyes before she gave into that kiss. This afternoon, the way her face lit up when she saw him—it was almost as if she was ready to confess the truth he saw in her eyes. He wanted so badly for her to love him because from the moment their lips touched in Paris, he had fallen completely in love with her. Even through the pain and the anger, he hadn't stopped, but now, he could feel her slipping away for good and didn't know if he could handle that.

Brooks would let her have the rest of the night. She'd put a lot of work into this, and she needed to see it through. But when it was done, he was going to do everything he could to show her what he already knew. Tate didn't need to be afraid anymore when she looked into his eyes. There would never be another pair staring back her more genuine, more sincere, and with more longing to have her than his.

~40~

The Ball of Hope was officially over. The lights had been turned back on, and the sea of black-tie attire had retreated out of the hotel. There was still dessert left over, and Genevieve was boxing it up. Delaney had insisted Tate had earned every sweet piece, so her team was to enjoy the leftovers for themselves.

Tate's interns helped to load the van, and Brooks was nowhere in sight. It had been at least an hour since she last saw him. She bowed her head at the thought he'd already gone home, but she tried not to let her disappointment overshadow her conquest.

"All right!" Genevieve clapped. "I think that's the last of it."

"Yup," Prue said. She and Layla had snuck in behind Tate. "The van is ready to go, and all the vendors are gone."

Tate reached out her arms and waved her hands to call her team closer. When they stepped in, she wrapped her arms around all of them, and they followed for a group hug.

"We did it!" Tate yelled into their makeshift circle. "Thank you all so much for the help tonight. You're all good to go. Don't forget to grab a box of goodies on the way out."

Layla and Prue didn't hesitate. They each swiped a box off the kitchen counter and, with their free hands, waved goodbye. Tate and Genevieve bent down underneath the counter to gather up what was left of their things.

"Well, boss...how does it feel?" Genevieve asked. She slung her arm around Tate's shoulder as they slowly sauntered toward the lobby. "I imagine pretty good, yeah?"

"Tate laughed. "Yeah, it feels pretty darn good."

Both girls took one last look over their shoulders. The Gateway Garden had been returned to the way it was when Tate had first walked into it. It was a blank canvas now for someone else.

Tate's smile faded slightly at the realization of how quickly her vision had turned into a memory. At every chance, she had she snapped a photo to make sure her starry night in Paris would never be forgotten. Most likely, she'd head home, slam her feet up on the coffee table, and scroll back and forth through them until her eyes no longer let her. It was surreal now, staring at an empty room, to think of what she had pulled off. Glancing over at Genevieve, who wore a similar look on her face, she could tell she wasn't alone in this. Her smile reappeared as Genevieve caught her eye, and they continued to walk through the hotel lobby out the front door.

"How about a celebratory drink before you head home?" Genevieve asked as they stood in the hotel lobby.

"Let's do it," Tate said.

The two of them walked past the lobby desk and out onto the stairs of the entrance. Tate hadn't taken more than a step before she noticed what was waiting for her outside.

Brooks turned around at the creaking of the door, and as soon as he recognized the bouncing head of brown curls, he shot up from the stairs where he had been sitting for almost an hour.

All three of them stood motionless. Genevieve's eyes traded places from Tate to Brooks, but both Tate and Brooks' eyes were locked on each other.

"Maybe a rain check for that drink, yeah?" Genevieve whispered as she stepped behind Tate to grab the door back into the lobby. "Hi, I'm Genevieve." She reached out her free hand, desperate to break the silence.

"Brooks." He reached out for her.

"His friends call him Leo." Tate took a step closer. She tilted her head to her shoulder and winked.

"I suppose I'll call you Leo then," Genevieve said. She pulled her hand out of his grasp. "I have a feeling we'll be great friends."

Brooks nodded, and Genevieve turned back to say her final goodbyes to Tate.

"I'll call you tomorrow."

"Sounds good." Tate leaned over and pulled Genevieve in for a hug. "Thanks again for everything."

Once Tate's hold loosened, Genevieve retreated back inside the hotel for the night.

Brooks moved closer, filling the space where Genevieve had stood only a second before.

"Were you waiting for me?" Tate asked.

"It's possible."

"Where's your date?" She smirked.

"She left me for some guy with better hair."

The red of Tate's lips pulled in Brooks' gaze. Everything around him turned to a blur as she swayed in front of him. Neither could stand the silence any longer. Their mouths opened, and both started to speak, but the sounds tangled in the air.

"You go first," Brooks said.

Tate cleared her throat. Her fingers fiddled with one of the bobby pins still sitting snug on top of her head, and she gathered her words in order.

"I'm really sorry," she began, "for what I said the other day. You were not a mistake." Brooks' eyes shot open at those words. "What happened between us...it scared me. It was as if, lying on the bed with you, I was undressed of all my fears and completely exposed to this unfamiliar sense of comfort. It felt too good to be true."

Brooks stepped closer to her, and she caught a twinkle in his eye. The light had hit it at the right angle.

"Tate..." He started to talk, but she interrupted.

"Wait. I need to say this before I lose my nerve. I've been absolutely terrified to open up my heart again, and then you came along. I used every reason I could think of to keep you at arm's length. Not because I was afraid you'd get in the way of my career, but because I could feel myself falling and I knew you...you were the one with the ability to catch me. That scares the hell out of me, but I don't want to be afraid anymore." Tate's eyelids fell closed at the feel of Brooks' hand softly sweeping against the back of her neck. Her body shivered underneath her dress.

"What are you saying?" he asked.

"I'm saying..." Tate's hands gripped the ends of his jacket and tugged him closer. "I love you, Brooks Leonardo Walker."

Along with those words, a heavy pant of air escaped Tate's lungs. Her chest was no longer heavy, and the way Brooks was staring into her eyes sent a wave of relief through her. He lowered his head so his forehead rested on hers.

"It's about time," he said.

Tate let out a giggle. Without a chance to retract, she reached out and pressed her hands on the stubble she'd been admiring all night.

There it was. Through those bright red lips were the words he'd been longing to hear. Brooks' fingers tangled in Tate's hair. The weight of her body against his chest invited him to keep going. He covered her smile with his lips. She whimpered. He held onto her with one hand, and the other waved behind him in search of the railing. When his fingers felt the cold metal, he leaned his weight against it.

Tate was still clinging tight to him. She pulled her lips from his and looked up into his eyes. Brooks placed three more short and quick kisses on her lips before saying anything.

"I love you too," he said. His eyes were only inches from hers. Brooks' heart was racing as fast as it did that night in Paris after he found the courage to leave his room for hers. Hearing those words come out of her mouth was like a long-awaited rainbow after a storm. He kissed her again.

"It's my turn now," he said. "I have something for you."

Tate looked down at the paper bag he was holding. It was thin. His hand covered most of it, leaving just enough room for her to grab it when he lifted it up to her. She pulled it into her chest.

"For me?"

"Yeah, a congratulatory gift," Brooks said. "Tonight was incredible. I wanted to give you something to remember it by."

"That is too kind of you." It took Tate a few tries to grasp the opening of the bag. Her nerves were taking over. Once she was able to calm herself enough, she reached inside. "Oh, Brooks! I can't believe... When did...?"

Her failure to form the right words was proof Brooks had made the right choice. Gripped tightly in Tate's hands was the book from the store in Cecil Court—the very one that inspired what she had pulled off tonight. On the cover was the outside of a café. In front of the window sat one single table. It was empty, but two coffee cups sat waiting for the couple standing next to it, peering through the window as they decided on their baked goods.

Tate clutched it to her chest as two single tears rolled down her cheeks. "Thank you." She leaned into him again. His lips parted and welcomed hers against them. "This is crazy," Tate said. "To think where we were only a month ago."

"That's what love is, right?" Brooks asked. Tate's head rested on his chest. "Love is crazy. It comes soaring into you when you least expect it. Like when you're walking out of a hotel door, and *bam*, this gorgeous woman runs into you with a cup full of fresh coffee."

"I didn't run into you! You ran into me!" Tate gave him a playful shove.

Brooks laughed. He was going to let her have this one. No matter what side of the story was told, it still ended the same way: a chance meeting between two strangers that turned into something they had never expected.

"You know I'll never let you live that down, right?" Tate laughed.

Brooks wrapped his arm snug around her, and they descended the stairs onto the cobblestone sidewalk.

"Yeah, I figured as much. How about we debate this over a drink or two? I know a great place that serves late-night chocolate martinis and coffee cocktails..."

"Oh, do you?"

Brooks nodded.

Tate had never done late-night at Primrose May, but a celebration martini sounded rather good after what she had pulled off that evening. "I suppose I can clear my evening for you, and then, of course, I could give you a ride home. It wouldn't be very ladylike of me to let you walk home alone in the dark."

"No, no, it wouldn't be, would it?" Brooks said.

Tate's eyelashes fluttered as she looked up at the one prominent dimple on his cheek. He swung his arm around her as the nightly breeze carried their laughter into the streets. Tate slid both of her arms around Brooks and pulled him into her as close as she could, her legs taking long strides to keep up with him. As they crossed the only busy street before May appeared, she looked up at him. Her eyes traced his strong profile down to his sultry lips. Brooks must have felt her stare pressing into him because, when they reached the other side of the street, he looked back down at her. Without warning, he stopped, swept her up in both arms, and lowered his lips to hers.

He pulled away only long enough to see Tate's reaction. Her eyes were still closed, and a soft smile glistened in her eyes as the streetlight shined upon her face. Then, he kissed her again—for longer this time. They were both oblivious to everyone passing by as their lips intertwined.

Brooks gently pulled away, but his gaze didn't leave Tate's.

"So, question for you," Brooks said, staring into her eyes. "Now that you've confessed your undying love for me...well...you know. Don't you think it's time to call me Leo now?

"I suppose I could give it a try...Leo." Tate liked the sound of it. "I thought only your friends called you Leo though. What if I don't want to be your friend?" Tate winked.

The creases in the corner of Brooks' eyes answered that question. He placed a kiss on Tate's forehead and shrugged as they started to walk again.

"Leo and Tate. It has a good ring to it doesn't it?" Brooks asked. "Maybe it's not just for friends after all."

"May not."

Tate's smile was still intact as the two of them, still holding tight to each other, blissfully headed back to Primrose May, where they once again would bond over two cups of coffee. This time, however, they'd make sure the only things falling were their two hearts for each other.

~41~
- *Four months later...*

Thanks to the Ball of Hope, Tate was busier than ever that summer. The event had almost doubled the number of charitable contributions from the year before. The success was in large part due to Tate's brilliant auction idea. Every single item had sold, and the painting from Pierre far surpassed the bid Delaney expected.

Tate woke up the morning after the event with a waterfall of text messages from Delaney. Clients were thrilled with the theme of the night, and some of them wanted to hire her right away. Genevieve was promoted to Event Lead, which she gladly accepted even with her growing influencer lifestyle. The flood of events pouring in allowed Tate to add two new assistants to her team.

By mid-August, Tate rarely had a weekend in her planner that didn't have something penciled in—except for this weekend coming up. She was so close to four whole days of no work and all play. All she had to do was get through this product launch party, and she was home free.

"How do we look on the dessert table?" She pressed the button on her walkie-talkie and lowered her lips to the microphone hanging from her shirt.

"We're pulling the rest of the cupcakes from the back now to restock."

"Thanks, Prue!"

Prue had graduated a few months after her first big event with Tate and was happy to take on the assistant role with Simple Charms Events. Layla had also accepted the position, but she still had another year of university left, and with summer in full swing she wouldn't be starting until September.

Tate stood with her hands folded in front of her next to the open bar. She peered through the final champagne toast of the night to find a familiar face staring back at her. He winked, and the corners of her lips rose. She cleared her throat and patted her hand against the warmth of her flushed cheeks.

Working with the man she now called Leo had ended up not being as difficult as Tate anticipated. This was the second event she'd booked where she worked with him in some capacity. It turned out Tate welcomed having someone on the other side she could count on. The clients trusted him, and he advocated for her. On the day of the first event, he'd treated her like she was anyone else in the room. Tonight, he was doing the same, but she knew when the night was over, it would be a different story.

Leo would say his goodbyes, shake hands, and wait for the crowd to die down. Tate would try to refuse his help when it came to overseeing the cleanup, but he wouldn't give in. Half-empty glasses of champagne lingered on the farm tables that were spread across the room. The crowd had dwindled, and Brooks was down to shaking one last hand before he sauntered over in Tate's direction.

"Well, we did it," Leo said. "We made it through."

"We sure did, Mr. Walker," Tate pulled the champagne glass from his hand. He tried to grab another from the table. She shook her head, and he jutted out his bottom lip. "No, sir. You go relax. This is my job."

"I'll have plenty of time to relax this weekend." Tate felt his hands brush across her hips. He squeezed them as he leaned over her shoulder and whispered in her ear, "Are you nervous?"

Tate swiped the centerpiece from the middle of the table. "To meet your parents?" she asked. "A little bit. I'm looking forward to it though, a weekend away, and a wedding where I don't have to wear one of these." She unclipped the microphone from her shirt and pulled the battery pack from her belt loop. "Now, you...go." She shoved her hand against Leo's solid bicep.

"You know I can't do that."

A heavy sigh escaped from between her lips. Pretty soon, she was going to have to add him to the payroll.

"Fine. Prue should be done packing the bags. If you want to grab those from her, I'll meet you both outside."

Leo placed his hand to his forehead in salute. Tate shook her head once again and bent down to pack the votive candles into her bag. She paused for a second to watch him as her hand clung to the zipper.

This weekend was going to be a big step in their relationship. For four months, they'd done the usual courtship. They'd gone out for drinks with friends and spent the occasional weeknight on her couch munching on takeout and watching old movies from the eighties. Sundays had become the day when she'd roll over to find Leo occupying the side of her bed that once lay empty. Tate always woke up before he did, and she liked it. She'd put on a pot of coffee and enjoy her first cup outside with a book until she heard the creak of the patio door. Leo would walk out with his cup of coffee and sit across from her. They'd enjoy about an hour or so of singing birds and rustling leaves before he'd leave her to her regular Sunday routine.

This weekend, however, Tate would be waking up to Leo more than one night in a row. That was new for them. On top of that, she'd be meeting his parents and seeing Garrett and Vera again as they pledged forever to each other. Her nerves piqued at the thought of it, but she was ready. Leo had erased the cracks Cameron left behind. Now, they were mere scars that documented her long-awaited journey to love. That was what this was: endless, elated, requited love, and it felt amazing. Tate had realized it that day in the dress shop, but watching him throw a bag full of event supplies over his shoulder solidified the depth. He could be anywhere else now, but he was there, helping her, because he felt the same way she did. Anywhere was better with him than without.

Tate looked forward to meeting his parents. A part of her was curious to see if she really was the missing piece to the family puzzle. With a zip of the bag and one final look around, she walked to the open doorway and flicked off the light. Her work was complete. Now, it was time for some fun.

~42~

The countryside offered a form of peace you couldn't find in London. There were rolling pastures, and an endless scope of greenery flowed into the horizon. Tate could see it all as she stared out the window of her hotel room.

In the courtyard below, people were walking in and out of the white tent in which Garrett and Vera's reception would take place. It was a short walk from the floral-covered gazebo where the ceremony would be. That was on the other side of the hotel. It overlooked the pond Tate remembered seeing when she and Leo first drove up.

"Hey, babe." She turned around to find Leo had emerged back into the room. His navy tie was hanging around his neck.

"Wanna tie this for me?"

Tate pursed her lips, and her eyes narrowed as she walked toward him. "This is the third time in two weeks you've ask me to do this." She wrapped her hands around the shiny strands of silk and tossed one side in front of the other. "Did you suddenly forget how?"

"I didn't forget, I just like when you do it." The words of his father flowed through his head as Tate grabbed the tie in her hand. *Criss cross, wrap around, throw it back, then pull it down.* He breathed in a hint of floral from her wrists as she pulled the final knot snug against his neck. It was similar to the roses he surprised her with a few weeks back, on the night they made their relationship official.

Tate patted her hands against the part of Leo's suit that hid his shoulders. "There," she said, "you're all set."

He lowered his head so that his lips could thank her. They were still the same shade of pale pink she'd touched to his chest when he woke up next to her that morning. That was the only thing left to complete Tate's wedding outfit. She had already slipped into her navy boatneck dress. It matched perfectly with Leo's suit and hit right above the knee. Tate was happy she went with that one and not the floor-length dress she originally had in mind. Summers weren't usually uncomfortable in Reading, but by the afternoon, the sun had already warmed the air a bit more than usual.

Leo held his hands at the base of Tate's neck. She could tell he approved from the longing look in his eyes. Her hands wrapped around his and she pulled him in for one more kiss. They had to get going. Leo's best man duties were calling. Tate was going to roam the hotel grounds for a bit before claiming one of the white folding chairs already lined up in front of the gazebo.

"Give me one minute," Tate said. She pinched her fingers against his chin before walking to her purse that lay on the bed and pulling out her trusty tube of red lipstick. She used her reflection to brush the color across her lips.

The whiteness of Tate's teeth was visible between her lips as they curled into a smile. Leo stood behind her. Through the mirror, she watched his eyes go wide as they locked on hers. This, right here, was what red lipstick dreams were made of.

Tate turned around, happy to see Leo still standing there. He wasn't a figment of her imagination that evaporated once she took her eyes off the glass.

He lifted his arm and wiggled his fingers toward her. "Are you ready?"

She gave him a firm nod. Each step of her nude heels brought her closer to him until she was finally able to reach. She embraced his warmth as she folded her fingers through his.

"I'm ready," she said. "Are you?"

"Oh, I've been ready." His hand tugged at hers until she was right by his side. "I've been waiting on you for a long time."

Tate smiled proudly with a kind sparkle in her eyes. The door closed behind them. Her fingers pressed tighter against his smooth skin as they walked down the hallway. She too had been waiting on him for a long time, and now that he was here, there was no way she was ever going to let him go.

...

THE END

Did you love Tate and Leo's story? I sure hope so! If you did, share the love by leaving a review over on Amazon and Goodreads!

Stay in touch! Come say hi to me on Instagram over @courtneygwrites

~ ACKNOWLEGEMENTS ~

I am so beyond grateful for the amazing beta readers I had on this project. Thank you, Lynn, Andrea, Sara and Samantha for helping this story reach its full potential. This book also came to the life with the help of my talented editor. Bryony it was such a pleasure working with you again!

There were a lot of late nights writing this novel and on days when I lost motivation, my fiancé was always there to cheer me on. Sam, thank you for believing in me and encouraging me to keep telling my stories. I'm the luckiest to have you by my side.

To all of my readers: your endless support is what makes this all worth it. You continue to read my stories and share them with your friends. I am forever appreciative of all of you.

~ Read more from Courtney ~

Tear Stained Beaches

In Kettlewood Island Haylie discovers a heartbreaking truth about her marriage, leaving her to decide if true strength means holding on or letting go

Holding on to Georgia

He has secrets. A past that haunts him. He's a tragic heartbreak waiting to happen. Call me crazy, but for some reason, I want to be the one who saves him.

Nashville Starlet Series

An unexpected spark ignites when Nashville's hottest country music blogger meets her match in a small-town songwriter.

About Courtney

I am a firm believer that we should never go a day without living our passions.

That's why the characters in my novels become your best friends and you turn the final pages of my books feeling empowered, overly caffeinated and on the search for your next adventure.

I grew up just outside of Rochester, NY where I have always had a lively imagination and a reach for the stars attitude.

When I was younger, I wanted to be a pirate. Yes, you read that right. My family used to spend their summers vacationing in the Thousand Islands where each year the town held a Pirate's Weekend. That's where my love of pirates began.

I also loved cheerleading and gymnastics. When my dreams of being a pirate and Olympic gymnast fell through, I turned to another love...writing.

As a creative, I have not only published multiple novels, but have appeared on TV shows like *Nashville*. If I can do anything in life, I hope to inspire others to dream big and believe in themselves because life is too short to wonder, "what if."

Learn more at www.courtneygiardina.com